SPACEFLIGHT TO A PREHISTORIC AGE

Earth sends a crack team of explorers to survey the natural resources of a wild and primitive planet—a parallel world still in a dinosaur-dominated Paleocene period. Accompanying them are four alien mantas, half-animal, half-fungoid creatures with the keenest senses in the universe—a gift which saves the mission from immediate disaster when an earthquake threatens the island they land on.

After sailing for weeks on a crude raft, they encounter a strange land where the mightiest beasts known to man still reign. There, amid the giant reptiles, they meet Orn, a man-size wingless bird whose unsurpassed racial memory enables him to tap into the mind of every creature in his evolutionary family tree. Inspired by this fantastic being, Cal, Veg, and Aquilon rebel against greedy powers—powers from Earth that crave the extinction of this bizarre and beautiful land.

ORN

>PIERS< ANTHONY

AVON
PUBLISHERS OF BARD, CAMELOT, DISCUS AND FLARE BOOKS

This book has been serialized in its
entirety in *Amazing Stories Magazine.*

AVON BOOKS
A division of
The Hearst Corporation
1790 Broadway
New York, New York 10019

First Avon Printing, November 1971

AVON TRADEMARK REG. U.S. PAT. OFF. AND IN OTHER
COUNTRIES, MARCA REGISTRADA, HECHO EN U.S.A.

Printed in the U.S.A.

WFH 20 19 18 17 16 15 14

I: ORN

Orn woke exhausted. His body was cold and somewhat sticky, and his muscles were uncertain. He could not remember how he had come here, but he knew it was not safe to yield to his confusion now.

Something was wrong. He lifted his head and forced open eyes that had been sealed shut by goo. At first the brightness hurt him; then it settled to a wan glow as his sensitive eyes protected themselves. He was in a cave, and it was half-light: the start or end of a day. That much he grasped, remembering the inanimate cycle.

He was sprawled awkwardly across cold stone. He wedged four sticky, clumsy limbs under his body ungracefully, then rose to stand with greater confidence on two.

Yes—in the gradually brightening light he made out the flat floor and naturally corrugated ceiling, both descending into darkness beyond him. Nearby was a voluminous tumble of dehydrated stalks: a nest, containing a single monstrous, elongated egg, and sticky fragments of another.

Orn brushed gingerly against the whole egg. Cold—nothing would hatch from this. Beyond it and the nest were rocks and bones and other debris of indeterminate origin. All dead.

He walked unsteadily toward the light, avoiding the scattered joints and droppings and teeth and dehydrated leaves and sticks that lined the track. The exertion warmed his body, and he began to feel better. But with this physical improvement his mind seemed to backslide, to lose coherence. Strange visions passed through his awareness, incredible peripheral memories that could not be his own, that faded as he became aware of them.

He relaxed, not attempting to scrutinize the twitchings of his brain, and then the pictures perversely took on a sharp focus.

Memory. It began far, far back in the half-light, wetter and warmer than since. He floated in a nutrient ocean and absorbed what he required through his spongy skin. He reached for the light, a hundred million years later, needing it . . . but recoiled, burned, finding it too fierce to approach. He had to wait, to adapt, and this did not come easily. He held his position and ate what he could and expanded his mass slowly, very slowly, a billion years slowly. But somehow the larger he grew, the greater became his hunger. He could not get enough nourishment. Never enough, never enough. . . .

The odd memory dissipated as he turned the corner and stood in the stronger light at the cave's mouth. Green shrubbery showed beyond, and the intense gray-white of the sky. This was morning: not the steamy dawn of twenty million years ago, but a chilly and empty rising of the sun.

The corpse of a mighty bird lay on the ground, astride the opening to the cave. In life it might have stood so tall as to brush the very ceiling, and it had a thick, slightly curved beak, stubby wings, and cruel, forward-reaching talons. Under the disarray of gray feathers the long strong muscles of the thighs still bunched, as though it had been running—or fighting—when it died. The powerful neck was twisted so that the head stared stiffly to the side, and dried blood fouled the upper plumes. One eye peered into the sun, the orb already shrunken with the dehydration of its tissues. Once-handsome tail feathers were broken off in the dirt.

There had been a desperate battle, and the bird had lost, but the victor had not paused to consume the flesh. This too was strange.

Looking at her—for he recognized the corpse as female as readily as he was coming to identify all the things he saw—Orn felt a vague alarm. He did not conjecture the meaning of his own awakening beside the abandoned nest of this creature, nor did he wonder what had vanquished

6

her. Instead he searched his troubled memory—and found the bird within.

Sixty to eighty million years ago the hot-bodied aves had completed their divergence from their rep ancestry, conserving the produce of their internal furnaces by means of scales lengthened into fluffy down. They lived in tall pines and rocky gullies, where it grew cold at night, and needed continuous warmth in order to stay alert and alive in those windy heights. They spread all four legs with strengthened coverts to add buoyancy, and leaped and glided to safety at the slightest provocation. For some of the predator reps could climb, and all were hungry. The tree-leaper who fell to the ground was dead, and not from the fall.

But soon one line of aves had grown too large to escape through the air, and while its light-boned, light-brained cousins ascended ever higher into the sky and pumped their expanding front wings and let the hind wings shrivel into claws, this nether line planted its hind limbs firmly in the dread earth and discarded flight. Here only the fleet of foot survived at all, and the strong of beak, and the firm of memory. They had to run at times, and fight at times, and to know without hesitation when each was appropriate in the stronghold of the reps.

They succeeded. They were able to forage in colder areas than the reps, and to travel at night. Other land-bound lines diverged.

All this Orn knew, his memory triggered by the need, by the sight of this ultimate bird. She was not a creature of terror to him, but of history, who had come fifty million years along her line to die so brutally before this cave. Orn did not sorrow for her; such was the nature of existence. The weak, the careless, the unlucky—these died and were replaced by others.

He stepped around the body and stood in the sun. A towering pine ascended from the nearby turf, as ancient and grand in its fashion as the bird. The ground was covered with tall ferns, and cycads shook their fronds in the light breeze. Similar plants had dominated the landscape for a very long time, Orn knew. Only recently had

7

others come to contest the land, and those others had not been very successful here.

He scratched the ground experimentally while the rising sun took the chill off the land. His digits were feeble and tender compared to the thick horned toes of the dead bird, but a few tentative scrapes exposed the underlying structure. Beneath the surface leaves and twigs and needles lay a spongy humus teeming with its own awakening life. He put one eye down and concentrated, bringing the miniature landscape into focus.

Here were cricks and roaches and black-shelled beets busily scavenging microscopic debris. Tiny springs, those wingless arths who jumped by flipping forked tails against the ground—these too scrambled for cover, disliking the sun.

Orn knew them. The arths had diverged very long ago, so far back that he had no memory of their early evolution. Somewhere—sometime in that hot sea as he struggled between the freezing darkness and the burning light and satisfied his compelling hunger by growing into an absorbtive cup, a cylinder, a blob with an internal gut, as he extruded fins and nascent flukes and swam erratically after game, and formed eyes to harness the light at last and gills to breathe the water and the lateral line system to navigate by—somewhere during that complex billion-year development that preceded his rise to land the little arths had taken their own mysterious but highly successful course. Now they crawled and flew and fashioned webs and hives and cocoons and burrows and lived their hasty lives in many-legged, many-winged, virtually mindless certainty. . . .

Orn moved on, observing everything but questioning nothing. Timorous hairy mams scooted from his path, afraid of him; these represented innocuous lines. He traveled a shallow valley that led gradually downward toward a body of water. Soft, flat vegetation of the new type crowded the edge of the water and floated on the surface, an increasing amount of it bearing flowers. Small fish, piscs, flashed where a streamlet flowed over naked stone and coursed between round mossy rocks; they

8

were an ancient and multiple line, and now and then one came to kiss the surface of the lake.

Once more Orn remembered: the flowing water was a different medium from the passive depths of the sea, as different in its fashion as air from land. The flaccid flesh of the calm ocean depths had had to develop a stiffened but flexible rod of gristle along its length, lest it be tumbled into danger by the new phenomenon of current. To this gristle the expanding muscle tissue was anchored; progress was no longer random but forward, against the flow. Before his line diverged from that of the piscs, they had invaded the less-habited regions up the current, and changed in the process. The spinal rod protected increasingly important nerves, for coordination had become essential; then the gristle hardened into cartilage and then into bone. The skeleton was the gift of flowing fresh water, and so the land had already affected life in the sea.

But the rivers of the past were fast and shallow, and they flowed from the bleak inhospitable mass of substance that formed the continent, and from time to time the ambitious swimmer was stranded in some stagnant pool. He had to gulp life from the surface, even as these fish in the lake did now, and hold the bubble in his mouth in an effort to absorb from it the breath that had left the water. But his mouth was now encumbered with jaws and teeth and tongue, all needed for feeding. Thus he was forced to develop a special cavity in the throat, a bag, a chamber—a lung. When the water of his isolated pool finally sank to nothing, his fins had to strengthen into four stout limbs to support the body against the gut-wrenching land gravity, and the new lungs sustained life entirely. It was a brief but awful trek, that first journey over the cruel land, and almost every fish who tried it perished; but that fraction who were not only determined and strong but fortunate as well—Orn's own line—won reprieve in a deeper, fresher pool.

Orn remembered the original home: the water. He remembered the gradually lengthening adventures over a land inhabited only by pulpy vegetation and rapidly scrambling arths, until most of his life was spent upon it and he was no longer a true fish. He remembered the

9

hardening of the rind around the soft eggs, until they withstood to some extent the ravages of sun and air. A small step, but significant, for it meant that the sea had let slip its last lingering hold. A complete life cycle could occur without the intervention of the ocean.

By the shore of the lake he found the body of the male bird. This one, too, had perished violently—but unlike his mate, he had taken his enemy with him. A long, powerful rep lay belly-up on the sand, its tail in water, its eyes two bloody sockets, its gut an open cavity. Gore on the beak and talons of the bird betrayed the savagery of its attack, here at the fringe of the rep's demesne; but the scattered feathers and blood on its breast showed that the teeth of the croc had not fastened on empty air.

Had the rep reached water before the bird attacked, the rep would have won the battle easily. But it had not, perhaps because of wounds inflicted by the female bird. Now all three combatants were food for the clustered flies.

The croc: as Orn gazed at it he comprehended the course it had taken since its ancestors branched away from his own, more recently than the fishes. His line had stayed on land in the trees before returning to the ground, climbing and leaping from branch to branch, becoming warm of body, omnivorous of diet, and highly specialized of brain. But the croc had returned part way to the water, hiding behind horny skin, preying on anything that fell in or strayed too near.

This time the croc had ventured too far from its region of strength, perhaps seeking to raid the enormous eggs in the cave nest while one bird was absent, thinking the remaining bird would not fight. . . .

Orn did not attempt to work out the details further in his mind. He was weak and tired and alone, and now ravenously hungry. His heritage of memory finally closed the gap between his evolution and himself, and he understood that there would be no outside help for his distress. He was a member of the most advanced species yet to tread the earth of this world—but he had nothing more to sustain him at the moment than his generalized body and the knowledge within him of the genesis of living things.

10

He did not pause to consider what would have happened had the croc reached the two eggs before the parent birds returned, or the happenstance that the elder egg had been on the verge of hatching the instant the fatal encounter took place. The mother's warmth had been taken away at the critical moment, forcing activity or death for the chick. He did not ponder the coincidence of destiny; he did not contemplate revenge. His mind was designed for far-reaching, comprehensive racial memory rather than true thought. Racial memory was his instrument of survival—a device like none ever employed by another species.

Orn shook out his stubby, still-featherless wings and advanced on the piled meat before him. Flies swarmed up as his beak chopped down. He was hungry, and there was no one to feed him.

II: AQUILON

For two days they orbited: three humans and seven mantas. The shell was tiny for ten occupants, the sanitary facilities embarrassingly unsophisticated and, the food monotonous. But the mantas were siblings who could range leagues or freeze in place for hours without suffering, and the human beings were two men and a woman said to be beautiful. Because the mantas were of fungoid metabolism (though this description was about as precise as "heated protoplasm" might be for the humans), their body processes complemented those of the humans, freshening the air to a certain extent. It was a tidy circumstance, though machine revitalization was still essential for oxygen.

Nevertheless, it was crowded.

By the time the shuttle came to grapple the capsule and haul it in entire for decontamination, the trio had talked out almost everything inconsequential.

The mantas faced each other in a ring, or perhaps a

seven-pointed star, or yet again a hemisphere, depending on how one viewed the topology of the shell's interior. Each gazed for a period of seconds into the eye of his opposite, three pairs engaged at all times, one individual sitting out. Then the pattern would shift for new combinations. What philosophies they contemplated so raptly Aquilon could not guess, but certainly something was being discussed at length. She cursed her female curiosity, but did not attempt to query a manta.

There was a jolt as the capsule was caught by the shuttle and braked. The spin that had provided a kind of gravity stopped, and they all had to cling to handholds to keep from somersaulting in free-fall. The mantas had no hands, but each had a mass approaching fifty pounds in normal gravity; they bounced against the wall and each other like so many huge rubber balls. She almost laughed.

"Prepare for decontamination," the speaker said.

Veg braced himself before the exit port, automatically assuming the lead for what promised to be an unpleasant procedure. Aquilon had been through it before, of course, as had the two men—but familiarity did not bring composure. Decontamination covered a good deal more than the external physique.

Watching Veg, Aquilon smiled, though not with her lips. She was tall for a woman, but Veg dwarfed her. He was as powerful a man as she had ever met, with one exception she preferred not to think about. She peered at his broad back through the mesh of blonde hair waving across her face in the free-fall. Who would normally suspect this two-fisted roughneck of compulsive passion for the well-being of all living creatures? Yet it was so. Only against men did Veg use his muscle, and then by way of demonstration, rather than coercion, except in rare instances.

She removed her gaze, and it fell naturally on the other man. Cal was superficially the opposite of Veg. He was tiny—hardly up to her own shoulder, and thin and weak. But his mind was frighteningly sharp, capable of appalling concepts, and he had the courage of his strange convictions. Cal seemed to fear death not at all; indeed, he seemed almost to worship it.

12

Aquilon loved both men. The physical side of her leaned toward Veg, the intellectual toward Cal. Yet it was Veg's intellectual example she followed now, for she had stopped eating meat, fish, and fowl. She needed something intangible that she had not been able to find or assess, except that it related to them. And both men believed they needed *her*—but the truth, it seemed to her, was that they needed each other, and she was only in the way. They had been good companions before she met them—better than they were now, though neither man spoke of the subtle, insidious change occurring. Could she abscond with Veg's body and Cal's mind? Was she selfish enough to interpose her femininity (more bluntly, her female-ness) between them, drawing to herself the life-preserving dialogue they had for each other?

It would be better if she stepped out of their lives entirely. If only she had the ability to devise a clean exit, and the emotional stamina to follow through. . . .

Now, she thought sadly. Now, during the decontamination. They segregated the sexes for that, thank God, and she could simply request a transfer to some other planet, and she would never see them again, even for a fond farewell. It would break her heart, but she had to do it.

"Cancel," said the speaker, and she jumped guiltily. The port remained sealed. "Your unit is to be transshipped entire. There will be no processing."

Veg looked about, perplexed. "This isn't SOP," he said.

Cal frowned. "That business below may have put us in a special category. One of their agents died—"

"Subble," she said tersely. "Subble died." She had only known the man, really, for four hours, and known him as an enemy. But it was as though a lover was gone.

"And the problem the manta represents is critical. They may have decided not to expose any of the station personnel to—"

"But what about the *Earth* germs?" Aquilon demanded. "Decon is both ways. We don't want to infect Nacre with—"

The communications screen glowed. A face appeared, supported by the lapels and insignia of the Space Police. "Your attention please. Your attention please."

13

"Does he mean us? Does he mean us?" Aquilon inquired mockingly in the same tone. She resented being treated impersonally.

"If they had television, why did they use the speaker all this time?" Veg wanted to know.

Cal smiled. "That's still the speaker. The picture has merely been added. It means we've been switched from voice to film."

"About time, after two days." Veg said, missing the irony.

The face on the screen frowned. "This is a live transmission. I am addressing you three in the capsule. I can hear you."

Veg closed his mouth, embarrassed at having been overheard. Aquilon had to suppress her smile. She almost envied him his essential simplicity.

"Please respond as I call your names," the man said. "Vachel E. Smith."

There was a silence. Aquilon noted Cal struggling similarly to void a smile. Veg did not like his proper name, and seldom answered to it. After the tedious confinement here, he was even less likely than usual to be tractable in the face of authority.

"Vachel E. Smith!" the official repeated impatiently.

"What's *your* name, noodlebrain?" Veg demanded. This time Aquilon did let out a noisy breath, attracting a momentary glance from the interrogator. She felt giddy, as though she were a schoolgirl testing the grouchy teacher. Confinement and near-free-fall could do that, particularly after the horror they had so recently experienced on Earth. They were all acting like gradeschoolers—but she felt like enjoying it while she could. It took her mind off what she would have to do.

The man in the screen brought up a clipboard and made a checkmark. "Deborah D. Hunt?"

Suddenly Aquilon appreciated Veg's ire. She had fallen out of the habit of using her own name since meeting Veg and Cal, and the derogatory nickname imposed on her during a childhood illness had become her badge of honor. She even signed her paintings with it. Now her real

14

name sounded strange and obnoxious, an epithet rather than an identification.

The officer made another check. "Calvin B. Potter?"

"Present," Cal said, not acceding to foolish gestures. "All present. What is your business with us?"

"Wait a minute," Aquilon cried mischievously. "You haven't checked off the others."

"Others?" The officer peered at her.

"The mantas. They're individuals too. As long as you're calling off names by remote control—"

Veg broke into a grin. "Yeah. Everyone gets on the roll. Call 'em off."

"The animals hardly qualify for—"

"I should advise you," Cal said to the screen, "that the mantas do comprehend human speech to a certain extent, even though they may not choose to acknowledge it. Actually, they are somewhat more civilized than we are, but their definitions differ from ours."

"That's *why* they're more civilized," Aquilon said.

The officer maintained his composure, obviously comprehending the ridicule. "I do not have names for the fungoids."

"It's very simple," Aquilon said, hoping her twinkle didn't show. "Each manta is represented by a characteristic symbol rather like a snowflake, no two alike. If you have an oscilloscope handy, they might feed in the patterns—" She hesitated, not wanting to confess how recently the trio had acquired this information. Cal had suspected it for some time, but it had taken Subble to break through and achieve complete communication—by whatever means would be forever a mystery. Now Subble and one manta were dead, but the other mantas demonstrated by their reactions that they understood a good deal of man's vocabulary and custom. The period in the capsule had brought out the eight names and a system for limited dialogue.

"If you will provide the names, I will add them to my roster," the officer said.

"Well, first there's the symbol of the line," she said brightly. "Of course it isn't exactly a line, but to our crude human perception that's the closest—"

15

"The name, please."

"Lin. Lin for Line."

One of the mantas bounced from one side of the capsule to the other, and ricocheted to the communication screen. Its single foot struck the oblong of light squarely.

The officer flinched. "Lin," he said, marking it down.

There was now a faint line across the screen, cut into the plastic by an unseen slash of the manta's whiplike tail. If Aquilon had had any doubt before about the ability of these creatures to understand human dialogue, this dispelled it. Intrigued, she strung out the game.

"Next we have the symbol of the circle, Circe. She's the one who stayed with me, and fed off the rats in the cellar-farm. Of course the mantas are all neuter, technically; only their spores have sex. But since she stayed with me, and *I'm* female—"

"Circe," the officer said, not rising to that particular bait. "The sorceress."

A second manta caromed off the screen. Behind it was left a neat circle. The juxtaposition of symbols made a bisected loop. "*Not* the sorceress," Aquilon said. "The circle, as you see it there." But she wondered whether the man's observation didn't have merit.

"And the triangle, Tri," she continued. The third manta added a triangle, its three points neatly touching the perimeter.

The officer allowed his mouth to fall open momentarily. This was impressive sleight of hand. He was not ready to believe that the mantas themselves were responsible for the geometric markings so accurately inscribed. "Tri," he said.

"And the diamond, Diam." The parallelogram was added to the figure.

Aquilon became serious. "Unfortunately the pentagram, Pent, is not with us. He—died. We don't know exactly how or why, but we think it has something to do with your agent Subble, who is also dead. You dropped a missile on the island and killed some citizens—"

Yes, she thought. The spores of the dead manta were in the atmosphere, threatening to contaminate all Earth and perhaps mutate its tame molds and fungi, harming its

16

food-protein industry. So a Florida resort area had been bombed in the attempt to eradicate those spores. It had not been pretty.

After that she didn't feel like playing the game any more, so Veg took over. "Hex," he said. "He was *my* manta, in the forest. The forest you burned to the ground—"

"I neither originate nor execute landside policy," the officer said primly. "Nor am I informed about it. I'm sure there was good reason for whatever action was taken."

"*Omnivore* reason," Aquilon muttered. The omnivore she meant was man, the most brutal killer known, and the only one who rationalized the misdeeds of his brother by pretending not to be responsible.

"And Star," Veg continued. "One of the six who stayed with Cal. And Oct, the last one."

The screen was now thickly crossed with lines, all geometric figures inscribed within the circle as though constructed by compass and straight edge. The officer's image came through as though he stood behind transparent stained glass.

"I believe I have all the names now," he said. "It is my duty to inform you ten that computer headquarters has recommended that you be assigned to a new mission. You will not be returning to Nacre."

Aquilon exchanged glances with the two men, and the mantas looked at each other. The harried officer was having the last laugh after all!

"In fact, you will not be visiting any of the listed planets, and it is unlikely that you will ever return to Earth. This is not to be considered an exile so much as—"

The voice continued, but Aquilon tuned it out internally, horrified. Banishment, not only from Earth but from all known colonies! So that was their punishment for the trouble the mantas had caused by their presence on Earth. She should have known that the powers that governed the planet would not destroy several billion dollars worth of development and landscape and wipe out a number of innocent lives, and then merely reprimand those who were to be the scapegoats. The trio had broken the law by importing unauthorized alien creatures to Earth, as many

17

travelers did. They had not intended any harm—but this time great harm had come.

No, she could not protest lifetime exile. Worse things were possible. She had wanted desperately to leave Earth again, yet now that her wish was being granted, she felt perversely nostalgic. She did not *like* Earth or feel at ease upon it—but it still was harsh to be denied it for life.

However, that did not really affect her decision to separate from the two men. That had made it impossible for her to go to Nacre anyway.

". . . first habitable alternate, as determined by soil, sea, and air samples," the officer was saying. She had missed something important! "But there are several problems. First, our connection is tenuous. We can ferry any amount of material over, but only when the phase is proper—and that's infrequent. Second, we can not alter the point of contact without risking complete severance, and it could take us a century to re-establish contact if we lost it now."

That didn't sound like ordinary space travel. But he had used the word "alternate." Could this mean—?

"And, unfortunately, this contact occurs under the ground. We have sent in borers to open passages to the surface, but another complication—"

She tried to pay attention, but her mind refused. An alternate world! This was exploration of an entirely different order. But if it were another Earth, why was it the "first habitable"? That implied that there were others unfit for human occupation. What true "Earth" could be unfit, except a devastated one? And even for another Earth, there should be decontamination processing; a virus virulent on one world should thrive on the other, if introduced.

No, she did not like the sound of this.

Cal's silent touch on her thigh jogged her to attention. He was not looking at her, and she would have supposed the contact to be accidental had she not known that nothing Cal ever did was accidental. Particularly not a goose with the thumb. She followed his gaze.

There was a map on the screen—a globe marked off with meridians of longitude and latitude, as though it were

18

the Earth proper. But the continents and great islands were strange; it was obviously a different world.

Cal touched her again. Then she understood. She unobtrusively brought out her pad and brush and quickly sketched the outlines of the map. As she worked, the geography was replaced by the face of the officer, but she held the prior image in her mind and continued to work on the picture, employing the trained short-term eidetic memory that helped make her the artist she was. Cal would have good reason for this subtle directive—reason he did not want the officer to know.

She put the finishing touches on the map as the dialogue continued, then quietly put the pad away. What secrets had Cal read in this seemingly routine illustration? She was now alive with female curiosity. But how would she learn, if she were to part from the two men now? For that matter, how would she deliver the map to Cal? She could not pass it over now without giving away the show.

"Your assignment is to enter this alternate and make casual survey of its flora, fauna, and, as far as practicable, its mineral resources. You'll be supplied from Earth, but there may be danger. You'll be expected to report—"

"Yeah, we know the route," Veg said. "We did it on Nacre, remember?"

The officer bore with this insolence. "Radio relay to the transfer point, where the recording will be brought back at such time as the phase permits, probably within two months. Analogous but not identical to your prior—" He paused. "I have just been informed that an excellent contact has developed in the past few minutes. Perfect phase, but it won't last long. We may have to wait a month for another, so we'll act immediately." He paused again, verifying instructions from an offscreen source. "The port will open. Move at once to the transmission chamber. Good luck."

Once more they exchanged glances. This was too sudden, too convenient; even Veg realized that. They were not being told something. Ordinarily the wheels of Earthly bureaucracy preferred a month to a minute for even a minor decision. Why should—

The port opened.

Before the humans could move, the mantas did. Three of them angled around Veg and launched through the hole, flaring into the flying shape as they emerged into the pressured connecting tube. There were no other spacelocks here; the passage entered the main station directly. The three were out of sight in a moment.

"What?" Veg exclaimed.

Then he piled out after them, determined to find out what they were doing. Cal and Aquilon followed. The four remaining mantas stayed in the shell, motionless.

Shouts and noises sounded ahead. Aquilon pulled herself along by the deep corrugations of the tube, floating after the men. She was surprised the mantas had been able to move so well in free-fall—though she realized, now that she thought about it, that it was air resistance that stabilized them, not gravity. They were like powered kites, perpetually tacking against the wind, except that they were doing the moving, not the air. One pushing foot, one sail—

There was gravity inside the station proper. A guard was rolling on the floor, clutching his hand. Aquilon stopped automatically to help him—and recognized the clean wound of a manta attack. The manta's tail was a deadly weapon, capable of indenting a television screen—or of severing the human hand from its wrist. In this instance the hand had only been cut. She saw the anesthetic gun on the floor and realized that the manta had merely disarmed the man. Few people could fire before a charging manta struck.

But why? Why had those three mantas bolted?

"They were going to ambush us," Veg said angrily, watching the guard. "Kill us out of hand—"

"Ridiculous," Cal snapped. Somewhere down the hall there was a continued commotion, and cries of anguish. "There are innumerable ways they could have dispatched us and the mantas without ever releasing us from the capsule, had they wanted to. Those three mantas provoked this."

"Then why did that bastard have his gun drawn?" Veg demanded. "He never could have reached it if he waited until he saw them."

20

He was right. The guard had to be waiting with the weapon ready, or he would have been struck down with it still in his holster. Or, more likely, not struck at all, since the manta would not have *had* to disarm him. But Cal was right too, for it was a sleep-gun, not a kill-gun.

Then she remembered: no deadly weapons were permitted in a normal orbiting station. The risk to personnel was too great, but that answered only the smallest part of it. The guard could have been instructed to stand by with weapon at the ready, just in case; that did not necessarily constitute aggressive intent. He would have tried to use it when he saw the horror shape of the manta coming at him, however.

She helped the guard to his feet. "Better get over to sick bay, mister. Your hand's laid open to the bone, and that's arterial bleeding. Next time remember: never point a weapon at a manta. They know what guns are, and their reflexes are faster than yours."

Dazed, the man departed. She wondered how it would have turned out had the guard been an agent. Agents' reflexes were super fast, and with the gun already drawn—but the mantas had obviously been ready for trouble. Could there have been such an encounter between Subble and Pent on the defunct island? Had Subble won, then been killed by the others? She really would have to inquire about that.

"I think we'd better get back to the capsule and wait," Cal said. "We weren't ambushed—but we weren't told the truth, either. I'm sure the mantas had reason for moving out like that. Notice how neatly executed it was—three took off, four sat tight."

They returned with alacrity. The four mantas remained, immobile as the fungi they were kin to. Somewhere in the bowels of the station a commotion continued, showing that the three were still on the rampage. The screen in the shell was still lighted, but now no face showed.

Cal faced the mantas. "All right, comrades—what is your purpose? Are we in immediate danger?"

One of the four flexed its tail twice, making a double snap: the signal for "no."

"Maybe they went berserk!" Veg cried. "Being cooped up for so long—"

Three snaps: question mark.

"Berserk," Cal explained, first to recognize the problem. "Going wild, acting unreasonably, making unnecessary trouble. A form of insanity."

Again the tail: no.

"Find out whom we're talking to," Aquilon suggested, wondering how long they would be allowed before station personnel closed in. "And who's left." She was not in the line of sight of the answering manta, but it made no difference. They had no ears, yet picked up human speech and other sounds quite nicely by seeing the compressions and rarefactions of the atmosphere that comprised sound. In effect, they could hear with their eyes—and very well, too.

Four snaps, answering her implied query. "Diam," she said recognizing the code. The four-sided symbol, the diamond.

Another manta moved: two snaps. "Circe," she said. "The two-sided symbol—inside and outside. I'm glad you're still here." It was a foolish sentiment, but it did seem to her that she could tell her erstwhile companion from the others, and that Circe had more personality, more feminine attributes.

A third snapped: six. "Hex," Veg said. "My pal. I knew it was you. You have more savvy than those others."

Personification, she thought.

And at last: seven. "Star."

"That means Lin, Tri, and Oct are gone," Cal said. "But we still don't know why. We weren't in physical danger—none that we weren't in all along, at least. They must have had a reason, just as the station personnel had one for rushing us. I think we'd better discover what that reason is. I wish we'd taught them Morse code."

"The mantas only learn what they choose to learn," Aquilon said. "We're lucky they communicate at all. They never did before."

"Your attention, please." It was the officer on the screen again. "There has been a disturbance."

"Now he tells us," Veg muttered.

22

"Your beasts attacked station personnel. We had understood they were tame."

"That's why you had guns on 'em," Veg said sarcastically. "Real brave."

"How can civilized individuals be 'tame'?" Aquilon demanded in her turn. "Do you have tame men, tame computers?" But she wondered. She *had* thought there had been an understanding with the mantas, and this breach of manners didn't jibe. Why had they done it?

"What happened to the three?" Cal asked, more practical.

"One is dead. The men cornered it with bayonets and stabbed it through the eye. The others—"

Aquilon flinched, knowing how terrible a wound of that type was to a manta. The eye constituted the substantial majority of its apperceptive mass; a blind manta was virtually a dead manta, except for the suffering.

"How many men dead?" Cal inquired softly.

"No fatalities. Our men are trained for trouble. Several lesser casualties, however—mostly cuts on the hands."

Thank God, she thought. The mantas weren't on a killing spree. They were merely trying to avoid capture. But again: why?

"We're in a hurry," the officer said. "Ordinarily there would be severe repercussions—but the phase is beginning to slip. Can you keep your remaining animals under control?"

"Yes," Cal said before anyone else could comment. Aquilon understood, then. The station personnel still thought the mantas were merely pets—dangerous when out of control, but basically subject to man's will. The demonstration of the manta's geometric ability had been deemed a stunt, no more. If these people realized the truth, after what had just happened—

And she had been trying to blab it out! She could have cost the lives of all the mantas!

That made one more reason to separate from this group, to go her own lonely way. They would survive better without her.

But Veg was hustling her along, and this time the

mantas followed docilely behind. They had made their move, whatever it was. She was unable to make hers.

She felt a terrible relief.

III: ORN

It was an island he dwelt on. Orn's explorations had long since verified that no exit from it existed for him, since he could not fly and did not care to swim. But his memory informed him that this bit of land, which he could cross many times in the course of a single day without fatigue, was not the total of the world. He was able to appreciate its recent history to a certain extent because there were evidences of many prior nestings of his species, and his memory suggested that land had been here several million years ago. Spot details, such as the cave he had hatched within, were too transitory to register; but the body of rock itself was stable enough to be familiar.

Orn's ancestors had ranged the entire continent, mapping its shifting configurations in the memory of fifty million years. Orn saw portions of the whole whenever he contemplated the local landscape. He was aware that this island was a tiny fringe of the great land mass, a part of it really, despite the gulf of sea cutting between them. The island rode the continent's western perimeter. He was aware too that the continent itself was moving, and had already traveled many times the breadth of the island, though slowly. Ponderous upheavals had split the original continent apart, fragmenting it. Though changing bridges of rock connected the new subcontinents, the last of these had severed hardly ten million years ago, isolating an entire ecological population. The influx of new species of animal from far regions had halted, ranging grounds had become comparatively restricted, and the increasing violence of the geography had led to the decline of certain established creatures and the sudden rise of others. The great reps had largely vacated the cool northern regions and the mountainous terrain, though they still predominated in the southern marshes. The tiny mams had overrun those deserted areas and, more importantly the orders of aves had flourished. A new balance of nature had occurred.

Orn's memory faded out for the most recent period. It required many generations for the racial record to become firmly established, so that he was clearest on the situation of five to twenty million years before. Prior to that period his memory became more general, being specific only in relation to his own line. Even much of that had faded as he grew farther away from the egg; he no longer remembered the impressions of swimming or conquering the land.

Some recent images were clear but uncertain, others foggy, and some so transient as to be meaningless. Had his parents lived, they would have educated him to the specifics of contemporary existence; memory was less important than example for day-to-day life. Lower creatures like the arths made do entirely on memory—but this would not do for himself. His own experiences would be added to that mass of memory already inscribed within his genes, strengthening some images infinitesimally and weakening others that were no longer applicable. His descendents would benefit accordingly.

The western section of this traveling subcontinent had buckled as it moved, tripping over the sea floor it overrode in its geologically precipitous traverse. An expansive shallow interior sea arm had drained away as the land wrinkled into a tremendous mountain range instead. Thus one natural barrier had been replaced by another, and the range was still rising as Orn's memory faded out. The flora had changed rapidly here; flowering plants had spread explosively over the highlands, leaving the old varieties to the warmer lowland coastlines.

Orn knew the geologic history of his present island mainly by extrapolation from precedent. This was a volcanic framework. It had risen out of the sea as the residue of frequent emissions of liquid stone and airborne ash. From a single cone it had grown to three, all feeding on that same restlessness inspired by the larger motion of the continent much as thunderstorms fed on the motions of

25

large air masses. Though two cones had subsided, the third and smallest still erupted periodically over the centuries. Orn had seen the traces of its erstwhile furies, recognizing the typical configurations though the vegetation now covered them richly. It was from its subterranean furnace that the heat had come to make the island pleasant; Orn's memory implied that the surrounding geography grew distressingly cold in winter—too cold for his kind to nest.

It was summer now, better than a year after his rude awakening here. Orn had grown to better than half the mass of the avian parents he had never known in life, whose rotting flesh had sustained him those first difficult days after hatching. They had done that for him, at least: given him food when he was too small to hunt effectively himself. Now his feathers had filled out comfortably, white around the neck and handsome gray on the breast, and his wings and tail were sturdy. He could twist his neck to reach any part of his body, and his beak was a respectable weapon. His thighs were well muscled for running, and his flesh well toned. He had grown up strong and fleet and smart; had it been otherwise, he would not have grown up at all, even in this protected locale.

He was aware that most birds of his type had parental care in the chick state, and were sheltered from the savagery of climate and predators. He had suffered, at first. But he was also aware that his particular parents had chosen their nesting site well; few really dangerous animals lived here. The croc that brought tragedy had come wandering from another isle, a loner, and with its demise the area had been rendered safe again. Occasionally Orn had seen another such croc swim by, but had hidden and it had not noticed him. Yes—his parents, by their sacrifice, had made it possible for him to survive even without their immediate care. They had been resourceful birds.

Once, he knew by the traces, many couples had nested here, and many eggs had hatched. Now he was alone; somehow his species had declined over the millennia along with the reps. Oh, there were birds on the island—more lines than ever before—but none of his own species. He did not wonder why the same circumstance that encouraged a general avian radiation simultaneously discouraged his particular line; he merely knew it was so. He did feel a general loss, a loneliness, and was from time to time disturbed by it.

Now, as he grew into his second year, he became aware of a more immediate problem. The island underpinning was building up to one of its periodic eruptions. He could feel the ground shuddering and swelling, and he could see and smell the increasing gases emerging from the active cone. He read the multiple signals: danger.

The other creatures were aware of it too, but largely helpless. Fish floated belly-up in ponds grown hot; tiny, warmbodied multis scrambled by day in the open, driven from their caved-in burrows. Birds hovered in the sky, afraid to perch for long on uncannily vibrating branches.

The aves at least could fly; Orn could not. Had he thought in those terms, he might have envied his distant cousins their ability to depart so readily. But he knew that physical escape was only part of it; their home was being destroyed as much as his own was. He paced the shore facing the mainland, peering at the mountainous vista so near by air, so far by water. He was not an efficient swimmer, and the sea had its own threats.

Yet even the mainland was restive. Dark clouds drifted above the mountains as other great cones vented their fury. There were tremors not of the island alone, but of the area, and the tide was off schedule.

He had to remove himself from this locale. He would not have chosen to travel in a half-grown state, but survival required it. He had to get across the water and away from the shore, and soon. But how?

Any decision he might have made became irrelevant. The crisis was on him even as he balked at the water.

A tremendous quake shook the island, making the ocean dance and the trees splinter and tumble. The ground lifted, dropped, and lifted again, throwing him violently to the side. As he scrambled back from the beach large cracks opened in the ground, grinding against each other noisily and spewing up gravel and mud. The sea pulled back momentarily, as though afraid; then it rushed at the beach in mighty waves, smashing into the

27

rocks and foliage there and foaming well beyond the normal high-tide limit. The water was brown, and where it passed a coating of mud and debris remained.

Then it was very quiet, but Orn knew that the island was doomed. His ancestors had tended to nest in similar places, and had met this situation before, and the warnings in his memory were lucid. He had to flee it, for there was no memory of those who had not done so; none of those had become his ancestor.

That memory also guided his course of action. He ran to the single river that wound down from the oldest and largest mountain and gathered token tributaries to itself. There should be trees in it now—floating trunks toppled by the quake and wrestled about by the current. He might board one there, where he could reach it, and ride it into the sea. With that extra mass and buoyancy he might achieve the crossing he could not hope to accomplish alone.

His trip was wasted. The river had been dammed by a mass of rock, and was already backing up into what would develop into a small lake. There were floating logs—but on the wrong side of that barrier.

Again the ground shook, less violently but more persistently than the last time. Before the vibration subsided there was a subterranean *snap*! followed by a different and, to Orn, more ominous type of rumbling.

Alarmed, he looked up at the tremendous elder mountain. His fear was justified: yellowish gas was rising from its weathered cone. The fire mountains never really died.

Even as he looked, a vent opened in the side of the cone and a monstrous belch of vapor emerged. It formed a bulging cloud, completely opaque, that gathered, swelled, and *rolled* down the incline toward the river. Behind it was conflagration: a swath of blistered rock, shorn of its former veneer of life.

The cloud was large—he could see the top of it even as it dipped into the gully of the river several miles upstream. He heard the hiss of boiling water, and in a moment saw the cloud expand enormously as water vapor distended it.

The mountain trembled again, roused into action by the

initial quake and now finished with the preliminaries. From the vent in its side poured a golden syrup, splashing down the smoking channel left by the cloud. Where it spread to touch the fringe of vegetation, flames erupted and smoke gouted up. The lava, like the gas, obliterated everything in its path except the ground itself.

Orn knew about this also. Perhaps the scarching molten rock would solidify and stop before reaching the sea, but probably more would come, overriding the first mass as it cooled, until the entire island lay buried beneath it and all life was gone.

Fire now raged through the forest, charging the air with its odors. Minor tremors continued. Tiny animals fled the forest and milled on the beach, doomed.

Orn waded into the water, knowing he could not afford to wait longer. There was a chance that the ocean predators would be frightened or confused by the shocks, or even stunned, so that he could swim across with no more than the water to contend with. A chance—but he entertained no unrealistic hopes.

The water appeared calm from a distance, but this was illusory. The surface had been churned into ugly foam. Hidden objects banged into his feet and chafed his legs, and the violent currents beneath the froth tugged strenuously at his balance. He flapped his wings, fouling them in the dirty spray, and held his beak high—but for nothing. He was soon swept off his feet and dunked in the grainy liquid.

He swam, using his legs as ballast and rudder, while paddling messily with his wings. Aquatic birds had webbed feet, but his own were clawed and virtually useless for propulsion in the water. Everything was wrong for him; he was poorly structured for swimming and had to hold his head low lest he capsize. That interfered with visibility. His nictitating membranes protected his eyes from the salt spume, but the constant dousing inhibited his breathing. He was not enjoying himself.

Storm clouds gathered overhead and wind whipped savagely across the surface. Orn rode the growing swells, up and down, up and down, fighting for equilibrium and orientation. The gusts of air were warm, not cool, and carried the stifling fumes of the volcano. Substance descended from the storm above—not rain but particles of rock-ash that chipped away at his feathers and smeared his plumage dark. Only his acute sense of direction kept him facing the invisible mainland.

Then his feet banged into something solid. For a moment he thought he had made it across, but his vector sense reminded him that this was impossible. But he was also far from the island. A sand bar must have developed since the crossings of his ancestors, for there was no hint of shallow water here in his memory. Full grown, the prior crossers had been more powerful swimmers and had made competent surveys of the local geography; there was a firm image of deep water here. The contours of the land and island had changed, fuzzing their images, but the depth of the water had been stable.

He stood, and the ocean fell away around him while the windborne fragments pelted down. A ridge of land ascended from the waves, mottled with fragments of seaweed.

No—this was no sand bar, though the bottom was not as deep as it had been at one time. Instead, the water was receding, laying bare the ocean floor.

He could walk to the other side, but he realized that the chances for his survival had just dropped again. To the earthquakes and volcanos had been added a third threat.

He trod upon an old-time coral reef, the shells now largely broken and compacted. Great sponges branched out of the crevices, and jellyfish lay sprawled helplessly. Most of the true fish had escaped with the water, but a few were wedged fatally in barnacle-encrusted declivities. Crabs scrambled frantically, their claws suddenly dead weights, and a starfish that had folded about a clam now found itself prey to circumstance.

This was a world less familiar to Orn, and despite the danger—or perhaps because he had given up hope of living when he realized what the dropping of the sea meant—he contemplated it avidly. There were many marine plants he had seldom tasted, even in memory, so many exotic forms of life. Many of them had changed little since his ancestral line left the water; others were quite

30

new. He had so little time to live; he wanted to learn as much as he could before he lost the opportunity forever.

He had been picking his way along, and had made incidental progress toward the shore while he observed all this. Now he began to give way to his reflexes, despite the uselessness of this. Behind him it was coming, as he had known it would: a massive swell of water traveling better than ten times his own maximum running speed. Around his feet the level was rising, seeping in quietly. But the major wave was another matter.

The wave would crush him; there was no way he could get out of its range in time, nor had there been since the water dropped. But the blind instinct for survival swept through his body at that sight, and he had to yield to it. He flapped his wings and stretched his neck forward, putting all his strength into the sprint, running over the ragged coral without regard for his feet. He could hear it now, as the giant wave tripped over the shallow island shelf, looming higher and higher. It had exchanged forward momentum for elevation, but still closed the gap rapidly.

That slowing of pace as it gained height had not been clear in his memory. He had more time than he had supposed, though still not enough. He kept running.

Suddenly the mainland beach was there, and he was scrambling across it. He charged into the brush, leaping over what he could and tunneling through the rest, heedless of the plumage torn out in the process. It was growing dark; the shadow of the wave was enveloping him. The breeze was suddenly chill—and it moved *toward* the water.

Still he ran, over rocks, around trees, up and away from the shore. He had expected the leaning wall of water to fall on him before this, ending everything, but that doom hovered, hovered.

And fell. It struck so abruptly that he wasn't aware of it until he found himself caught up and hurled forward, completely inundated and helpless. It was as though he were drowning in a fierce ocean current—but as he was whirled about, he saw a landscape in the sky, falling sideways.

Then he was sinking through increasingly tenuous foam, losing support yet not really falling. He flapped his wings and felt froth splashing against them. His rump landed hard, and he clutched at foliage with his beak, afraid of being sucked back out to sea though the alternative was to be dashed against the ground and crushed.

But he had already landed, and was no longer moving. Somehow he had survived the blast, through no doing of his own.

The water continued to subside, leaving him on a green island. He was dizzy but whole—and on the mainland! He looked about.

He was perched on the stout upper foliage of a broken-topped fir, six times his own height above the ground.

IV: VEG

They were in a cavern—not a natural one. Solid rock had been melted to form an irregular chamber, in whose wall was set the receiving focus. Below that entrance were scattered boxes of supplies, as though they had simply been dumped without supervision.

Just the way the seven of them had been, Veg thought. It was a pretty unimpressive way to begin a mission.

"No receiver, since this is what might be termed a probability shift," Cal observed. He seemed to have worked it all out already. He always knew the score before the game got started. "The effect would resemble that of a spurting firehose: it can affect the volume in front of the nozzle, but not very much behind it. They must have fired a heat-beam through and melted out a cylindrical cavity. Then supplies, never risking any men...."

The mantas were already spreading out. One had found a drill hole projecting straight up, and was shining its eye into it; another poked into a dark horizontal recess.

"But where did all the stone go?" Aquilon asked. "Solid or melted, it can't just disappear."

"Not if they reverse the flow and suck it out through the aperture—or rather, let its own gaseous pressure drive it through. A ticklish operation, but feasible, it would seem."

Veg followed the manta—Hex, he was sure—beyond the tumble of supplies, his flash beam flicking about. A yard-high tube curved away into darkness. "No sense sitting around until our air runs out," he called back.

Aquilon joined him, seeming to agree. They were committed; it was pointless to procrastinate. A new adventure beckoned.

"That would be the corkscrew leading to the surface," Cal said. "The small vertical shaft would have been intended to provide air, but of course that failed. I imagine they used it to fire up the observation rocket instead, then let it seal over again. There's a fair amount of work ahead before we leave this region."

Veg moved along, knowing Cal was probably right, but disinclined to dawdle while the tunnel lay unexplored. He did not suffer from claustrophobia, but did prefer open range when available. He slung the flash around his neck and proceeded on hands and knees. He could hear Aquilon following, and wished he had a pretext to glance back at her in that position. She was a well-structured woman.

The passage curved steadily to the left. He soon lost his orientation, retaining only the nebulous impression that he had navigated at least one complete circle. His knees were chafed; there was not room to go on hands and feet. But with Aquilon behind (and not complaining about *her* knees), he could not hesitate. Hex had long since disappeared ahead, managing to travel nicely in the confined tube.

The loops were interminable. The officer, noodlebrain, had said something about using a borer to cut through the rock, but he hadn't hinted at the distance! Veg was beginning to feel constrained.

At last he came up to the manta Hex, who was humped before a metal barrier. This was a plug that filled the tunnel almost completely, rimmed by a rubberlike flashing that squeezed tight against the circular wall. In the center of the plug was a dial and knob resembling the face of a combination lock. That was all.

"What's the matter, slowpoke?" Aquilon inquired. It meant nothing negative and nothing positive, but he felt a certain happy tension whenever she addressed him, especially with a friendly teasing comment like this.

"Can't get around Hex," he said, straightening so that there was room for her to squirm up beside him. She did, moving lithely—but the process still entailed a certain amount of contortion and physical abrasion. As if anything as rounded and resiliant as Aquilon's torso could abrade in any but an esthetic sense. Esthetic? Least of all that!

"That's not Hex," she said. "That's Circe."

What a woman she was! Since he had met her, Veg had lost interest in the fleshy shells that masqueraded as human femininity. He had not realized how deeply Aquilon affected him until they had parted, after Nacre. On Nacre, home planet of the mantas, he had bantered with her in the midst of mystery and danger, thinking it no more than a passing fancy; but back on Earth when the trio split up in order to protect the growing mantas—

"Wake up, vegetable," she said, snapping her fingers under his nose. Even those were slender and shapely. "I said you had the wrong manta."

"You're crazy," he mumbled, embarrassed at the chain of thought her nearness had started. Yet what other thoughts were possible when she was this close?

"And you claimed you knew your own manta!" She dismissed the matter as though it were settled (as probably it was; he hadn't identified the manta that surely) and peered ahead. "Must be an air-lock." Her lovely face with its tangled blonde hair was so close to his that her breath caressed his cheek. The skin stretched over the delicate curve of her chin, close enough to kiss. She lay on her left side, he on his right.

Dolt that he was, he hadn't realized how strongly he felt about her until that government agent, Subble, had tricked him into the admission, after beating him in fair fight. . . .

"There must be some way to open it," she continued, oblivious to his turbulent yearnings. "Is that a combination lock?"

"Maybe." There had been no element of flirtation in her contact. She was unaware of the electrifying effect of a perfect breast as it touched a man, even sheathed as hers was by layers of clothing. Once it had seemed that she returned his developing interest, but obviously that had passed. She did not need to say a thing; her indifference to his maleness was manifest in so many little ways. He was a friend, not a man friend.

"Let me try it." She brought her right arm up, threading it between them and reached for the dial. As she twisted, Veg was treated to a scenic view of her right breast flexing under the coverall in response to the motion of her arm.

A woman with a mind, yes. But not one of the pinched genius types. He had regarded the gender with a certain veiled contempt in earlier years, to be appreciated in purely physical fashion—until he discovered in Aquilon what a woman could be. A *complete* woman. She had said she did not eat meat any more. . . .

Yet of course he had little to offer a real woman. He appreciated intellect without being intellectual himself, much as a working man appreciated wealth without possessing it. And no windfall income could rectify *that*.

There was a click, and Circe moved aside somewhat. "I've got it," Aquilon exclaimed. "It's not really a combination, just a kind of safety catch. I'll have it open in a moment."

Her eyes, as she peered up, were gray-blue; her lips, as she talked, compelling. "Moment," she had said—that word like two kisses strung together.

"Careful." It was Cal, behind them, startling them both. "Remember, we're under water."

Aquilon's hand froze on the knob. "Water!" she exclaimed, as though she hadn't known.

"That's right, I forgot!" Veg said, taken aback. He imagined a torrent of salty liquid smashing in, washing them down the tube as though it were a drainpipe, swirling them in among the boxes of supplies like so many

35

drowned rats. What would they do without Cal's innate caution?

"That would be the borer," Cal said, shining his own light between them. Grotesque shadows blotted out most of the beam. "Probably it is watertight, and of course we'll use it as an exit-lock, once we have our diving suits on. But it would be wise to verify—"

"The borer?" Aquilon asked.

"My dear, I fear you were not paying proper attention to that attendant's lecture," Cal said reprovingly, and her fair skin colored slightly in the angled beam. Veg saw it then: if she had real interest in either man, it was Cal. Cal, with his brain, was the trouble. A woman without a mind looked for a strong man or a handsome one; a woman *with* a mind looked for an intelligent man. The kind of woman Veg could appreciate was also the kind who would naturally prefer Cal. Cal was only small and weak when you looked at him, never when you listened to him.

The borer, as Cal explained for Aquilon's benefit (and for Veg's too—he had not paid proper attention to Noodlebrain's lecture either), was a tractorlike device with a diamond-surfaced bit that ground into rock and pulverized it. The dust and chunks were blown back down through the tube for disposal. In this instance the borer had been stopped the moment its nose projected into the water, so as not to flood the passage. It could be entered by reopening the sealed exhaust section, and also by the service gate set into its side. The dial in its rear would indicate internal pressure and the proper setting would activate the water pump and evacuate the interior as required.

In the end Veg had to back away so Cal could pass him and Aquilon and Circe and come up to manipulate the control. Veg felt as though he had been demoted—but it was good that *someone* here knew what he was doing! The thought of all that sea water pouring in—

"Clear," Cal announced. He clicked the dial. "Should come open now—"

It didn't. Cal manipulated the knob again, puzzled, but still nothing happened.

36

"Must be jammed," Veg said. "Want me to—?"

"There's no handhold," Aquilon pointed out. "No way to yank. Unless the dial can be—"

She was right. He remembered the featureless wall of metal. And obviously it would be unwise to tug too hard at the knob. He pictured delicate wiring tearing, tumblers jamming, so that the group was sealed in permanently behind a ruined mechanism. A fine report to take back to Earth: "Sorry—the door was stuck!"

But if the connection to Earth was out of phase, or whatever that problem was, they could stay cooped up in the worm-bore for weeks or months. How much canned air did they have?

"I'm afraid Veg is right," Cal said after another fruitless minute. "It is jammed. It should open but it doesn't."

"We could try it again in a few hours," Aquilon said without enthusiasm.

"And let it rust even worse?" Veg demanded. He put one large hand on Aquilon's slim ankle and tugged gently. "Back off, both of you. And Circe too. I'll get it open!"

The others allowed themselves to be bullied away from the barrier, and Veg came up. Circe retreated a little, so that he had an entire segment of the tunnel to himself. He braced, brought back his arm, and slammed his fist sidewise into the panel beside the dial.

It was that simple. The metal gave. Opposite the dial a semicircular section swung out, spraying flecks of dirt into his face, and cold water gushed forth.

"Oops!" Aquilon exclaimed as she got soaked.

But it was only the token backlash of inanimate perversity. Veg had won the round and the way was open. He blinked his eyes clear and caught the panel. It rotated around a vertical column, the dial set in its center, leaving a vent about a foot wide on either side. Wires trailed from the backside into the body of the borer.

"I must admit you have your uses," Cal said, coming up. "Now this should slide out—"

The borer chamber was about eight feet long, with a bank of dials on the far wall. Beyond it, Cal explained, was the motor, and beyond that the drill itself—now projecting harmlessly into the water. Along the sides of the compartment were indentations for the caterpillar housings, making the available space quite narrow.

"We'll have to haul our supplies to this point, then ferry them through the lock," Cal said. "The outside man will have to wear a diving suit. According to soundings and the record of the photographic rocket, we're only two hundred feet below the surface of the water, so it shouldn't be too difficult. Still, it might be wise to climb to the top and take a sighting, before we commit ourselves too far."

"Climb?" Aquilon inquired from behind the manta. "Don't you mean *swim* to the top?"

"Swimming would be risky until we know more about the local currents," Cal explained. "And the suits are weighted. We'll send up a balloon and climb the ladder that anchors it to the borer. If we spot land, we'll *walk* to it—across the bottom."

Aquilon was silent, and Veg appreciated the reason. On Nacre, Cal had been near death, and the other two had assumed the leadership and organized the trek from the wreck of their vehicle back to the camp. Now Cal was healthy, and it was evident that he was the natural leader of this trio. It simply took some getting used to.

There was a winch in the borer, powered electrically with cartridge capacitors. They removed it and got organized on an assembly-line basis. Cal connected the line to objects in the proper sequence, Aquilon ran the winch from a location just below the borer, and Veg was outside man. The line was actually doubled, passing through a pulley at the base of the tunnel so that it was not necessary to reset it by hand after each haul. But because of the narrowness and curvature of the passage, they had decided to run only one load at a time; a break or jam would be awkward to fix otherwise.

The diving suit was rather like a space suit, but built to resist pressure at key points rather than to contain it. It was quite heavy. He got it on, then had to squeeze himself into an uncomfortable knot inside the borer and push closed the panel. It sealed into place as Aquilon worked the knob control. Then water began to flow in through a vent in the floor. It entered with some force, splashing against him and collecting in a puddle beneath, as though

38

he were lying in a filling bathtub. As the water rose up around his faceplate he began to feel that claustrophobia he thought he didn't suffer from. He knew he couldn't drown in the sealed suit, but the suggestion was powerful. He couldn't move, he couldn't escape; he had to lie here and let the liquid claim him! One leak. . . .

Once the chamber was full the effect vanished. It was the sight of the advancing water line that did it, he decided. Now he was floating and felt comfortable.

He tried the side port. At first it wouldn't open, and he realized that the pressure hadn't equalized yet. He tried again after a short wait, and it yielded readily. It swung out, a blister of metal, and he peered into the darkness beyond.

He activated the suit's helmet light and looked again. The beam struck through cloudy water and faded in the distance. Like foggy Nacre, he thought; and this must be what the manta's vision was like: just a tunnel of light in the opacity. A manta could not see anything that wasn't directly in front of its eye. But it certainly saw everything that *was* in front. Even sound waves. . . .

He pried himself out of the borer, feeling like old-time toothpaste inching from the tube. The borer manufacturer had not had a man of his dimensions in mind!

At last he stood beside the borer. The suit seemed light now, and he was glad for the weights that kept him gently anchored. He knew that without that ballast he would be borne helplessly to the surface by the buoyancy of the air encasing him in the suit. And without that shield of air he would be pretty cold in this water, not to mention squashed and suffocated. He had to admit that things had been pretty well planned.

He looked about. Cal had been right about the position of the borer: its gleaming blades projected into the water, reflecting the beam of his helmet in a spray of light. How much diamond had gone to coat that massive screw?

Beyond the borer was the floor of the ocean. He was surprised to discover that it was not level here, but hilly; somehow he had visualized the depths as similar to the surface—flat with small waves. The borer projected from a steeply slanting face of rock. Had the slant been the other way, the machine would have had to grind a long way farther before emerging. He saw some small fish, but could not identify their type; certainly they were not like the ones he knew. All in all, the unfamiliar detail made him uneasy; he expected oddities on some far planet, but here in the water he had no proper emotional framework.

He was startled by a knocking from within the borer. Three taps: their joint human-manta code for question. Aquilon wanted to know how he was doing.

He tapped back once, affirmatively, and pushed closed the port. He heard the click as it locked in place. The evacuation pump started up, and he saw the seaweedlike growths wave as the water was spouted out of the bottom aperture.

In a few minutes bubbles emerged, the current stopped, and assorted rumblings emanated from the interior of the unit. Then there came a banging, not a signal; Aquilon was pounding on the panel, trying to open it.

In a sudden mental illumination he understood the problem: the air forced into the chamber to evacuate the sea water had to be under high pressure. Once the water was out, that pressure remained; it had nowhere to go. And the bulkhead to the tunnel was designed to open only when the pressures were equalized, in and out, to prevent leakage.

There should be a valve to release the surplus pressure within the chamber, once the water was out. Probably it had gotten plugged. He had pounded open the panel by sheer force, but Aquilon did not have his strength.

Here he was with both the muscle and the insight— where neither could be applied to the problem. How were they going to get the supplies through?

A large, sleek fish nosed up to him. Veg cast about for some weapon, but had none. Anyway, he had no idea whether this creature was dangerous. It must weigh more than he did—or *would* weigh more, out of the water. What would he do if it attacked?

It did not attack. It merely continued to snuff him and the borer as though curious. He wished he could identify it, in case it were a shark. But he didn't want to be on the defensive if it turned out to be some entirely innocuous or even friendly prowler.

There was a deeper *thunk!* and under his hand the metal shook. The fist jerked back, alarmed. What had happened? He tried to pry open the port, but it was tight, as of course it would be. Whatever had happened inside—had happened. There was nothing he could do.

"What's your opinion, Sam?" he asked the fish. He doubted that any sound left his helmet, however.

Then bubbles shot up from the top pipe, and he knew that it was all right. The water cycle was starting over.

This was too much for Sam, however. The big fish coursed away into the obscurity of the surrounding ocean.

Before long the bubbles stopped. He tried the port again, and it opened. He aimed his light within. There was a cylinder, a roll of nylon-cord ladder, and a balled balloon. He took them out, wondering how Aquilon had gotten around the pressure problem.

He tied one end of the cord to the borer, looping it around just below the bubble chimney. He threaded the other end through a gross needle eye in the base of the balloon and knotted it tight. Finally he hooked the nozzle of the tank into the balloon and fastened it in place. He turned the tank's cock.

Helium gas whistled coldly into the balloon. The ball unrolled as though it were a Halloween toy and inflated into a yard-long tongue, then became a long gourd, then a watermelon. It began to lift the tank, hauling up on the nozzle.

Hastily Veg flung another loop of the ladder around the borer and clung to it. The balloon dragged the tank up to the limit of its play, twelve feet above the borer, and held it there.

Stupid! He had forgotten that the thing would rise as soon as it was inflated, and he had made no preparations. As though a ball of helium, light enough to lift a dirigible in air, would sit still under water. . . .

Expansion leveled off when the balloon was about a yard in diameter. Veg climbed up the ladder, now taut, and tied off the sphere, letting the tank drift down. He watched the flow of bubbles from the borer's chimney go by within a foot of him. Then he descended to the floor and wrestled with the segment of ladder he had tide to the borer. It was too rigid to move.

Meanwhile the next cycle had been completed. He gave up on the ladder and opened the port.

A head poked out, followed by a body that was feminine even through the crude folds of the suit. Aquilon had joined him.

She glanced around, shining her headlight, entranced as he had been by the scene. Then she saw the tangled ladder.

She could have spoken to him by touching her helmet to his—or maybe even directly through the water, since this was *not* a vacuum between them—but did not, to his relief. His stupidity was obvious. He'd had no idea the pull would be so strong with such a small balloon.

Together they worked the ladder over the body of the borer, seeking to pass it off the end. Suddenly Aquilon stopped, pointing to the diamond-edged drill. Of course! Friction against that could sever the rope, or at least damage it and make it unsafe.

Aquilon tried another ploy. She picked up the slack length of the ladder between the first and second loops and began pushing it under the borer. Veg saw what she was doing and assisted. The idea was to carry the slack around the borer, so that the second loop would in effect be brought adjacent to the first, allowing all the intervening ladder to ascend to the surface. The cord was very fine, and there appeared to be well over two hundred feet of it—more than enough.

They bunched it up and shoved—and abruptly the whole length of it was rasping through, and the balloon was rising out of sight. They stood back and watched it. Veg appreciated how narrowly they had missed making another mistake: had a hand been caught when the rope let go—

The motion stopped, and there was slack at last in the main line. Quickly they re-anchored it so that the ladder was vertical and firm; then Veg began to climb. Belatedly he realized that he could have had a free ride up, had he clung to a rising rung. Now he had the easy but tedious job of mounting it step by step.

By step. He lost count of the rungs somewhere between sixty and eighty, not certain whether he had skipped seventy or repeated it. The water around him was featureless; even Sam the fish would have been welcome company. Was he really ascending, or just working a treadmill through nothing?

At last he reached the top. The balloon floated amid a choppy sea, and white clouds decorated the blue sky spreading overhead.

He looked out over the waves, standing with his feet hooked into the top rung of the ladder and his arm about the bobbing balloon. He saw—more waves.

He craned his head about.

Behind him, perhaps within a mile, perhaps much less, was a mountain.

Veg smiled, let go the balloon, and drifted down toward the floor of the ocean, mission accomplished.

V: ORN

It was a strange world he ranged. The familiar palms and cycads were rare, their places taken by burgeoning flat-leaved, flowering trees and bushes. He knew these newer plants, but here they thrived in unprecedented profusion, dominating the landscape rather than occupying their occasional nooks, and that was hard to accept readily. His reflexes were wrong for this, his expectations constantly in error, and that upset him. The mighty firs still stood in thick forests—but these forests were smaller than they had been. Ferns were still common, but stunted; if their form was little changed from those of his twenty-million-year memory, this was small comfort.

Orn did not speculate on the meaning of these changes.

He was concerned with what had been and what existed now, not with what it might portend. Every object he saw evoked its peculiar history, clear with the vision of countless generations of his observant forebears. Change was in fact uncomfortable for him—but he had been forced by his orphan status and the pressure of invincible events to adapt more readily than had his ancestors. Perhaps his very isolation had facilitated his survival, for had he been trained in the usual fashion by careful parents he might not have had the initiative to escape the island when that became necessary.

He was familiar with the mainland as it had existed many millions of years before, and was hungry for fresh information. But this normally would have meant slight changes in geography, flora and fauna, instead of the catastrophic alterations in all three he actually discovered. These flowering plants—never had anything leaped into prominence so explosively before.

Orn was hungry physically, too. His appetite was unspecialized, omnivorous. Leaves, fruits, mams, arths, occasional gulps of water, pebbles to aid digestion—whatever had food value could be his meal, provided it was not poisonous. But he lacked the imagination to search actively for specific meals. He ate whatever was available.

He scratched away the dried, mottled leaves beneath his feet. His two front toes had long sharp claws, while the rear toes that bore much of his weight were stubby and solid, the claws more like hoofs.

Yes—the little arths were there, just as they had been on the island. The land had changed; the soil had not. Some flying aves fed exclusively on the tasty arths, and so could he if he could only find enough. But these vanished even as he uncovered them. He required more substantial food for his travels. And he had to travel, for he knew that the lull in the volcanic activity was temporary.

Orn's beak was not adapted to snare the fast scrambling creatures, but he scratched again and ran out the sticky tip of his tongue to spear several before they found cover. They were delicious as they passed into his crop—but such a meager repast only intensified his hunger.

44

He straightened up, casting about for prey that would satisfy him for many hours. Hunting was difficult in this unfamiliar territory. He listened.

From far above came the cry of one of his primitive cousins, a flying bird. Orn looked up and saw it swoop over the trees, searching out the flying arths. He flapped his wings experimentally, momentarily wishing he could do likewise. Many hundreds of lines rode the air now, more than ever before. But this had been impossible for his own line for so long that he had only the dimmest specific memories of flying. His wings were mainly for display and defense now; the weight of his large head, with its burden of memories, prevented him from even jumping high, let alone flying.

Another, gentler sound came to him. It was the trickle of water over naked stone. A stream!

Orn found it immediately. He stood at its brink and studied the narrow channels as the bright liquid coursed between the rocks, then plunged his beak into it and drank. Unlike his cousins, he was able to suck in water without lifting his head to swallow. But he did not need the voluminous quantities that poured through the little systems of the mams. *They* survived by tanking up sufficient liquid to last them for a reasonable period in spite of copious urination; *he* survived by being efficient. That was one reason his line was superior to theirs, apart from the factor of memory.

Small fish flashed by, reminding him fleetingly of the swimming stage of his ancestral line. The notion of feeding on creatures like those he had derived from did not disturb him; in fact, he rather cherished the connection. He stalked upstream in quest of a pool that might contain fish large enough to be worthwhile.

Something moved nearby. Orn swiveled his neck to fix one eye on it, and spied the disappearing tail of a good-sized snake. This line of reps had recently dispensed with legs and became slithering creatures. He had eaten a few on the island, but this one was fatter and longer. He pounced on it, pinning its head with one foot while his beak cut through the neck.

The raw segments of it were cool and juicy and delightful as they collected inside him, assuaging his hunger.

Highlands existed where he remembered swamps, and the drainage of the landscape had changed. The nights inland were cool, the days hot. Orn, in the days of travel away from the treacherous volcanoes, was finally able to set aside his expectations and accept what he found, and his emotional distress diminished.

Birds were everywhere, none intelligent but in other respects more advanced than those of his memory. They swooped cleverly through the air and swam in the small, cold ponds. The families of arths were fabulously abundant. And the little warm hairy juicy mams had emerged from their tunnels and hideaways to tread boldly in the open, overrunning forest and glade.

Orn found a number of the mams easy prey. The largest were hardly a danger to him, and most were so small he could swallow them in a few bites, wasting only a few hot drops of their substance. It was not that they were not cautious, but that the larger ones did not seem to expect trouble from a bird. This allowed him to get quite close before they took proper alarm, and a quick neat pounce usually brought him a pleasant meal. The mams learned quickly, however, and he found them to be much more wary of him after one or two of their number had been taken from any particular assemblage. But since he was traveling, this hardly interfered. He had never eaten better.

He continued to feel a vague disturbance, however. Something was missing—but he could not identify it until such time as he actually saw it. He knew that life was too easy for him here; that there should be more danger. But again—he had to experience that danger to identify it. His memory was very long, but also very selective.

Gradually he overcame his initial difficulty in appreciating the new forms of animal. Had his ancestors watched these creatures evolve for a thousand thousand generations, the picture would have been strong. A million consecutive lives, each life a single, momentary picture:

46

the whole making a composite creature. But this single flash was too brief for him to assimilate properly, even though it occurred in the present and consisted of many hours and days. His ancestors had been confined beyond the rising mountains recently, making too few forays through the changing passes and over the moving continent to form the necessary pictures of the fast-changing animals.

But some few lines were clear. The cautious marsups were little changed. The plant-feeding multis were more difficult, for they were larger and more diverse now, making a jump in the memory pattern. Some he had come to know on the island, and that helped him make the adjustment. But the arth-eaters had diverged prodigiously, feeding on the vast numbers the flowering plants supported. Now there were many major lines, few of which retained their original nature—and these creatures with small pasts were largely invisible to him.

This was dangerous, as he realized almost too late.

The thing was coming at him before he comprehended its menace—much as he had come at careless small prey. This was a mam, but almost as massive as himself, and far more ferocious than he had come to expect. Vaguely he fathomed its ancestry: one of the lines of tiny tree-dwelling insectivores that expanded their scope to feed as well on nuts and carrion, quivering as the tread of giant reps shook the ground. Somehow these unprepossessing midgets had descended to take over the reps' terrain, and now were becoming large and bold themselves.

For a moment Orn seemed to grasp what had bothered him most about this land, but he was allowed no time to fix on it. The adjustment to the present creature was too rapid. He did not have its entirety in mind, and so did not know how to handle it. Rapid thinking was not his forte; he depended on the reflexes engendered by millions of years of experience. Given time, he could adapt to this situation, though with difficulty—but the animal was attacking *now*.

Its tiny claws of Orn's memory had become talons worthy of an ave; its teeth, though small, were thick and

47

sharp. It moved with a sinuous grace almost like that of a snake, yet it carried its bulk on four muscular legs, and was capable of alarming speed.

A killer mam.

He countered as it pounced. He spread his wings, squawked, and jumped to the side, stabbing forward with his beak. His pattern was clumsy because of the oddity of the creature; had it been a rep of similar size he would have scored upon an eye socket. But his action caused it to veer off, and he had a momentary respite while it slowed, turned, and came back.

Classify it as a new creature, Orn decided. Once it had been an insectivore, but now it was a carnivore, a creo. Its legs were springy, its snout blunt, and it used its feet for fighting as well as its teeth. It was as alert and swift as Orn himself—not astonishing in a warm-bodied mam, but horrifying considering its grotesque size.

If only he could *see* it! But his ancestral images simply did not match the immediacy; his memories were too far out of phase to be meaningful at once. He had to guess at much of the creo's nature, and he was not good at such extrapolation.

Had the mam been familiar, he should have been able to defeat it in combat. He was, after all, Orn. But as it was, he would be its meal.

It sprang. Inspired in an uncharacteristic fashion, Orn visualized it as a running rep of similar mass, and reacted accordingly. He brought up one foot, spread his wings for balance, and struck for the tender nostril.

His blow missed, since this creo was faster than a rep and had a shorter snout. But his talon caught it in the neck and raked a bloody furrow across its hairy hide— something the scales of the rep would have prevented. He followed up with another beak stab at its eye, and scored on its pointed, flabby ear.

The creo howled and snapped sidewise, but Orn was out of its reach already. He brought his foot up again, and this time caught it in the muscular jaw with the downstroke. Flesh tore from its cheek as his claw carried through; blood and hot saliva sprayed out. Again it snapped side-wise, toward the injury—and because that was exactly

48

what a rep would have done, Orn was prepared once more. His beak speared its eyeball and penetrated its brain, killing it abruptly.

Again Orn struck, reacting to the greater life tenacity of the rep, and had its belly torn open before he realized that it wasn't fighting any more.

He stood back then and gazed at it, knowing that he had been fortunate to survive. Had he not summoned an image that enabled him to fight *something* efficiently, creo would now be looking down at his own corpse.

But he did not waste undue time in contemplation. He finished the work of dissection, studying each soft organ as he consumed it, and when his crop was full he had some better understanding of this mam. Should he have to fight another, he would be better prepared. But he would not battle another voluntarily—not this agile, clawed, toothed monster! Better to avoid creo and all large mams.

But it did make an excellent meal.

VI: CAL

Cal lay in the bore hole, his light off, just below the winch. Circe stood above it. He doubted that the mantas had anything resembling human sentiments, and certainly they were sexless. But it did seem that Circe was female, and that she looked out for Aquilon's interests. The other mantas remained below, taking no part in the human activity, sitting beside the supplies like so many toadstools. Circe had stayed with Aquilon throughout, the only one never to leave her, and there was now a certain flavor of Aquilon about this manta. Perhaps some manta lottery had decided which one would associate with which human—but Cal suspected something more than that.

It was too easy to personify all the mantas. Actually they were alien; indeed, in some ways man was more closely related to the birds, snakes, or spiders than to these third-kingdom sentients of Nacre. On that far planet a germ plasm of something akin to slime mold had evolved into complex, motile forms, superseding the entire animal kingdom. The internal chemistry of the Nacre creatures remained largely a matter of conjecture, since their bodily energies came from breaking down organic substances, not building them up. The mantas were the pinnacle of fungoid evolution in much the way man was the end result of animal evolution on Earth—so far. The astonishing thing was how closely the two species resembled each other in areas that counted. Man had two eyes; the manta had one. Man had a powerful brain; the manta had a lesser brain, but was able to communicate more effectively. Man was omnivorous, the manta carnivorous, in relation to its framework. Strictly speaking, all the creatures of Nacre had been herbivorous until man arrived there, since there had been no animal kingdom to prey on.

Yet these were picayune distinctions. Converging evolution had brought the two species to the point where they had more in common with each other than with a number of the variants of their own lines. It was as though nature had intended them to meet and coexist.

But why had those three mantas made their suicidal dash for freedom? They must have understood a good part of the official's presentation, and so been aware that no harm would come to them, even though they were not to be returned to Nacre.

Not to be returned to Nacre.

He lay there, chagrined at his own obtuseness. Of course the manta would rebel at such a sentence of exile! Even the human trio had not been happy on Earth, crowded and sick as mankind was; how could they have supposed the mantas would like it any better? Sparsely settled Nacre was the best place for the mantas. They must have eagerly awaited the chance to go home, after learning the ways of man and establishing a line of communication. To have had that expectation, that dream, so rudely canceled. . . .

But only three had bolted.

"Circe," he said.

The manta made a tail-snap noise: It seemed strange to

50

speak in the darkness and have her respond, when he knew she heard with her eye. But the darkness was to his eyes only; the mantas generated their own illumination in the ultra-violet range, so were independent of outside sources. Circe could see his speech.

"Did you seven agree that three of your number would make the break?"

Three snaps: question.

He had phrased it in too complicated a fashion. He tried again: "Lin, Tri, Oct—you knew?"

One snap: yes.

So it had been planned. The mantas had had ample opportunity to work out a detailed plan of attack, since the full power of each mind was channeled through the single eye. A man might require a full hour to convey a single nuance of feeling, and even then not succeed; but the mantas could project it all in a fraction of a second. They were not more intelligent than man, merely more efficient.

"You—sent them?" He had to keep it simple. Perhaps the manta vocabulary was still small. Perhaps they did not ordinarily think in word forms. He suspected that the manta's capability in theoretical matters was considerably smaller than man's. The same efficiency that promoted communication also militated against high intelligence. Man's brain had not evolved appreciably since he achieved competent verbal communication because there had no longer been a competitive advantage in higher intelligence. He had risen above the hurdle that isolated him socially, and so achieved the stability of water flowing over a dam. Barriers were necessary to progress; neither water nor brain capacity rose without compulsion. That was the way of nature, a mere permutation of physics. The ant had remained virtually unchanged for millions of years, once it achieved a satisfactory social organization; it did not need size or intelligence, so had not achieved them. Man did not need *more* size or intelligence than he had. Why should the manta differ in this respect?

Circe had answered with another snap. Yes, three had been selected to make the attempt, while four played it safe.

It did make sense, tactically. "Who died?"

Three snaps, followed by eight. So *two* had died: Tri and Oct. Cal wondered how Circe knew. Had the spores of the decedents already circulated through the station before the others left?

That was another thing about the mantas. They reproduced by spores, and the spores were released only at death. Microscopic in size, those spores could be filtered out of the air only with difficulty. Now two sets of them suffused the station. That meant that individual male and female spores could mate with their opposite numbers, to develop with luck into new mantas. Provided they found omnivores to ride on. . . .

There was going to be real trouble aboard that station! Cal could not evoke much regret; his sympathy was with the mantas. But it would not be wise to count on much assistance from the station soon. The personnel would be very busy at first, very angry later.

"Lin escaped?"

Yes.

So Lin would, circumstance permitting, go free. Perhaps he would actually manage to hitchhike back to Nacre and report to the manta society there. That would probably mean even more serious trouble for Earth. After all, the visiting mantas had seen the planet in all its squalor and savagery, and mantas had died. But he couldn't help hoping that Lin made it. In many respects the manta society was admirable compared to that of Earth.

There was a *thunk!* from outside, transmitted through the layers of metal. That would be the outer port closing. Aquilon was coming back.

He turned on the light and watched the panel, though he knew it would be a few minutes before the evacuation cycle finished. Aquilon affected him that way, making him yearn to catch the earliest possible glimpse of her. She was such a lovely creature, the first woman who had ever treated him as a man, and he loved her. While not brilliant, she possessed more than the average sensitivity. This showed in her artwork. Perhaps it was her painting that he loved, rather than herself. Certainly she was not for him physically—he knew that, whether she was aware of it or not. The physical, the sexual part—he lacked the capacity and the desire, largely. Oh, there were times ... but it was the intellectual side that intrigued him, and he was attracted less to Aquilon's comely physique than to her female mystique.

Still, he liked to look at her.

The dial showed the completion of the cycle. "Go to it, Circe," he said.

The manta leaped and bounced off the panel. The impact of the single foot jarred it open. Air exploded into the tunnel, creating a kind of shock wave but not hurting anything. They would have to do something about that inoperative pressure-equalization valve; this was a cumbersome way to open the chamber.

Aquilon crawled in, unfastening her helmet as she came toward him. "There's land!" she said, her beautiful face alight. "Veg climbed up and saw it. An island, we think—but within a mile."

"Good," he said, feeling enormous relief. He had not realized until this moment how important that was to him. Land, even an island, meant that they could be independent, at least to some extent, of the tunnel and its supplies. Independent of Earth. They could not suddenly be recalled by angry station personnel, or wiped out by a heat-beam fired through the aperture. And the mantas would be safe.

The map he had had Aquilon sketch had not been detailed enough to show the configuration of land and water within a hundred miles of the aperture, so the issue had been in doubt. If the significence of that map dawned too soon upon the military organizers of this expedition, there would also be trouble. It tied in, in fact, with the ramifications of the mantas' violence at the station. He and Veg and Aquilon and the four mantas particularly were in dire peril—until they got far away from here.

Aquilon completed the removal of her suit, folding it carefully and placing the bulky, weighted wad beside the winch. Her coverall clung to her economically; she was sleek and strong. "We might as well move out what we'll need, for now," she said. "I'd like to spend the day on land."

Yes—she understood, at least intuitively, the need for a prompt exodus. Wordlessly he crawled down the worm-bore, so that he could hook up the next box.

It was an island, swept by steady west winds. A small beach well laden with shells gave way to an interior spread of massed palmetto. A number of off-brown birds nested in that tangle, feeding on the surrounding insects and sea life of the beach. Cal watched them, but was unable to identify their specific species. They had beaks and feathers and birdlike ways, but matched no genus of his experience. Most were not really good flyers; they were too heavy for their size, and had to rest often. He wondered how they had reached this island. Storm-blown, perhaps—and then could not escape it.

The insects and arachnids, on the other hand, were familiar. Flies buzzed about the foliage and inspected the human visitors hungrily. Some were mosquitolike, some wasplike. A drab butterfly skirted his display and moved on. A black-armored beetle mounted a spire of driftwood. In the trees he had spotted the trailing lines of spiders, too. Liquid repellent discouraged most of the biters, however.

Crabs and snails occupied the salty perimeter, and schools of small fish traversed the shallows. Both air and sea were warm and clean. Cal was invigorated by the surf as he waded in and bent to pick up an assortment of shells. There was something about the smell of the sea. . . .

In due course he had a basketful of hardware. He brought it to the beach, cleared off a section of sand, and arranged the shells in neat columns by type. Some were flat, some spiral; some were drab, others ornate. He turned each over, contemplating it, and bit by bit an incredulous excitement grew in him. First the hint of the map, now this confirmation. . . .

He thought for a moment, his heart beating with unaccustomed vigor. Then he proceeded to the supply depot they had set up near the brush and picked up his voice-typer. He selected a shell and began dictating.

Cal laid out his last shell and spoke into his typer:

"phylum *Mollusca*, class *Pelecypoda*, order *Taxodonta*, suborder *Arcacea*, family—forget it, I'll have to look it up. Call it an Arca, two-inch diameter, mint condition." He smiled privately and paused to review his display affectionately: a score of clam shells. Taxodonts, with their small numerous hinge teeth; a number of Dysodonta, like assorted scallops; burrowing Desmodonta; a single weird Pachyodont; several unclassified. These shells offered only a rough guide to this world, since the pelecypods as a class had diversified early and evolved thereafter quite conservatively. In four hundred million years of Earth's history there had been only nominal modifications of most orders.

He moved a few paces to the gastropod display. Here there was much greater variety, for the shells were coiled, ridged, and spired diversely, and several were very pretty. But these too were not definitive for his purpose.

It was, in fact, mainly what was missing that fascinated him. There were very few cephalopods. He had searched diligently and come up with only two shells, both belemnites. That was highly significant, for the cephalopods had dominated the seas of Earth for three hundred million years before suffering certain selective but drastic extinctions. The belemnites had given way to their squidlike cousins—but the geological period in which belemnites had existed in the *absence* of ammonites was restricted.

The picture described by his carefully ordered collection of shells was remarkable. He was not properly versed, without his reference texts, in every detail of invertebrate fossilography; but he was certain that coincidence did not stretch this far. The fauna of the shallows here matched those of Earth, order for order, and probably species for species. Not contemporary Earth, no. Not truly ancient Earth, either. But definitely Earth.

In fact, the evidence of the sea shells reinforced that of Aquilon's map in exactly the way he had incredulously anticipated. He had recognized its configuration without daring to believe it, and suppressed his burgeoning excitement. The Earth authorities, unused to paleogeographical perspective, had apparently missed its significance. Now he looked at shells that suggested either a preposterous coincidence of convergent evolution, or—

Or they stood upon an island in the oceans of an Earth of sixty-five million years past. No—not *an* Earth—

The Earth.

Aquilon walked up the beach, resplendent in a one-piece bathing suit. It covered more of her flesh than certain contemporary fashions would have, on or off the beach; but she was perfect in it. Her hair in the sun was almost white, in contrast with the black of the suit, while her skin already showed an enhancing tan.

"Have to come in before I burn," she said, joining him in the shade of the display tent. "And I'd better catch up on illustration, too." She brought out her brush—somehow she was never without it—and began sketching the shells of the display.

Should he tell her what he had discovered? No—not right away. It would only disturb her unnecessarily. Time travel, after all. . . .

"This is Earth, isn't it," she said calmly as she sketched.

"Yes." So much for feminine histrionics. Would he ever fully understand this woman? "How did you know?"

"Your silence, mostly. You should have been exclaiming over divergencies and parallels, since this is by any reckoning a sharply Earthlike world. If it were a true parallel, it would be contemporary, and even *I* can tell it isn't. And you knew something when you had me sketch the map— yet you never spoke of it again. When I thought about it, I realized that there was a certain familiarity about that map, as though it were a gross distortion of the geography we have today. Earth might once have looked like that, millions of years ago—and you would be the first to spot it. But you shut up—and you're wound up like one of these shells."

Had he shown his tension so obviously? "You've been apprenticed to an agent, I suspect."

She did not reply. Low blow, he realized then. The agent Subble had made an impression on her, how much of one he was only gradually coming to appreciate. Best to move off that topic. "Does Veg know?" he inquired.

"Maybe. It doesn't matter much to him, though. When is this—the Permian?"

"Off by two hundred million years, 'Quilon. It's the Paleocene."

"The Paleocene," she mused, placing it. "Dawn of the age of mammals, if my girlhood schooling does not betray my aging memory. Vice versa, I mean. I think we should have been safer in the Permian, though."

"Oh, there are few dangerous landbound forms in this epoch. With the reptiles decimated—"

"Safer from paradox, I meant."

There was that. Could their actions here affect the evolution of man? It seemed incredible, yet—

"What are these?" she inquired, her brush moving and rendering as of its own volition. Shape, shade, and color were artistically duplicated, the pigments flowing from the brush in response to subtle signals from her fingers, without dipping, without rinsing.

It was an abrupt change of subject, but he accepted the shift with relief. "Phylum *Mollusca*—or as Veg would say, shellfish."

"You underestimate him, difficult as that is to do at times. He calls them clams and conks."

"He's right. The hinged shells are pelecypods, commonly known as clams. Most of the others are gastropods—Greek *gaster*, meaning stomach, and *pous*, foot. This army really does march on its stomach—"

"Like the manta," she said.

Cal paused, surprised. "Yes indeed. Strange that that similarity hadn't occurred to me."

"But the mantas don't carry their houses on their backs." She turned over a gastropod shell in order to get a new view for sketching. "I studied tetrapodal anatomy, but I'm beginning to wish I'd learned more about sea life. These shells are beautiful."

"Anything you paint is beautiful."

She ignored that. "What do the live animals look like?"

"Like snails. That's what they are. As they grow larger, they add on to their domiciles, forming the spirals you see. Because the result is really a horn—an expanding tube—it is possible to sound a note on the empty shell,

57

when it is properly prepared. Thus Veg's conch, or 'conk'. He'd have trouble sounding a blast on an ammonite, though."

"Which of these are ammonites?"

"None. They're extinct. That's one reason I know this is the Paleocene and not the Cretaceous period."

"How can you be sure? Maybe you just didn't happen to scoop up any ammonites." She was teasing him, anticipating his reply.

He made it anyway, enjoying her smile. *Any* dialogue with Aquilon was pleasant. "My dear, you are asking for a tedious narration of marine paleontology—"

"Oops—not that!" She continued painting.

"The major distinction between the shells of the gastropods and those of the cephalopods is compartmentalization. The snail shells are hollow throughout, forming a single valve; but those of the cephalopods—"

"You forgot to tell me what cephalopods are," she said. "What do *they* look like, in life?"

"Squids in shells. Your snails and clams are sluggish in the mature state, but the cephalopods are active. They have keen eyesight and are strong swimmers, despite their hardware. They have a number of tentacles around the mouth. The cephalopods as a class have been abundant and important in the seas for well over three hundred million years, and are the only invertebrates able to compete actively with the ocean vertebrates. The giant squid—"

"But you were talking about shellfish, not squids!"

"*Mollusca.* Some wear their shells outside, some inside. The squid's shell is vestigial and internal, so you're not aware of it. The ammonite shell is external and, as I was *about* to explain, chambered. Segments of the interior are walled off as the creature grows, and these are filled with gas to make the dead weight more manageable. A sophisticated, highly successful format—and the ammonites were virtual rulers of the sea for a length of time that makes the tenure of the great reptiles on land seem brief. Yet the ammonites suffered a series of calamitous decimations, marking off the Triassic, Jurassic, and Cretaceous periods, and finally became extinct just before this Paleocene epoch. Their passing is, to my mind, a more subtle and significant mystery than that of the complex of reptilian orders that claims popular attention. In fact, the ammonites passed at about the same time as the dinosaurs."

"The same time," Aquilon repeated, seeming to appreciate the significance of that. "But some reptiles did survive, and some mollusks." She had finished her painting.

"A few reptiles like the lizards, snakes, and crocodiles. And turtles. But none of the ammonites, only the related but more primitive Nautiloids. They have the septa in the shell—simple, saucer-shaped partitions—but with comparatively unimaginative convolution. The ammonites in their time developed extraordinary elaborate fluting, and with much greater variety."

"We shouldn't stay here," she said, evidently tired of paleontology at last, "on the island."

"I've hardly begun to catalog—"

"Circe says something is happening."

He studied her, realizing that she was seriously concerned, and had only listened to him in order to have time to settle her own thoughts. Circe was her manta, just as Hex was Veg's, and news from that source had to be taken seriously.

"Can you be more specific?"

"We don't have the terms, the words. But it's something big. She doesn't know whether it's dangerous, but it might be. Something about the water."

"Storm?"

"I don't think so. And we'd know about that ourselves, wouldn't we?"

"We should. We have a fair selection of meteorological instruments. The barometer doesn't indicate trouble, and we'd have some advance warning if a hurricane were coming. Enough to retreat to the undersea tube, I'd think. Could the water be polluted in some way?"

"We'd know about that too, wouldn't we? What would pollute it, here?"

He shrugged. "What indeed, without man's machine age. Perhaps I should question Circe directly."

He could tell by her attitude that this was exactly what she'd had in mind. Aquilon put two fingers to her mouth and delivered a piercing whistle, astonishing him. In a moment the disk shape of a traveling manta rounded the curve of the island, moving at a good thirty miles per hour over the water. Circe.

"What's this I hear about the water?" Cal inquired as the creature came to rest before him.

Circe did not move or snap her tail, but Aquilon responded. "She doesn't know what you mean, Cal."

"There is something wrong with the water," he said, making it a statement.

Now Circe snapped her tail twice: no.

"Something *will be* wrong."

Three snaps: question.

"The water will change."

Yes.

"Warmer."

No.

"Colder."

No.

"Higher."

Yes.

Suddenly it clicked. "A wave!"

Yes.

"Tsunami!"

Question.

"A big wave caused by movements of the land. Very big."

Yes.

"How soon? One day?"

No.

"Sooner?"

Yes.

"Twelve hours?"

No.

"How many hours?"

Six snaps of the tail.

Cal stood up. "Get Veg. We have to get off this island in a hurry. We have just about time to batten down before it hits."

Circe was up and away, though he had been addressing Aquilon. That was just as well; the manta could spread the news more efficiently.

60

But Veg, when notified, threw an unexpected block. "No. I'd rather ride it out right here. I don't want to go back in the can."

"It would only be for a day or so," Cal explained, but privately he shared the big man's reluctance. They joked about Veg's obtuseness, but he generally knew what was going on. And by this time the spore problem at the orbiting station would be in full swing, and the personnel could be in a very bad mood. "Until the danger is over. Then we can resume work here."

"Well, I've been thinking," Veg said. "Out here in the sun and spray, no problems, no people crowding together, not even rationed cutting rights. I like it. It's the way a man is meant to live. Down there—we'd be walking back into the tin can, squeezed tight. That's what the trouble is back on Earth. Crowded. Here it's good; there it's bad. I don't want to go back. At all. Not even for a day."

Oh-oh. When Veg "thought something out" he could be obstinate, and the irony was that Cal agreed almost entirely. It was possible that they would be in greater danger in the tunnel than on the island, though from a different source. But at least they could remain near the borer exit. "Let me explain what a tsunami is," he said carefully. This was for Aquilon's benefit too, to be certain everyone knew what the choices were. "An Earthquake or erupting volcano can do enormous damage on land, but if it is in or near the sea it acts in a different way. It makes a wave—a shift in the level of the water, a number of inches or feet. This wave travels at a rate governed by the amount of the disturbance and the depth of the water; it is a top-to-bottom matter, not just a surface ripple like those the wind makes. In deep water its forward velocity can exceed six hundred miles per hour. Because the vertical displacement is proportionately small, ships at sea may not even be aware of the tsunami's passage—but once it strikes the shallows, its full impact is felt. Forward momentum is converted to vertical displacement. The water can rise up in a wall a hundred feet high, and demolish shore installations with its impact.

"Now we don't know how bad this one is—but this is a small island without any really high land. A large wave could inundate it completely. Back on Earth such waves used to kill thousands and carry ships miles inland. Here—"

"Only three people, and four mantas," Aquilon said. "Hardly worth its while."

Veg retained that determined expression. "You said ships could ride it out."

"Ships in deep water, yes. Not those too near the shore."

"How about a raft?"

"A raft!" Aquilon repeated, becoming interested.

"The matter is academic," Cal pointed out. "We don't have a raft—unless you're thinking of the emergency balloon-type craft. I wouldn't care to risk it. One puncture—"

"How about a log raft? Good solid timbers, rudder, cabin, sail—"

So that was what Veg had been doing! Trust an out-doorsman to put his talent to work. "All right, Veg. Let's see it."

The raft floated in a cove on the far side of the island, about twelve feet wide and twenty long, fashioned of stout, round palm logs bound together by nylon cord set into notches. In the center was a cabin six feet square, and from the center of that rose a ten-foot mast of sturdy bamboo.

"Haven't made the sail yet," Veg admitted. "But she has a six-foot keel and the cabin's tight. I call her the *Nacre*."

"And you hope to ride out a tsunami in this?" Cal shook his head, though he was impressed with his friend's accomplishment.

"Why not? You said ships wouldn't even notice the wave. *Nacre*'s unsinkable. And we have to look about this world sometime."

"It seems reasonable to me," Aquilon said.

Cal tried to marshal his objections, but saw that he had already been outvoted. Or was he compensating for his own unreasonable desire to get far away from the works of Earth-contemporary? Or could he actually *want* to reach some area of this world where their actions might prejudice the development of the primates, and therefore abolish man from the globe entirely? No, the paradox inherent made that notion ridiculous. "I hope there is a survivor to tell the tale," he said morosely.

It required four hours of strenuous group labor to load their supplies and tie everything down. Cal had to agree that it would not have been feasible to convey everything to the undersea tunnel in that period. They would have had to sustain a serious loss of supplies, unless the wave were minor. But Circe could probably not have detected the advance tremors of a minor one. Perhaps this raft, fragile as it seemed, *was* the best alternative. But with only two hours to reach deep water, and no sail—

They boarded and pushed off without ceremony. Veg poled the craft out from the island while Cal and Aquilon paddled as well as they were able with splayed palm-flower pods, and the four mantas circled on the water. Cal was glad he had recovered enough of his strength to make a decent show of it. Six months ago he would not have been able to lift the crude oar, let alone use it effectively. He owed his resurgence to Nacre—the planet, not the raft—that had been inhospitable to man's physique but excellent for his spirit.

No —the planet had been no more than the locale. The benefit had been due to the friendship of two people—*these* two people—that had faced him back toward life.

He continued to row. His arms were tired, but the thought of that approaching wave kept him working. How *had* the mantas known of the tsunami? They could not have detected a shock wave in the water, because the wave *was* the shock. Yet he was sure they were correct, for they did not make mistakes of that nature. Something important would happen with the water, and if not a wave it was because he had misinterpreted Circe's message. There must have been a vibration that their peculiar eyesight had picked up, or a radiation typical of large land movements. Something that not only signaled trouble, but allowed the mantas to judge its time of arrival.

There was still much to learn about these fungus companions. And much to learn about tsunamis.

All loose equipment was in the cabin, and that tiny enclosure was tied together and sealed as well as limited time and resource permitted; but Cal retained grave doubts about the outcome of this jaunt. He was not afraid of death—actually, he rather approved of it as a natural institution—but disliked contemplating the premature termination of the young lives of those who had befriended him. And there was the group's mission to be considered: the charting of life on this Paleocene planet. Better to die after the mysteries of this world had been fathomed and the report made; then the effort would not have been wasted.

Veg took over Cal's oar as soon as they were out of poling depth, and Cal moved gratefully to the rudder. This was little more than a paddle tied between two projecting logs, and in view of the *Nacre*'s overall clumsiness seemed almost useless. But they did make steady if tedious progress toward the open sea.

They had hardly gotten far enough before their time was up. Cal had carefully directed them away from the direction Circe indicated for the oncoming tsunami, so that the island stood between them and it. He hoped they would thereby escape the worst of it even though the water was still too shallow for safety. The swell should bear them *away* from land, rather than into the turbulence of the shallows.

The time came—and nothing happened. "False alarm," Aquilon announced, sounding uncertain whether to be annoyed or relieved.

"Not necessarily so," Cal cautioned her. "The first signs of the typical tsunami are inconspicuous. A very small rise in the water level, followed by a deeper trough. But the second or third real wave shows its full mischief. Keep paddling."

Aquilon looked dubiously at the serene island behind them. "I somehow thought a tidal wave was a tall wall of water striking without warning," she said.

"That may be true enough, for those on land who aren't alert for the signals. Of course 'tidal wave' is a misnomer. The phenomenon has nothing to do with the tides."

Veg kept paddling.

Fifteen minutes passed placidly. They nudged farther into the ocean.

"Are you *sure*—?" Aquilon inquired.

"Of course I'm not sure," he told her. "It is possible that we misunderstood what Circe was trying to tell us. It is also true that most tsunamis are not serious affairs; that depends on the severity of the incitation and its distance from the observer's position."

"Now he tells us," Veg muttered.

"However, Circe was alarmed, and I suspect she had good reason," Cal said. "Because of the masses of water involved, the waves may be over a hundred miles apart. I wouldn't count the danger as over until a couple more hours pass."

Veg shrugged and kept working on his oar. "Quietest calamity I ever survived."

The four mantas had been ranging out, then returning to the raft to rest. They seemed to require frequent quiescence. Cal had never had the opportunity to watch them in action for days at a time like this, and it was instructive. On Earth he had found them a secluded island to camp out on, and had seen them only occasionally thereafter. There had never been a laboratory analysis of their metabolism, but he suspected that it was not conducive to sustained energy output of the level of Earthly animals. They were cold-blooded, for one thing. Not that their body fluid resembled blood in any chemical way, or that it was actually cool—but it did suggest a basic conservation of energy. Cold temperature inhibited them; that was probably the main reason the majority had elected to stay with him in the subtropics, on Earth. They were saprophytes, feeding on the breakdown of organic matter; to what extent did temperature affect their chemistry? Or were they inhibited now because they were primed to spore upon death—a state that must be equivalent to pregnancy in a mammal? The mantas he had seen die on Nacre had not spored, since their deaths had been unexpected and they had not been primed.

Now they were resting. Fatigue, boredom—or in preparation for some unusual stress ahead? It pained him to be so ignorant.

Forty minutes after the scheduled arrival of the tsunami, Veg saw something. He stopped rowing and watched. The others, noting his reaction, did the same.

65

It was as though a weathered mountain were rising on the horizon behind the island. The water humped up grotesquely, its main height concealed by the island foliage. Even so, the swell was not really striking; the highest point could not be much more than thirty feet above sea norm.

"We could have weathered that," Veg remarked.

Cal kept his peace. He knew what was coming, and his mind's eye augmented the visible traces. The wave was rising on the shallows leading up to the island, the same submarine slant they had walked up from the tunnel. From the look of it, there was a fairly extensive submerged reef angling across the path of the tsunami shock wave.

Near the island the rolling swell became a peaked wave at last, showing a tumbling white crest and emitting an increasing roar. The water formed into a vertical wall—he heard Aquilon's intake of breath—and crashed over the green landscape. A cloud of spume went up, as though a tremendous explosion had sundered the island. A rainbow appeared in the sky, tribute to the water sprayed high into the atmosphere.

"We could have weathered that!" Aquilon said, mimicking Veg's remark without malicious intent.

Then the misty wake was upon them. White foam surged by the raft, lifting it precariously and causing the logs to shift against each other, and bits of island debris bobbed about.

The swell subsided and they viewed the island again. From this distance it seemed unchanged, but Cal knew that terrible havoc had been wreaked there. The mantas' warning had been valid.

Reminded, he turned to check on their otherworld associates. Circe, Diam, Hex, and Star stood on the roof of the cabin looking miserable. They would have had difficulty running over this wave; its changing configuration and bubbly surface could easily have inundated them. Though a manta could "walk" on water, it could not swim within it, except for very brief scoops at speed. A manta had to keep moving swiftly or stop entirely, when the surface was liquid. These four needed the raft more than the humans did in this instance.

Yet they could have avoided the problem nicely by traveling over deep water, where the swell of the tsunami was mild. Did they feel an emotional loyalty to the human party? It always came back to what he did not know about them. Right now, however, his job was this planet, not manta.

In due course the second wave crashed over the isle. Others followed at about twenty-minute intervals, but the worst was over. The raft had saved the party.

"I believe it is safe to return now," Cal said at last.

"Why?" Veg asked.

Cal looked at him, so tousled and sweaty and strong. "Are you implying that the raft is better than a land base?" The notion was foolish; there was not room to spread his shells or keep them secure, let alone acquire more.

"I'm implying we can't travel far on an island."

"Travel! These winds are obviously seasonal. Once we drift from this vicinity, we'll be unable to return for months."

Veg nodded.

So it was coming into the open already: the decision to mutiny, to break contact with the Earth authorities. Not completely, for the radio equipment could keep them in touch. But since they would be unable to return if so directed. . . .

Veg wanted simply to isolate himself from a hateful influence, and Cal understood this entirely too well. Yet he could not so casually justify the abrogation of the mission. They were not here on any vacation, and too obvious a balk could trigger the trouble already building for them.

In addition, if this were Paleocene Earth, the consequence of activity on the mainland could ramify appallingly. What *about* the paradoxes of time travel? They had not yet done anything significant, for their traces on the island would have been wiped out by the tsunami—but such good fortune could not be perpetual. What would happen when some action of theirs threatened to change the nature of their own reality? Such paradox was patently impossible—but the situation could be extremely delicate.

"It seems to me we would have to move about a bit to gather information," Aquilon said. "For a proper report, I mean. We should at least map the continents—"

"Map the continents!" Cal knew she meant the floral and faunal features, since they already had the map, but still it was an excuse. "That would take a full-fledged survey party several years with a cartographic satellite. And we already know what they would find."

"That reminds me," she said. "That map. How did you know—"

"I'd have to go into paleogeography to explain that. It—"

"Summarize it," Veg said, irritated. He was holding his paddle and seemed anxious to use it, rather than talking. But Aquilon must have brought up this matter now in order to make sure Veg knew about it.

Summarize the concept of drifting continents? Cal sighed inwardly. It had to be done, though, and now did seem to be the time. Now—before they committed themselves to the mainland. "Well ... the crust of the Earth may seem solid and permanent to us today, but in fact it is boiling and moving steadily. Like the surface of a pot of cooking oatmeal (he saw they didn't comprehend the allusion, but let it stand), it bubbles up in some regions and cools and solidifies and sinks down in creases elsewhere. Segments of the more solid, lighter material float, collecting above the creases until large masses are built up by this action. These are the continents—or rather, the single continent, that formed billions of years ago, then broke up as the convection patterns changed, drifted, reformed. Two hundred and fifty million years ago there were two great continents, two halves separated by narrow seas: Laurasia in the north, Gondwanaland in the south. These broke up into the present continents, and changes are still occurring. In time the Americas may complete their journey across the oceans and rejoin the main land mass from the other side—"

"Watch it," Veg said. "You're theorizing."

"Now I remember!" Aquilon said. "They verified the

continental drift by checking the magnetism of the ocean floor. The metal in the rocks that bubbled up was aligned with the magnetic poles as the material cooled and hardened, so there was a record, and they could tell where it had been when."

"Something like that," Cal agreed, surprised that she had made the connection. "There were other ways to corroborate the phenomenon, too. Computer analysis showed how certain continents, such as Australia and Antarctica, made a precise fit despite being separated by two thousand miles of water. The underlying strata also matched. All over the world, the changing continental geography could be interpolated to show the configuration for any particular period. The map I had you sketch strongly suggested the Paleocene epoch, since the major continents as we know them had only recently severed from the main masses and remained relatively close together."

"So where are we now—on Earth?" Veg asked.

"Our island here is some distance off the coast of what will be known as California. In our time Western America has overridden one of the Pacific rifts and so developed the San Andreas Fault, a source of regular earthquakes. This has been an active area of the world for some time, and no doubt this tsunami stems from—"

"We can't just sit here talking," Veg grumbled. "There might be another wave."

"And we really should take a look at California," Aquilon said. "The westerlies should take us right there, and I could paint some of the animal life for your report."

Cal perceived that she had an ulterior motive. She didn't truly comprehend something until she painted it, and she was intrigued by the notion of treading the soils of the past. She was not concerned about paradox.

"We aren't operating as an isolated party," he said. "There could be consequences—"

"Maybe we should take a vote," Veg suggested.

Cal already knew the outcome of that. Trust the group to revert to elementary democracy in this wilderness world. The others were not trained to appreciate the enormous fund of information available on the single island, or to anticipate the vagaries of seemingly steady wind. It would be far safer to remain here, and more efficient. Though there *was* that matter of the spores in the station . . . and he could not outvote the two of them.

"Four out of seven?" Cal inquired.

Veg and Aquilon exchanged glances. They had not thought of this. If the precedent of voting on key decisions were established, the precedent of including the mantas as franchised individuals would also be in force.

"Manta suffrage," Aquilon murmured.

In the course of a difficult discussion the nature of the voting concept and practice was conveyed to the mantas: each entity to cast his ballot, the minority amenable to the will of the majority. Cal wondered whether the fungoid creatures really understood. They could easily cast a bloc vote. Should they have been considered as a single entity, one vote for the group of them? Too late now.

Cal called off the names in alphabetical order. Each voter would advance to the bow if he wished to travel on the raft, and to the stern if he wished to remain based on the island.

" 'Quilon." She stepped to the bow, and the tally stood one to nothing, raft.

"Cal." After he spoke his own name, he moved to the rear. The truth was that he did want to explore, and to get away from Earth's influence—but he did not want to alarm the others by giving his reasons, or to have it on record that he approved the jaunt. There were sometimes distinct advantages to a split decision, particularly when the results would be recorded and evaluated by unfriendly officials.

"Circe." Here was the test: which way would the manta jump?

Circe hopped to join Aquilon. Two to one.

"Diam." This could decide it, for Veg surely wanted to explore, and that would make a majority.

Diam bounded into the air, shaking the raft by the force of his takeoff, flared, and came down beside Cal. Two to two—and they were *not* bloc voting!

"Hex." That was Veg's companion. But if Circe had

70

joined Aquilon from personal sentiment, Hex could not do the same, for Veg had not yet formally committed himself.

Hex joined the bow party, and it was three to two. The outcome was no longer in doubt, but the vote had to be officially completed.

"Star." Star had stayed with Cal throughout, as had Diam. Would he choose accordingly, as a matter of academic curiosity?

Star did. Three to three.

"Veg." And of course Veg went forward. The issue had been decided, and—what was far more significant—the mantas had voted as individuals.

The party of seven was about to travel, and Cal was glad.

VII: ORN

Time was long, yet it was nothing, for he only wandered and grew. He crossed inland mountains—the kind that developed from shifts and buckles of the ground, rather than from ash and lava—and plains and swamps, bearing east. Though he ran his limit each day, stopping only to feed himself, the summer was waning before he reached the new ocean formed from the widening chasm between land fragments. He had verified his general map: this land was now far away from its origin, and was still moving.

Increasing cold nudged him south. Many things had changed, and much of the landscape differed substantially from that of his memory, but that was the way of the Earth. It always changed, as the waves on the seas changed, and so had to be resurveyed periodically for posterity.

The mams were everywhere. Small primes twittered in the occasional grassy areas, burrowing for grubs and tubers, and some peered at him from trees with great round eyes. They were generally fragile and shy, yet numerous; he fed on them frequently. Every so often he brought down a dino, horned, but clumsy and not very bright. This creature tended to become absorbed in his browsing and not be alert for danger.

There were also a number of snakes, and many liz and small amphibs, all feeding on the plentiful arths. And Orn did too, tearing open anthills with relish and picking up the scurrying morsels with his gluey tongue. Never in his memory had there been such regular feasting!

Aves filled the trees, benefitting even more from the arth supply. The birds had become more diverse than ever, and were now excellent fliers. Several lines swam in the ponds and rivers, and others ran along the ground as he did, though none of these were closely allied to him. His line had been landbound longer, and during more dangerous times; thus he was larger and swifter than these newcomers. Many of the others would never have been able to survive attack by a running rep.

Winter promised to be far more severe than his prior one on the island. Orn continued driving south, making good progress; yet the cold stalked him. There was nowhere he could set up a regular abode. He could withstand freezing temperatures for short periods, but this sapped his strength. His plumage was not thick enough to protect him against a prolonged siege, even though many smaller birds endured winter well enough. He was becoming tired of perpetual travel; he was almost full-grown now, and beginning to respond to developing urges for other things.

He did not recognize in himself the nesting impulse, for only the sight of a nubile female of his species would clarify that. But he carried on with increasing and undefined hunger, hurrying somewhere while wanting to stay where he was. It was not only the onrushing season that disturbed him.

At last his southward progress was blocked by mountains. They were volcanic, and therefore to be treated with respect and fear. He trotted west, seeking a way around them, but was met after a day by a great ocean.

He had crossed the continent again, intersecting the coastline here where the land mass narrowed. He had either to give up or to proceed on through this region; the nights of the inland area had become far too cold now for his comfort.

The range extended into the sea, the individual summits diminishing to islands and finally reefs. These isles would be warm, he knew—but Orn did not care to set up residence in such a precarious locale again. He could abide a quiescent volcano, or an island, but not the combination. That was too much of a trap.

So it had to be the land route. He had no memory of the territory ahead; the configurations of this landscape had shifted too rapidly and drastically in the past few million years. The wall of volcanoes was new, certainly—and if any prospective ancestor had penetrated it, that bird had never emerged to sire his line thereafter. Sometimes what Orn could not remember spoke as eloquently as what he could.

He found a promising avenue a few mountains from the coast and moved in. It was a pass of a sort—a fissure between two of the lesser peaks, overgrown with bracken and a tough new strain of grass. Some water trickled along it, but not enough; he risked thirst here. But better that than the other flow—of liquid stone.

The mountains were dead. He could read their histories as he passed, observing the remnants of ancient lava fields and mounded ash. The sides of the gully were weathered and overgrown with brush. He made a foray up one slope and brought down a young, slow-footed ambly who had strayed into this inhospitable region. He severed its jugular with a single contraction of his beak muscles, and fed quickly on the warm carcass. There was far more meat than he could consume at one time, but he had to tolerate the waste this time because of the need to save his strength for the climb ahead. An arduous, tedious search for small prey at this time would have worn him down, though ordinarily he killed no larger than his hunger, however vulnerable the prey.

The air was cold as he fed, and the warmth of the flesh

73

he swallowed was fleeting. Almost, he desired a little more activity in the old fire cones. Almost.

In the morning he outran the cleft and crossed the steep side of the smaller mountain, stiffening his feathers against the chill wind that struck at this height. Then he was over the pass, and it was warmer on the other side. Too much so: he smelled the fumes of an active volcano.

There was no way to avoid it. The cold of the heights forced him to seek the lowest valleys, and from the great basin ahead rose the live cone. Fires danced upon its rim, reflected from the hanging clouds above it, and as Orn approached the ground quivered ominously.

It took him a full day to skirt it, and he watched its every malignant gesture. This was not a lava mountain; this one was the more deadly gas and ash type. No plants grew near it. Yet he found arths amid the tumbled rocks of its perimeter, and one semi-stagnant pond, so his hunger and thirst were partially abated.

On the southern slope the volcano caught him. Monstrous gases swirled out of its cruel orifice, forming a burgeoning cloud that glowed of its own accord. As night came this cloud drifted south—following Orn. As it gained on him, slow-moving as it seemed, the thing began to rain: a downpour of incandescent droplets that accumulated voluminously on the ground.

Orn fled before it, knowing that the smallest touch of that fiery storm meant annihilation. He did escape—but his retreat had been sealed off. He could not know what lay ahead, but death lay behind.

Exhausted, he perched at last upon a jagged boulder and slept nervously amid the drifting fringe gases of the storm. In all that murky region there was nothing alive but him.

Next day he came across a spring of boiling water. Where it overflowed into a basin and cooled sufficiently, he washed the cutting grime from his feathers and felt clean again. Once more there were arths; he scratched for grubs and had a partial meal.

After that there was more even ground, and he made good time though the unusually rough turf abraded his feet. The rocks were warm, and not entirely from the sun, with many heated ponds. He washed cautiously and drank the richly flavored water dubiously, but found no fish. He avoided the boiling mud and steaming fumaroles, and particularly the active cones.

It was an awful landscape, jagged in the distance, bare and dead up close. He longed for the end of it, but feared that there was no end. He felt too vulnerable without his memory to guide him.

Gradually the land leveled into a desert, and though Orn made excellent time here, he had to go without food and water for two days. Because of his rapid metabolism a third day would finish him. Not at once, but by crippling him and thus preventing any possible escape. Yet he also lacked the resources to retreat. He pushed on. There was nothing else to do.

Though the evening brought relief from the ambient heat, this was scant consolation. The cold was severe, and he had to roost on the ground and half bury himself in dust as a hedge against it. Now he had no way to cleanse his feathers properly or to slake his terrible thirst. He almost felt like a mam, the way this territory wrung the moisture from his body; but no mam could have traveled this far.

On the second morning he lay stiffly for a time, waiting for the sun to restore what energy it might to his body. His flesh, under the battered and poorly insulating feathers, was dehydrated—yet he knew that the day would soon dry it out farther. Would it be more comfortable to rouse himself for the terminal effort, or to lie here and let death visit him peacefully?

Across the brightening desert he saw the sunlight stab at a rising wisp of mist, giving it momentary brilliance as the beam refracted. This was the single instant of the day that these barrens had beauty, however slight.

Then his memory informed him what mist meant. Orn lurched to his feet, flapping his stubby wings in his eagerness, and staggered forward. He was weak, his feet were bruised, his muscles hurting, and he doubted that he could crack even a hard nut with his beak—but he covered the ground.

There was a gully where the mist had been. Within this

depression was a cleft similar to the one he had followed into these badlands. And at the bottom of this crevice was a tiny flow of water.

Orn dug a pit in the sand with his broken talons and set his head in it. He lay there and the water trickled over his tongue.

He remained there all day, and by night he was not thirsty any more.

He followed the riven gully down, too hungry now to sleep. A quarter day's trek below his point of interception the first stunted vegetation appeared. He dug it out in the dark and swallowed it, hoping to find nutritious grubs within. He had not recovered enough to be able to tell by smell. Then he relaxed.

The following day was better. The cleft, at first only a few wingspans across, broadened out into a winding canyon, and creeping foliage covered its shadowed sides. It was hot, but not nearly as bad as the burning desert. The minuscule water had been reinforced from offshoot crevices and gathered into a running brook. Orn traveled slowly and recovered his strength.

At last there was enough water pooled for a proper washing, and he bathed with delight. Once more he could fluff out his feathers and protect himself better from cold.

But on the second day he climbed the canyon wall and poked his head over the rim and spied—a steaming mountain. He was not out of the volcano belt yet; the desert and cleft had been only a hiatus.

The canyon widened out and finally the water in it leveled and became salty. He was back at the sea.

But with a difference. He had passed the first major belt of mountains and reached a warmer area. He might be able to make a winter nest in a burrow by the water, within the protected canyon, and feed on fish.

Then he discovered the underground river.

It opened into the canyon wall: a squat tunnel from which warm water poured. He braced himself against its gentle current and entered the cavern. Light spilled from natural vents in the ceiling, and he saw stone columns he recognized as typical of such places. His ancestors had often

76

stayed in caves. This was better, much better; he could winter here in comfort, going outside only for forage.

Unless other animals—predators—had the same notion.

Orn sniffed the slowly moving air. The worst came to him then, hidden before by the lingering insensitivity left over from his desert thirst: the rank odor of a large rep.

He sought out the source, alert for rapid retreat. Not all reps were inimical, and this smell was borderline.

He found it lying half-submerged. It was a Para, five times Orn's own length and many times as massive. Its four feet were webbed for efficient swimming, and its tail was long and powerful. There was no armor on its body. Its head was equipped with a large scooplike bill that Orn remembered was used to delve into the soft muck of shallow ponds. It had a monstrous bony crest that projected back so far that it effectively doubled the length of the head. Through this process the nasal passages ran, and to it the hot blood of the active animal was pumped for cooling in the heat of the day. Too much heat was deadly to reps, and the large ones had trouble dissipating it; thus this evaporative cooling system gave the Para an advantage over his cousins. Neither exertion nor noon sunlight was likely to harm him.

Nevertheless, the Para was dead, its flesh rotting.

This was a creature of the old type. Orn had not seen such a rep in anything but memory before, except for the crocs, but it was familiar in a way the tiny mams were not. Paras were among those reps who had dominated the world for much of his memory, and who until this moment had seemed to be absent from it.

Yet something had killed it. Not an animal enemy, for the creature was unmarked except for those bruises typical of inanimate encounters, and post-mortem infestation. Not thirst or hunger, for it was sleek and in potable water.

If this superbly equipped animal had succumbed within this cavern, far more its natural habitat than Orn's, how could Orn expect to survive?

Better to brave the dangers he knew, than to subject himself to the sordid and fatal mystery of this place. He would have to continue his journey.

VIII: AQUILON

They sailed due east. The *Nacre*'s yardwork was crude—
a wedge of rubberoid sheeting buttressed by palm fronds
suspended on half a dozen transverse bamboo poles,
vaguely in the manner of a Chinese junk. Nothing better
had been available. It would have taken them weeks to
form a suitable sail from natural materials, and they
might not have held the wind any better than this cut-and-
stretched balloon material.

When Veg wanted to slow progress, he let out a support-
ive rope and the sail collapsed in a mess of sticks; when
he wanted full power, he hauled it back up, using all his
brute strength.

It functioned, anyway. When the breeze was stiff,
Aquilon judged that they made as much as five knots.
Ordinarily the rate was more like two. Thus they traversed
from fifty to a hundred miles per day, for the *Nacre* never
rested. Respectable progress!

The sea air was balmy, the day clear. But the perpetually rolling waves lifted the raft, tilted it, dropped it, and
lifted it again interminably, and very soon Aquilon was
feeling more than queasy. She was sure the men had a
similar complaint. She felt sorry for Cal, hanging bravely
to a rope knotted around a log. Not only did he seem to
be in continual peril of being washed overboard—that was
why he had the rope—but he looked quite sick. Veg didn't
complain, but he hadn't eaten all day. Aquilon herself had
simply puked into the water and felt better for a while—
until being blessed with the dry heaves. She wondered
whether the mantas, perched in the cabin shade, had
equivalent difficulties.

She tried to distract herself by watching the sights. The
heaving seascape was no help at all, but she found she
could see a good deal by donning her diving mask, immers-

ing her head, and peering down through the water. Once she learned the trick of compensating for the flexing façade of the surface.

The sea, at first glance so desolate, was actually full of life. Aquilon had some familiarity with fish, having painted them many times and she had also done a number of dissections for anatomical illustrations. The species here were not identical to those she knew, but they fell into similar patterns, and some were so close she was sure only an ichthyologist would be able to differentiate the types. A school of herring drifted directly under the raft, flanked by a shark she couldn't quite see. Then a four-foot tuna cut across, and suddenly several flying fish broke surface and skated over the water, their fins spread like the wings of insects. Half an hour later she spied several cod, then some jacks, and finally a great lone swordfish fully eight feet long.

She lifted her head at last and doffed the mask, deciding that her seasickness was coming under control. It was late afternoon. The two men seemed listless, perhaps dulled by the monotony of the waves. Veg was spume-flecked; Cal now leaned against the cabin. The four mantas remained where they had been. They would not venture forth in direct sunlight, of course; that was too rough on their eyes.

"Tennis, anyone?" she inquired with mock cheer. "Or maybe supper?"

But no one replied, and she wasn't hungry herself. There were supplies on board for several days, so foraging from the sea was not necessary. Yet.

She pondered this, since she was already feeling dismal. Suppose the map were wrong, and California was not within three or four hundred miles? Suppose they had to remain on the raft for two weeks? By then the stored food would run out, and the canned water. If they were to survive, they would have to fish, consuming the flesh and grinding out fish-body fluids to drink. It was feasible; they all knew the techniques, and the necessary equipment was part of the life-raft package. But Veg would not touch fish, himself, and might refuse to bring in any for the others. She could do it herself—but she now shared Veg's

79

viewpoint to a considerable extent, though her rationale was different, and wasn't sure she cared to go back to an omnivorous diet. It would make her feel unclean. Would she eat fish if she got hungry enough, and drink fish juice? Would she kill another living, feeling creature in order to slake her own needs? She didn't know—but the feeling that she *might* made her feel again.

What value was a moral standard, if it disappeared the moment it became inconvenient or uncomfortable?

They took turns sleeping, one at a time—not from any urge for privacy but to insure that two were always alert to the vagaries of the sea. Their collective motion sickness was responsible for the pessimistic outlook for the voyage, she was sure, but meanwhile caution was their only resource.

She lay alone in the cabin, listening to the slap of the waves against the logs and trying to ignore the swells of brine that inundated the nethermost centimeter of her torso at irregular intervals. In time, she knew, she would acquire the reflex to hold her breath even in her sleep for those essential seconds, and would not even notice the involuntary baths. Human beings were adaptable; that was why they survived.

Survival. It seemed to have less to recommend it recently. How blithely she had cast her ballot in favor of this stomach-wringing journey! Cal, at least, had foreseen what it entailed. One overruled his judgment at one's peril. Now it was far too late to change course; the force of air driving them along would not permit it. With this clumsy vehicle they could not hope to tack into the wind effectively—and even if they could, it would take twice as long (at best!) to return to their island as the outward trip had taken. There was no way to escape at least another day of oceanic violence.

Yet she was dead tired, and sleep had to come. The mantas seemed to be comfortable enough on the cabin roof, so why couldn't she be likewise here? Gradually she acclimatized and passed into a fitful dream state interspersed with ten-second cold shocks as the pseudo-tide touched her again and again.

She found herself—no, not back in her cosy Earth apartment, for that physical comfort was empty in the face of the intellectual horror on which it rested. She did not like Earth; she had no fond memories to bind her to it. Space meant more to her, Nacre meant more, and the easy, sexless companionship of these two men. Her dream was of current matters, her nearest approach to joy: the day and night just passed on the island.

She stood conversing with Cal, and he was taller and stronger than in life, and simultaneously she painted the shells of his collection. They were ammonite fossils, extinct just yesterday, geologically speaking—extinct, that is, barely ten million years ago. And her picture grew as she filled in the color; it swelled and became real, and then she was walking into it, or rather swimming, for it was a living ocean habitat. All around her floated the cephalopods, their shells coiled, straight, or indecisive. Most were small, but some were large—fist-sized, even head-sized, their tentacles spread out hungrily, fifty or a hundred for each individual, plus the two larger feeder tentacles.

She was stroking lithely, but these clumsy-seeming mollusks were more agile. Their bodies matched the specific gravity of the water so that they neither lifted nor sank involuntarily, and they moved rapidly backward as they jetted water from their hyponomes. She could not catch any in her hands, try as she might. Soon she gave up the attempt, and then they drifted confidently closer to her, shells sparkling iridescently.

It was a wonderland of bright living coral and sponge and jellyfish and crabs and forestlike seaweed, with the abundant 'bony' fish circulating everywhere. But the cephalopods dominated the scene—small squids shooting past in shoals, almost indistinguishable from fish at that velocity. There were also the relatives of the cephalopods: the belemnites, and the nautiloids and ammonites. The mollusks did not swim in the manner of vertebrates, however; they all moved by that same jet propulsion, using their finlike members only for guidance. The belemnites were cigar-shaped shells completely surrounded by flesh, almost like little manta rays with backbones fused.

They were feeding now, culling animalcules and tiny fishes from the water with their myriad tentacles and bearing them in to the mouth parts. Their big round eyes stared at her as she went along. The individuals were getting larger; some were more than a foot in diameter across the coiled shell, and their short tentacles were six inches.

Their shells were varied, but nowhere did the markings of the septa show. She remembered that Cal had explained about that: the sutures were the internal joining places of the septa, analogous to the dark rings inside a poorly washed coffee cup. They did not ordinarily show externally. Where the septum, or disk blocking off a segment of the interior was flat, the suture merely ringed the inside of the shell. But the more advanced ammonites had fluted sutures, reflecting a convoluted septum. She visualized the situation, using a straight shell for convenience rather than a normal coiled one:

LIVE   FLAT   FLUTED

The sutures became more and more complex as the ammonoids developed, until in the middle Cretaceous they were phenomenal. Loops formed within loops, resembling the profile of elaborate branching coral.

Aquilon contemplated an ammonite fully eighteen inches in diameter, tentacles as long as her hand reaching out from it. The creature was impressive in much the manner of a monstrous spider. She waved her hand at it, and it snapped back into its shell, closing its hood over its head. She laughed, making bubbles in the water (where did she find air to breathe? she wondered fleetingly, but this was immaterial) and waited for the cephalopod to lift its anterior portcullis and peep out again. So much like a hermit crab, she thought—only this was a hermit octopus, who constructed its own shell.

"Take me to your leader," she said as its eyes reappeared.

The ammonite nodded with its entire body and jetted away, its tentacles streaming behind. She followed, not really surprised.

Through bays and inlets of coral they swam, by algae-covered rocks and sea moss like green waving hair, and now and then a stray brown kelp anchored to the bottom with its top held near the surface by small bladders of gas. Purple, green, orange, solid or tenuous, the shallow-water plants decorated the reef. Starfish crowded near vaselike sponges, and beautiful but dangerous sea anemones perched on stones or the backs of crabs. Green spiked sea urchins and dark sand dollars dotted the bottom sand (where sand occurred), and green lobsters gestured with their terrible pincers. She had to swerve to avoid a giant ancient horseshoe crab. And the bivalves—they were everywhere!

She longed to stop and begin painting—but then she would lose the guide, for that fast-jetting mollusk gave her no time to lag. Tragedy!

Then, abruptly, she faced it: a coiled ammonite shell over six feet in diameter. Her guide was gone, perhaps afraid for its own safety, and she was on her own.

The tremendous hood hoisted up, a gateway almost as tall as she was in that position. Yellow tentacles snaked out, writhing toward her. She was frightened now, but she stood her ground as well as her buoyancy permitted. An eye the size of a small saucer fixed on her.

"Yes?" the king of the ammonites said. No bubbles rose, for it was not an air breather.

She didn't want to admit that its speech surprised her, so she asked it an inane question. "Are your sutures fluted?"

A hundred tentacles formed a frown. "Are they fluted, *what*?"

She blushed. "Are they fluted, *Your Majesty*?"

The frown writhed into neutrality. "Honeyshell," King

Ammon said, "my sutures are royally fluted and convoluted, each in the shape of a finely crafted crown. Would you care to examine them from the inside?" Its purple tentacles were extending toward her, each a yard long, and its mouth pried itself open.

"No," she said quickly, backpedaling.

"One does not," Ammon remarked slowly, "say no to the king." Several of its red tentacles were coiling around projections in the coral reef, as though ready to pull the entire shell forward suddenly.

"I meant—" She cast about for the proper phraseology. "Your Majesty, I meant that I could never think of doubting the statement of the king so it would be insulting to suggest any closer inspection, Your Majesty."

The tentacles relaxed while Ammon considered. "There is that." Somehow she had the impression the king was disappointed. Now he was green.

"What I came to ask," she said humbly, "was why? Why do you need such a complex pattern, when no one can admire it . . . from the outside?"

"*I* can admire it very well from the inside—and my opinion is the only one that matters. And I am hungry."

"Hungry?" She didn't make the connection, unless this were a hint that she should get farther out of range. But the king surely could move through the water faster than she, and he had so many appendages! Brown, at the moment.

"I perceive you do not comprehend the way of the ammonite," Ammon remarked. "You vertebrates are powerful but clumsy. You have only four or five extremities, one or two colors, and your shell is obscure."

"We do our best to live with our handicaps," she said.

"Actually, you're decent enough, for a lower species," Ammon admitted graciously. "It behooves me to educate you. Pay attention: our primitive ancestors, the Nautiloids, had simplistic septums, hardly more than dismal disks, and so their sutures were aconvolute. They scrounged and scavenged after a fashion, gobbling down anything they could catch, and doubtless made a living of sorts. But we ammonites learned the secret of specialization: by varying the size of the space between the torso and the outermost septum, the early ammonite was able to change his specific gravity. Larger air pocket (actually a unique gas—but you would not comprehend the secret formula), and he floated; smaller, and he sank. Do you understand?"

"Oh, yes," she said. "That would be a big advantage in swimming, since you could maintain any level without effort."

"Hm." King Ammon did not seem to be entirely pleased. "Just so. Now with a flat septum there is not much purchase, since the body is anchored only at the rim and the siphuncle. You know what the siphuncle is, of course?"

"No, sir," she said.

"Hm." The mollusk was pleased this time. "That is the cord of flesh that passes through the septa and chambers of the shell, right back to the very end. Have to keep in touch, you know. I suppose your tail is a clumsy effort in that direction. At any rate, a convoluted septum, matching the configuration of the body surface, is a more effective base for adjustment of the volume of that gaseous partition. So we ammonites have superior depth control. That enables us to feed more effectively, among other things."

"How clever!" Aquilon exclaimed. "I can see how you grew so large. But what do you eat?"

"Zilch, naturally. What else would a sapient species bother to consume?"

"I don't think we vertebrates are that advanced. I don't even know what zilch is."

Ammon's tentacles writhed and went rainbow at this astonishing confession of ignorance, but he courteously refrained from remarking on it. "Call it a type of marine fungus. There are quite a number of varieties, and naturally each ammonite species specializes on one. I imbibe nothing less than Royal Zilch, for example. No other creature can feed thereon!"

"By kingly decree?" She had not realized that ammonites were so finicky.

"By no means, though it is an interesting thought. No lesser creature has the physical capability to capture a Royal Zilch, let alone to assimilate it. It is necessary to lock on to its depth and duplicate its evasive course precisely, or all is lost. One mistake, and the zilch eats *you*."

Oh. "That's why your convolutions are so important. Your hunting is dangerous."

"Yes. I can, among other feats, navigate to an accuracy of two millimeters, plus or minus 15 percent, while interpenetrating the zilch with seventy-three tentacles." Gray members waved proudly. "And I've seldom been slashed."

This was beginning to sound like doubletalk to Aquilon. But she remained entirely too close to the king to risk contradicting him directly. He might yet develop an appetite for bipedal vertebrate à la blonde. "I'm amazed you can coordinate so well."

"Your amazement is entirely proper, my dear. You, with your mere five or six appendages, can hardly appreciate the magnitude of the task. And every unit has to be under specific control. The nervous system this entails— you know what a brain is?"

"I think so."

"Hm. Well, I have a sizable brain. As a matter of fact, the convolutions of my septa merely reflect the configuration of the surface lobes of my brain, which are naturally housed deep within my shell for proper protection. It is my advanced brain that sets me off from all other species; nothing like it exists elsewhere, nothing ever has, nothing ever will. That is why I am king."

Aquilon searched for some suitable comment.

Suddenly Ammon turned orange and lifted grandly in the water. She had supposed him bottom-bound because of his size, but he moved with exactly the control he had claimed, smoothly and powerfully. "There's one!"

She peered about anxiously. "One what?"

"One Royal Zilch. My meal!" And the king jetted off.

Now she saw his prey, a flat gray shape. "No!" she cried with sudden horror. "That's Circe!"

But the chase was already on, the monster cephalopod shooting backwards in pursuit of the fleeing manta. She knew how helpless the mantas were in water, and foresaw only one outcome of this chase. "No!" she cried again, desperately, but the bubbles merely rose upward from her mouth, carrying her protest snared within them.

She woke with a mouthful of sea water, her body soaking and shivering, and she still felt sick. She clambered out into the chill breeze. It was 4:00 A.M., or close enough, and time for her shift on watch to begin.

Veg had the four-to-eight sleep, and she didn't envy him his attempt in the watery cabin. The mantas wisely remained on the roof, seemingly oblivious to the continual spray. A gentle phosphorescence showed the outlines of the rolling waves, and the wind continued unabated. Now that she was fully awake and erect, she found the chill night breeze refreshing.

There was not much to do. Veg had lashed the rudder and cut the sail to a quarter spread, and the *Nacre* was stable. They had merely to remain alert and act quickly if anything untoward happened. She did not expect to see more than routine waves, however.

"Cal," she ventured.

"Yes, 'Quilon," he said immediately. He did not sound tired, though he could not have had any better rest than she had had, during his turn in the cabin. This was a rough vigil for him. The fact that he was able to bear up at all meant that he had gained strength considerably since Nacre. That was reassuring.

"The ammonites—could they have been intelligent?"

She was afraid as she said it that he would laugh; but he was silent for a time, considering it. She waited for him, feeling the damp air in her hair, the vibrations of the shifting logs underfoot. No, Cal was not the one to laugh at a foolish question; he always took in the larger framework, the reason behind the statement.

"Highly unlikely, if you mean in any advanced manner. They had neither the size nor the metabolism to support extensive brain tissue, and water is a poor environment for intellectual activity. It—"

"I mean—the big ones. As big as us."

"Most ammonites were quite small, by human standards. But yes, in the late Mesozoic some did achieve considerable size. I believe the largest had a shell six and a half feet in diameter. However—"

"That's the one!"

He glanced toward her in the dark; she could tell this by the changing sound of his voice. "Actually, we know very little about their biology or life habits. The soft parts are not ordinarily preserved in fossils, and even if they were, there would be doubt about such things as color and temperament. But still, there are considerable objections to your thesis."

"In short, no," she said, smiling. She liked to smile, even when no one could see; it was a talent she had not always had. "Try this: could they have eaten a kind of swimming fungus exclusively, and become extinct when it disappeared?"

"One would then have to explain the abrupt extinction of the fungus," he pointed out.

"Maybe it emigrated to Nacre ..." But this was another dead end. It had been quite convincing in her dream, but it lacked that conviction here. The mystery remained, nagging her: why had so highly successful a subclass as the *Ammonoidea*, virtually rulers of the sea during the Cretaceous period, become abruptly extinct? Survived only by its far more primitive relative, the pearly nautilus. ...

"What, if I may inquire into such a personal matter, brought the status of the cephalopods to mind? I had understood these were not of paramount interest to you."

"You showed me those shells and explained, and I—had a dream," she said. "A foolish, waterlogged vision . . . if you care to listen."

"Oh, I have enormous respect for dreams," he said, surprising her. "Their primary purpose is to sort, assess, and file the accumulated experience of the preceding few hours. Without them we would soon all be thoroughly pyschotic, particularly on so-called contemporary Earth. Adapting to this Paleocene framework is difficult, but have you noticed how much less wearing it is intellectually than was merely *existing* on Earth? So it is not surprising that your dreams reflect the change. They are reaching out into the unbounded, as your mind responds to this release."

The odd thing was that he was right. She had longed to return to Nacre, because of the relief it offered from the tensions of home—but this world served the purpose just as well. She would rather be battered, seasick, and in fear for her life *here,* than safe and comfortable *there.*

But it was not entirely the freedom from Earth that was responsible, she knew. Cal, Veg, the mantas—she loved them all, and they all loved her, and Earth had nothing to match that.

She told Cal in detail about colorful King Ammon, and both laughed and it was good, and her seasickness dissipated.

At eight, daylight over the water, Veg came up to relieve Cal. "Do snails have false teeth?" he inquired groggily. "I had this dream—"

Direct sunlight hustled the mantas back inside the cabin, the solar radiation too hard on them. There had been tree shade on the island, and irregular cloud cover; apart from that they tended toward the night. It was not that they were naturally nocturnal; but high noon on the planet Nacre was solid fog, and the beam of the sun never touched their skins. These four were more resistant to hard light than were their kin on Nacre, for they had been raised on Earth—but environment could modify their heredity only so much. They could survive sunlight here, but not comfortably and not long.

The day swept on, the wind abating only momentarily. Her heart pounded pusillanimously during such hesitations, anticipating the consequence of a prolonged delay in mid-ocean. What use would land within a hundred miles be, if they had to *row* the clumsy craft there? And should the wind shift. . . .

At dusk, windchapped and tired, they watched the mantas come out and glide over the water, their pumping feet invisible as they moved at speed. How clearly this illustrated the fact that mantas did not perambulate or fly or swim! They jumped, and their flat bodies braced against the air in the manner of a kite or airplane wing, providing control. They either sat still and lumplike, or traveled at from thirty to a hundred miles per hour; they could not "walk." They were beautiful.

And they were hungry. Circling near the raft, they lashed at surfacing fish. She heard the whip-snap of their tails striking water, and saw the spreading blood. Cal brought out a long-handled hook Aquilon hadn't known was aboard and hauled the carcasses in. He spread them on the deck, and one by one the mantas came in to feed. Circe first—and Aquilon watched her chip the fish up into small chunks with her deadly tail, then settle on top of the mess for assimilation. Cal had placed a section of sail over the logs so that the fluids of this process would not be lost.

Veg did not watch, and neither, after a moment, did Aquilon. They all understood the necessity of feeding the mantas, and knew that the creatures could not digest anything but raw meat, and would not touch any but the flesh of omnivorous creatures—but this proximity was appalling. Circe had fed on rats in the theoretically aseptic far-cellar of Aquilon's Earth apartment building, and this had been accomplished privately. No doubt Hex had similarly isolated himself from Veg in the forest at feeding time. Now it was hard to accept physically what they had known intellectually. Only Cal seemed unaffected—and of course he had foreseen this problem too.

Aquilon called herself a hypocrite, but still did not watch. Perhaps it was because she knew herself to be a member of an omnivorous species—evolved to eat anything, and to kill wantonly. Whatever brutality was involved in the manta's existence was redoubled for man's. What could she accomplish, deciding to stop eating flesh after indulging for a lifetime, and spawned from millions of years ancestry of flesh eaters? Years would be required to expel the tainted protoplasm from her body, and the memory would never be expunged. Yet how could she kill, now that she comprehended the inherent evil of the action?

She felt sick again. Damn her subjectivity!

In five days they spotted land.

"There she blows!" Veg sang out happily.

"That's land ho!" Aquilon corrected him. "Fine lookout *you'd* make."

But she was immensely relieved, and knew the others were too. Diminished appetites had extended their stores of food, but the men were looking lean and the limit had been coming distressingly near. Their camaraderie had never been tested by real hunger. Certainly it would have been ugly—a compulsive meat-eater, a vegetarian, and a woman wavering unprettily between, and nothing but fish. . . .

But she was relieved because of the change in scenery, too. The sea, after the first day, had become monotonous; it had seemed as though they were sailing nowhere, accomplishing nothing.

The *Nacre* tacked clumsily along the shoreline, seeking an appropriate landing. Aquilon could not be certain whether it was mainland or merely a large island, but it was obviously suitable for foraging and camping. No smog.

"No really formidable land animals on Earth during the Paleocene epoch," Cal remarked, as though to reassure them.

"Good for Paleo," Veg said.

"Paleo?"

"Here. You want to call this world Epoch instead?"

Cal did not argue. Veg tended to identify things simply, and the names stuck. Henceforth this planet would be Paleo.

Soon a calm inlet opened, and Veg guided the craft so neatly into the cove that she knew it was blind luck. She watched for a suitable beach, wondering whether this was San Francisco Bay. Probably not; everything could have changed. Palms were in view, and conifers, and populous deciduous trees. Birds flitted through the branches, uttering harsh notes. Insects swarmed. Flowers of many types waved in the breeze.

"Look—fungus!" she exclaimed, spying a giant puffball. For a moment she thought of Nacre again, the planet of fungi. But Paleo, really, was better, for here the sun could shine. In fact, she was coming to realize that Nacre itself had represented little more than an escape from Earth for her; there was nothing inherently appealing about it other-wise, except for the mantas. And it was not the *planet* Earth that soured her, but the human culture that infested it. Yes, yes—Paleo was better.

The raft drifted close. The bottom of the bay was clear now, small fish hovering placidly. The smell of woods and earth came to her as the wind subsided, cut off by the land. The soil-loam-humus *cleanness* of it filled her with longing.

Veg touched her arm, and she looked up with a start.

Near the shore stood two hairy animals. They were four-footed, thickset and toothy, with long tails and blunt multiple-hoofed feet. Small tusks projected from their mouths, and their eyes were tiny. The overall aspect was like that of a hippopotamus—except that they were far too small. The highest point of the back was no more than a yard off the ground.

"Amblypods," Cal remarked without surprise. "*Cory-phodon*, probably. Typical Paleocene fauna."

"Yeah, typical," Veg muttered. "You never saw it be-fore, but you know all about it."

Cal smiled. "Merely a matter of a decent paleontologi-cal grounding. I don't really know very much, but I'm familiar with the general lines. The amblypods are distinc-tive. One of the later forms, *Uintatherium*, had the bulk of an elephant, with three pairs of horns on his—"

"You figure any of those are around here?"

"Of course not. *Uintatherium* was Eocene. He could no more show up in a Paleocene landscape than could a dinosaur."

Veg's eyes ranged over the forest. "I sure would laugh if a dinosaur poked his head over the hill while you were saying that. You're so sure of yourself."

Cal smiled again, complacently. "When that happens, you'll certainly be entitled to your mirth. The shellfish I studied on the island were decisive."

Veg shook his head and guided the raft to shore. Aquilon noticed irrelevantly that his face was filling out with blond beard. The amblypods, startled by the in-trusion, trotted off, soon to be lost in the forest.

Smoothly the *Nacre* glided in, cutting the gap to land to twenty feet, fifteen, ten—

And jarred to a halt, dumping Veg and Aquilon into the water. "Oops, struck bottom," Veg said sheepishly. "Wasn't thinking."

"Wasn't *thinking*," she exclaimed, cupping a splash of water at him violently. But she was so glad to touch solid land that she didn't care. The sea was hip-deep on her here, and she waded ashore gleefully, pulling strings of seaweed from her torso.

Veg, meanwhile, went back to fetch a rope and haul the craft about by hand. Cal, never careless about his footing, had held his place, and helped unwind the coil. Soon they had the raft hitched loosely to a mangrove trunk.

Aquilon wandered inland, content for the moment merely to absorb the sights and smells of this richly primitive world. Ferns grew thickly on the ground, and she recognized several species of bush and tree: sycamore, holly, persimmon, willow, poplar, magnolia. Mosses sprouted profusely, and mushrooms were common; but she saw no grass, to her surprise. Still, there had been bamboo on the island, and that was a form of grass.

Something launched itself from a shrub ahead, and she jumped in alarm. It was a brown streak that sailed through the air, away from her. She caught a glimpse of extended limbs, a web of skin, an oblong shape. Then it was gone; she heard the rustle of its ascent in other foliage. It was not a bird.

"Planetetherium," Cal said behind her. "Primitive insectivore, one of the prime mammalian stocks. A glider."

"Yes ..." she said, seeming to remember it from her studies. She really had no excuse to be ignorant of mammalian lines, but time and other considerations had let her knowledge fade. Cal, with his appalling intellect, seemed never to forget a thing.

"Perhaps you should change," Cal suggested, "before you become uncomfortable."

She looked down at herself. Her clothing was plastered against her body, and she knew the salt would chafe as the moisture evaporated. Cal was right, as always.

Yet the air was pleasant, and despite the shade of the

trees there was no chill. She wished she could simply remove her clothes and glide nymphlike through glade and fern, free of all encumbrance.

"Why not?" she said rhetorically. She began to strip, handing her wet garments to Cal stage by stage. He made no comment, and did not avert his gaze.

So she ran, nymphlike, through glade and fern. It was every bit as glorious as she had imagined, except for a thorn that got in her foot. She had shed the restraints of civilization with her clothing, and was whole again.

Veg's mouth dropped open appreciatively as she burst upon him, but he said no more than Cal had.

The *Nacre* was tight against the shore: Veg's muscle had come into play Her dry apparel was aboard, but she hesitated to seek it. Wouldn't it be better if they *all* were to—

No. Sexual tensions existed among them already at a barely submerged level. It would be criminally foolish to do anything to heighten them needlessly. Subdued, she boarded the raft and dressed.

They spent the night on the raft, anchored just offshore. There might be no dangerous species, but they preferred a little more time for acclimation.

In the morning the insects and birds were clustered thickly on the shore. The first were familiar, the second strange. Several large gray sea fowl swam around the raft, diving for fish. Aquilon stood on the deck and painted them, intrigued by their fearlessness. Were there no significant predators on the water? Or was the raft so unusual as to be taken for an artifact of nature? Or did they know instinctively who was a threat and who was not?

Veg brought the *Nacre* to shore again and tied up. This time there was no premature jolt. She wondered whether he had scouted the bottom to locate a suitable channel for the keel, or whether he had excavated one himself.

They ventured inland several miles, as a party. Here were oaks, beeches, walnuts, and squirrellike creatures sporting in them. Occasional tufts of grass sprouted in the hilly country, where the thickly growing trees permitted.

So it *was* present, but not well established. Ratlike creatures skittered away as the human party approached.

"Were there true rodents in the Paleocene?" Aquilon inquired.

"Not to speak of," Cal said. "These are probably ancestral primates."

"Primates!" She was shocked.

"Before the true rodents developed, the primitive primates occupied that niche. They descended from trees, like most mammals, and took to the opening fields. But there wasn't enough grass, as you can see; it occupies a minor ecological niche until the Miocene epoch, when widespread dry plains developed. And the primates weren't completely committed. So the true rodents eventually drove them back into the trees, this time to stay. The primates never were very successful."

"Except for man . . ."

"A minor exception, paleontologically. Man happened to wobble back and forth between field and forest just enough to remain more generalized than most of his contemporaries. If he hadn't been lucky and clever, he would not have survived."

"I see." She wasn't certain how serious he was.

"Quite often it is the less specialized creature that pulls through," he continued blithely. "Conditions change, and the species fully adapted to a particular environment may have to change in a hurry or perish. Often it can't adapt. But the generalized species can jump either way. So although it seldom dominates, it may outlast those who do. Probably that explains the marginal success of the primitive nautilus, while the specialized and dominant ammonite vanished."

She had never thought of it quite that way. Man—as an unspecialized, lucky, but clever species, thrown into prominence by accident of circumstance. . . .

A large running bird with yellow tail feathers appeared and scooped up a careless mammal that resembled a kangaroo rat. The bird, a good two feet tall, passed quite close to them before passing out of sight. Aquilon wondered whether the rat could have been an ancestor of hers, then chided herself: dead, it could not have sired much. At any rate, it would be foolish to interfere. Suicidally foolish, possibly, for *any* change in the life patterns here might affect those of her own time.

"The birds showed considerably more promise, initially," Cal said. "Actually, throughout the Cenozoic until the present, they have dominated Earth, reckoned in the normal manner."

"By number of species," she said. "So I understand. But diversity isn't everything, fortunately."

"Fortunately?"

"You don't approve of man winning out?"

"I believe the world would have endured more amicably without him. It is not good to have a single species run amuck."

She saw that he meant it. She thought of contemporary Earth, and understood his point. Paleo was clean, unspoiled. Better that it remain that way, paradox aside.

The next few days they ranged more widely. They encountered more amblypods, and both doglike and catlike carnivores. The pursuers, Cal explained, had long snouts for reaching out on the run; the hide-and-pouncers had sharp claws for holding and slashing, and short snouts. The ambushers buried their dung, to mute the giveaway odor; the chasers did not bother. The physical properties of what were later to be canines and felines and ursines were not random. Another line was the fairly substantial *Dinocerata*, ancestors to the monster *Uintatherium* of the later epoch. But all these mammals were stupid, compared to those that were to evolve; none would have survived readily on Earth of fifty million years later. She painted them all, and Cal made many notes on his voicetyper. She learned to ignore the monotonous murmur of his descriptions as he made his entries.

This was a warm paradise—but she became restless. There was nothing, really, to *do*. It had been nice to dream of a life without responsibility or danger or discomfort, but the actuality palled rapidly. It was late summer, and a number of the trees bore small fruit, and there were berries and edible tubers. Food was not a serious problem. She talked with Veg and Cal, but knew them both too well already, and she did not care to get too personal lest it come down abruptly to the male-female problem. She had not decided between them, yet; that was what restrained her, she decided.

"Going to get cold," Veg observed. "Fall's coming."

Of course he was right. They didn't know their exact location, and it probably could not be matched precisely to a modern-Earth geography anyway, but the number of deciduous trees said things about the seasons. There might be no actual snow here in winter, or there might be several feet of it—but it would be cold enough to make leaves turn and drop. They would have to prepare for the worst, or—"Let's go south!" she cried. "To the tropics, where it is warm all year round. Explore. Travel. Survey."

"You sound as though we're staying here indefinitely," Cal remarked, but there was something funny about the way he said it. *He's afraid of something*, she thought, and that made her uneasy. Was it that a long-term residence would force them to revert farther toward the natural state, mating and homemaking? Or that doing so would upset the existing balance of nature and imperil the status quo on Earth, because of the paradox effect? Her inclination was to ignore that; somehow she doubted that what they did *here* could affect Earth *there*, whatever the theory might be. And if it did—well, so be it.

"Actually, there appears to be more than enough data on hand to render a report on Paleo," Cal continued.

She felt the skin along her forearms tightening—a nervous reaction once more common than now. She *had* forgotten, or tried to forget, their assigned mission. The truth was that she viewed the prospective return to Earth, or whatever other mission awaited next, with misgiving bordering on alarm. She liked Paleo, bored though she had been with it a moment ago. She liked its wildness— "In wildness is the preservation of the world," she remembered from somewhere—and she would far rather tackle its problems than those of Earth society.

But they had little excuse to tarry longer. The onset of winter could be of little concern to them if they were to return to the station and report. Their radio equipment

97

was in good order, and they could find the way by homing in on the master unit remaining in the tunnel.

But she was sure, now, that Cal did not want to go back, though she also knew it would be useless to challenge him on that. He comprehended something she did not, something that worried him deeply, but that he chose to keep to himself. He might allow himself to be persuaded to travel south—or somewhere, anywhere but back—if she could provide a strong enough pretext.

Yet she did not care to admit her true feelings yet. How did Veg stand?

"Can't sail back against the wind," Veg said. "More likely sink, tacking the whole way, and it'd take us a month in clear weather. Going to get hungry on the way."

Bless him! She felt a surge of special affection for the big, simple man, so naïve in manner but practical in action. They *couldn't* go back without enormous preparation.

"Of course," Cal said, unperturbed. "I was thinking of a radio report. We can not make a physical return until the wind shifts with the season—though that may occur any day now."

That did not reassure her particularly, though she wasn't sure why. Cal seemed to be agreeing to some procrastination, and a radio report would keep them officially on duty.

"I thought your report came at the end," Veg said.

"Not necessarily. We were to determine the status of the planet, then put the report on record for the next in-phase connection to Earth. It was presumed that these various delays would make the report wait for a month or two, perhaps longer. But we've done the job. This is definitely Paleocene. All the fauna and flora check. We have exceeded coincidence by a millionfold; this can not be a foreign planet."

"How about the geography?"

"I explained about that. Their map seems accurate, and it *is*—"

"We could follow the coast a little and find out, maybe," Veg said. "Make sure there isn't some out-of-place continent, or something."

Clumsy, clumsy, she thought. That tack would never work.

Cal smiled ruefully. "In other words, you're voting with 'Quilon again."

Was he *asking* to be outvoted? What was on his mind?

Veg shrugged, missing the implication. "There's time to kill, and maybe we'll learn something new for your report. Better than sitting around here waiting for the wind."

"That's a transparent appeal to the researcher in me," Cal said. "You know I don't like to make a premature statement, and so long as the possibility exists of discovering something significant—" He sighed. "All right. I know how the mantas feel. They all want to remain here indefinitely. So a full vote would change nothing. We'll leave one of the two radios here under cover and mark the place. That way, if anything happens to the raft, I'll still be able to make my report."

Aquilon smiled uneasily. Cal had yielded almost too readily.

They sailed by day, tacking along the shore and covering about twenty miles before searching out a harbor for the night. It was good to be moving again, even though there was now no tangible destination.

A month passed like the breath of the breeze, and it was good. Gradually the curve of the continent brought them around so that they were sailing south-southeast and largely before the shifting wind. They had come perhaps eight hundred miles, and only verified that the Paleocene landscape was remarkably uniform, though she realized that this could be because their progress south roughly matched that of the coming fall season.

The mantas rode the raft the first few days, then took to traveling on land. They would disappear in the morning and reappear at the new camp in the evening. Sometimes only one or two would show up, the others ranging elsewhere for days at a time. Yes, they liked Paleo!

It was Circe who broke the lull, bringing news to Aquilon just before dusk. "Mountains? Tall ones?" Aquilon inquired, reading the manta's responses so readily now that it was almost the same as human dialogue. "Unusual? Snow-capped? And—"

She spoke to the others, excitedly. "It seems there are extremely large mountains about two hundred miles south of us. Twenty thousand feet, or more. They form a virtually solid wall, and a number are actively volcanic. The mantas can't get past, on land, because of the cold, and they don't trust the water route either."

"How can an active volcano have snow on it?" Veg demanded. "It's hot, isn't it—or else the snow would put it out."

"Silly! Volcanoes aren't on fire," she reproved him. "One could shoot off in a snowstorm—or underwater, as many do." But she was thrilled. They were finally coming up to something atypical, something not suggested by the map or Cal's knowledge of Paleocene geography. Massive, active volcanoes, shoulder to shoulder, in America.

The mantas had been ranging far ahead, scouting the territory, yet had been balked by these, both on land and water. A mighty barrier indeed, for the manta's traveling range was good.

"If that's the region the tsunami originated from," Cal said, "we had better approach it with exceeding caution."

Aquilon nodded soberly, but she was singing inside. This promised to be an unforgettable experience—and that, despite all the undertones, was a thing she ardently craved.

IX: ORN

The mountains were high, and chill winds swept through the pass. The range was new; Orn's memory of the landscape of this tropical section of the subcontinent indicated a flat plain sometimes submerged by an inlet of the ocean. Natural forces had come into play in unusual fashion to bring this orogeny where none had occurred before. Yet it was possible that his mental map was inaccurate, for this was at the fringe of it. None of his ancestors had gone far beyond this place, having been stopped by the sea. The range, and whatever land might lie beyond it, must have risen complete out of that ocean in the past few million years.

Orn would have turned back and sought another route, but it had been a long, difficult climb, game was scarce, and he was hungry. Prey might be near ahead; it certainly was not near behind. He ran on, generating new warmth to replace what the wind tore from him. If the lie of this pass were typical, the descent would begin soon.

It did. As Orn passed the ridge, the weather changed. The cold dry air became cold damp air that steadily warmed as he went lower. The stinging snow became ice mist, then rain.

He adjusted his wings to shed as much water as possible in their oil-starved state and went on. He wanted to reach the lowlands by nightfall, and fill his crop. The vegetation was increasing, but the ferns and palmetto bore no fruit.

It was getting warm. Orn recognized the type of soil underfoot. Volcanic in origin. This alerted him; he knew firsthand, and many times over, how dangerous volcanism was. Instead of getting out of it, he was going deeper in.

There seemed to be more regions of such activity than ever in the past, and had his mind worked that way Orn would have wondered what the world was coming to. Great changes were taking place all over the land mass, apart from the revisions of plant and animal life. It continued to be unsettling.

He came across a streamlet, and followed it down rapidly. Dusk was coming. Just as it became almost too dark to forage by sight, he found a shallow pond stocked with fat lazy fish, teleos. He jumped in with both feet and scooped two out before they took alarm.

He fed well and spent the night in a dense mag tree. The hazard of the mountain range had been overcome.

In the clear morning Orn looked out over the landscape. The stream fell away in a series of rapids and finally disappeared in a tangled mass of vegetation at the

101

foot of the slope. A short distance beyond that lay the shore of a wide shallow lake. Many thickly overgrown islands spotted it, and portions were little more than liquid swamp. Far in the distance across that water rose another ridge of mountains.

The valley was hot. Jets of steam plumed from the bay nearest the live volcanoes and thick mists hung over much of the lake.

The valley was flat. Nothing stood taller than the height of the trees, and the majority of it was open water. It was, on the whole, familiar: this was the landscape of twenty million years ago, sharpest in his memory, though in greatly reduced scale.

He followed the stream down. Rushes and horsetails grew at the edges of its shallows, and leafed plants bordered it everywhere. Tufts of grass were present high on the mountainside, but disappeared in the lowland, unable to compete there. Orn did not miss it; grass was tough and tasteless stuff and its seeds were too small for his appetite.

As the land leveled out, Orn lost sight of the overall valley. He discovered that it was not as flat as it had seemed from above; mist had filled in irregularities, concealing banks and gulleys and gorges. The stream plunged into a mass of tall trees. A few were of the seasonal leaf-dropping variety that had taken over the continent of the north, but most were the memory-familiar ginks and firs. Here full-sized fern trees prospered, and many treelike varieties of cycad.

Game was especially plentiful. The little primes peeked out from the branches of the larger leafed trees and liz were abundant on the turf. Flying arths hummed everywhere.

He cut away from the river that was degenerating into swamp, and shortly came out on a bushy plateau punctuated by short barrel-bodied cycads and shrublike angios. Moss covered the occasional rocks. He trotted after a particularly large four-winged drag, not with any real hope of catching it but content to explore this wonderful, unexpected reincarnation of familiarity. Any pretext would do.

A huge, low shape rose before him. Orn was almost

upon it before he was aware, having allowed pursuit of the winger to take up more of his attention than was wise. He had become careless, in this season of innocuous animals. He had smelled no large mam, so had relaxed. Foolishly.

It was a rep—a big one. It was not as tall as Orn, but that was because this creature's whole body was spread out against the ground. Its head was low and armored with bony scales, and four toothlike horns projected sidewise. Similar scales extended the length of the body, making the back a broad impervious trunk. Stout spikes lined each side, some as long as Orn's beak and as wickedly curved. The tail was a blunt, solid mass of bone.

Orn remembered immediately. This was an Anky, one of the lines of great reps. It was four times his own length and disproportionately heavy and powerful, but no aggressive threat to him. Its massive armor was defensive, and it was a herbivore.

This was the second giant land rep he had seen here. The first had been in the cavern, mysteriously dead, but this one was healthy. Orn did not concern himself with the complex ramifications of his discovery, but did understand that where there was one live monster there were likely to be more. His relaxing reflexes were brought once more to full functioning, and he looked around alertly and somewhat furtively.

The Anky, slow-witted, became aware of him, and flexed its tail. Orn leaped back. A single sweep of that bludgeon could destroy him, were he so careless as to step within its range. The Anky was harmless—but normal precautions had to be taken. It could kill without meaning to.

The Anky took a slow step forward, the muscles in its short thick legs making the scales bulge outward. It was curious about him, in its dull way. He could easily outrun it, but preferred not to. Guided by a memory functioning for the first time the way it should, Orn stood still. The Anky hesitated, then lost interest and took another mouthful of leaves from the nearest shrub. What did not move and did not smell threatening did not exist as a danger to it. Anky had forgotten him.

Orn moved on, alarming the rep again. This time he was not concerned; he had verified the reliability of his memory, and would trust it within this valley. The sun was high now; the mists had cleared and the brush ahead thinned out into a field of low ferns.

A herd of large animals came into view, grazing peacefully. Orn recognized these too: Tricers. Larger than the ones his ancestors had known, more horny—but also harmless, for him, when undisturbed.

He approached them cautiously, but they took no notice of him. Nearest was a large bull as long as the Anky, but taller than Orn, with a monstrous shield projecting from the back of the head. Three heavy-duty horns curved slightly downward from the region of eyes and nose, and mighty muscles flexed as it swung its head about. This was an animal no sensible creature tampered with.

Orn skirted the herd of fifty or more individuals and traveled on toward the main lake. The turf became spongy and the horsetails tall. And, significantly, the small birds became silent.

A head appeared above the mixed foliage. Orn jumped, spreading his wings in a reflex, that had nothing to do with flying. He recognized this rep, too—and now he was in for trouble. This was a Struth.

The Struth was about Orn's own height, and rather similar in physique at first glance. It stood on long slender hind legs, and its small head topped a sinuous neck. It was omnivorous, but did not attack large prey. Its diet consisted of arths, aves, mams, and anything else that offered, such as eggs or fruit. It was fleet.

The resemblance to Orn ended about there, for the Struth had small forelimbs in lieu of wings, and a strong fleshy tail in place of Orn's tuft of feathers, and a mottled smooth skin and a much uglier beak. Its body, like that of any rep, varied in temperature with the heat of the day.

But its similarities to Orn were enough to constitute a problem, for the two shared, to a considerable extent, an ecological niche. They were direct competitors.

Orn had never physically encountered a Struth before, but his memory covered all of this. The rep, possessing some faint hint of the species recollection so highly developed in Orn, knew the competitor instinctively. They were not enemies in the sense of predator/prey, but the one could not tolerate the other in his foraging ground. The rival for food had to be driven off.

The Struth, despite the similarity in size, outmassed Orn considerably, for it had fat and muscle where he had down and quill. It was fresh, while he was lean from the difficult trek over wasteland and mountain. In the chill of night or height, Orn would have contested with it nevertheless, for his warm body did not become lethargic as the temperature dropped. His reactions there would be faster, his blows surer, his perceptions more accurate.

But this was the heat of the day, and of the lowland, and the rep was at its best in its home territory. Orn, in these circumstances, would be foolish to fight it now.

The Struth was aware of its advantage. It charged.

Neither bravery nor cowardice were concepts in Orn's lexicon. He battled when it behooved him to, and avoided trouble at other times. He fled.

The Struth had routed its rival—but was not bright enough to realize it yet. The chase, once commenced, had to continue until it terminated forcefully in some fashion.

Orn was a swift runner, as he had to be as a landbound bird. But the terrain was new to him in detail, and the somewhat marshy ground was poor footing for his claws. He started with a fair lead, but the rep was gaining. This pursuit might be pointless for *it*—but it could also be fatal for *him*.

Orn dodged to the side, seeking to avoid the Tricer herd. The Struth cut across the angle, narrowing the gap between them rapidly. Only five body-lengths separated them now.

It would be useless to seek out the water and wade into it; the rep would merely follow, making better progress because of its solidity. Orn could swim on the surface, as the Struth could not—but deep water was dangerous for other reasons. He would need time to scout it out thoroughly before trusting himself to it, regardless of the chase.

The ground became mucky, inhibiting him more. The wet sand and clinging mud encumbered his feet, slowing him down critically and tiring him rapidly. It interfered with the Struth too, but not as much. The gap was down to three body-lengths.

Orn ran on, not exhausted but straining to his utmost. Soon he would have to stand and fight—and unless he were unrealistically fortunate, the outcome would be the same as that of the chase. He could hurt the rep, perhaps cripple it—but could not expect to overcome it.

A single bull Tricer grazed in the cycads at the edge of an inlet of marsh. Orn saw that in his haste he had trapped himself: ahead and to one side was a bubbling swamp that he dared not enter unprepared, even granted the time to do so, and to the other side was the massive horned herbivore. He had nowhere to go.

Except—

He did it, hearing the Struth one length behind. He lunged toward the bull as though to impale himself on the ferocious horns.

The Tricer looked up, huge and stupid. A green strand dangled from its beak. Its tiny eyes were obscured by the two vicious horns overshadowing them, and the semicircular flange of head armor stood higher than Orn himself. Yes, a most dangerous creature—but slow to initiate business. Its eyesight was not good, so it judged a potential enemy primarily by size and smell—and did not fear birds. Provided that it recognized them in time.

Orn ran up to it, fluttering his wings and squawking so that his avian affinity was quite clear—to almost any creature. He passed within a wingspan of the Tricer's head ... and the bull merely stood there, attempting to make up its mind.

The Struth, however, did not dare try such a stunt. It was a hunter, and therefore not completely dense. Though too small to be a threat to the bull, it was too large to be tolerated by the herd. Orn saw the juvenile Tricers sporting near their dams. Actually, few reps guarded their eggs or protected their own young, but those infants who stayed with the herd tended to survive more readily than those who wandered free, so the effect was much the same. No—no predator was welcome here.

But the Struth, intent on the chase, did not sheer off in

106

time. It approached the bull moments after Orn passed: just time enough for the monster to make up his mind. The Tricer sniffed, snorted, and whipped his terrible shield about, making ready to charge.

Already the Struth realized what was happening. The delay had been in implementation rather than cognizance. Now it halted and pulled back, the bull following. Finally the Struth ran back the way it had come, its original mission forgotten. The Tricer pursued it a few paces, then stopped and resumed grazing. The episode was over, and Orn was safe.

Just as well. He had had no real quarrel with the Struth, and was happy to honor its territorial integrity. His only concern had been to protect himself.

He walked through the herd unmolested. This was good, because it gave him respite, but he could not remain here indefinitely. A Tricer cow might absent-mindedly step on him. And if anything should happen to alarm the herd, to send it milling or stampeding, he could be crushed between the bruising bodies.

Yet where was he to go? This was a pleasant and memory-familiar valley in type if not in detail, and he could reside here comfortably for some time. But it did not have that something which had increasingly urged him on.

He left the herd and struck for the mountain range that defined the valley. There at least he could find arths and fish to satisfy his returning hunger, and probably that elevation was free of large predators. With this return of the old world had come the old dangers. He had allowed himself to become used to sleeping safely, and until he recovered his proper nocturnal reflexes he did not dare to sleep amid the reps. Though he could not visualize these until he saw them, he was aware that far more dangerous creatures prowled this valley than the ones he had encountered so far.

This, at least, was the gist of the diffuse array of thoughts Orn had as he climbed the slope.

He returned to the descending river and the volcanic soil, because these were now familiar. Familiarity was life to him. There was danger from the heated earth and the rumbling mountain, but this known hazard militated against *unknown* hazards. The volcanic threat applied to *all* creatures particularly the reps, and the environment was in fact more hostile to them than to him. He would utilize it until a larger area had been properly scouted.

He encountered no more of the large reps, though his sensitive eyes and nose picked up their profuse traces. There were numbers of them, mostly young, but these hid from him. The valley was not really more crowded than the surrounding areas beyond the badlands; it merely seemed that way because its denizens tended to be larger and more familiar. There were small mams in far greater abundance in the north country, while the huge reps were comparatively sparse. A few crocs, a few snakes. What had happened, there?

He dined on fish again, and splashed the clear water over his feathers, refreshing them. Time had passed, and now it was afternoon. He began to search for an appropriate lodging for the night. He preferred not to roost directly on the ground, but an ascent into a tree was impractical, here where the trees were stunted and scarce. Possibly a good thicket of thorns—

This was a serious matter, and Orn undertook his search carefully. He was looking for a permanent roost—one he could depend on during the entire period of his stay within this valley. Later he might develop other roosts, so that he could canvass more distant sections of the valley without having to make a long trek back; but this first refuge was essential.

The sun dipped toward the far side, making the range there thrust up in silhouette, and the clouds became pink. But still he had not found a suitable spot.

The ground was becoming warm again, signal of another subterranean furnace ahead, or at least a vent from the depths. It was as though the entire range were riddled with hot conduits. Orn became nervous, reminded again of what could happen in such terrain. He did not think of it at other times; the immediacy, as always, conjured the painful image. Yet he felt there was a certain security in water. Though the river channel might shift, it was protection against actual fire.

Accordingly, he followed an offshoot of the stream up toward its snowy source. He could, if necessary, spend this night in the coldest heights. The reps certainly would not be there. But this would not be comfortable, and it was too far away from the valley proper to be convenient as a regular thing.

He came across a waterfall, as the sun touched the far mountains. The brook passed over an outcropping of hard rock, forming a pool above and another below, and splayed in a shallow falling sheet between the two. The drop was somewhat more than Orn's standing height, but the force of the water was not great.

He recognized the construction. Behind such a sheet of water would be a concavity, where the less durable substrata melted away in the course of millennia. This was the way, in the life cycle of rivers. Sometimes there was space enough underneath for a large bird to roost.

Orn braced himself and poked his beak into the waterfall. The cold water split, and his head went on through. There was space—but no adequate footing. In an emergency he might grasp one slanting ridge of rock with one foot, and hang on to the carved backwall with his beak, but certainly not by preference. This was not his roost.

Then something activated every perception and conjured a barrage of images, one tumbling over the other in unique confusion. Orn snapped back his head and stood rocking in the spuming water, sorting it out while his wings fluttered spasmodically.

The thing he had been unknowingly searching for—the nameless mission—the object of his quest—

Excitement! For he had seen the traces of a prior occupant of that emergency roost. The scrape of claw, the mark of beak—

The unmistakable spoor of another bird of his species. Another "Orn"—his own age, and female.

X: VEG

It was a truly awesome range: scarred volcanic cones set almost adjacent to each other to form a wall, seemingly solid, extending right into the sea. The ambient fumes suggested that the volcanic activity continued beneath the water, too, and there were very few fish.

"I don't understand this," Cal lamented. "This should be about where Baja California terminates, or will terminate, on our globe. This formation, to put it euphemistically, is atypical."

Veg maneuvered the *Nacre* into deep water, unconcerned with that aspect. He could see why the mantas hadn't fooled with this section; it was a real wasteland.

The mountains were followed by much more active cones. An almost impenetrable fog of gas and floating ash obscured portions of the shore. After that came desert, rent by jagged rifts. They drew the raft in only enough to view the desolation under strange foul clouds, and did not touch land.

At one point the wind reversed, pushing the *Nacre* far out to sea before he could angle it back. The smell was appalling. They had to tie shirts over their heads to keep the stinging particles out of eyes and lungs. The four mantas huddled inside the cabin, no more comfortable, though of course they did not need to breathe.

After days and nights of this another range appeared, even more massive and imposing than the first. Its oceanic barriers extended far out, becoming mighty reefs with jigsaw-puzzle elevations poking through the surface. It was as though grotesque statues stood upon the water, mocking Jesus Christ.

Twice the *Nacre* was snagged, forcing them to disembark and struggle waist-deep in the gritty fluid to free it. But there were some few fish here, and corals, and crabs,

110

and barnacles. To their dismay, they had to wear shoes in the water, for the fish had teeth and the crabs pincers, and the coral was sharp.

"But where there's life, there's hope," Aquilon said. Veg didn't think it was funny, but agreed that some sea life was better than none, for things must be about to ease up.

At last they spied deep water—but had virtually to portage across a final band of shallows. The solid raft, even without their weight or that of the mantas, projected too far down to make navigation easy, and it was crushingly heavy to haul about by hand. The palm wood had become waterlogged, making it worse. Veg had to dive under and remove the keel, and even so the raft caught on every conceivable piece of reef. He braced his feet against the rocklike coral foundation and hauled on the front rope, while Cal and Aquilon pried with poles.

Busy as he was, he couldn't help noticing Aquilon's anatomy as she strained at the raft. Her shapely legs were bare from the water level up to her brief shorts, and her midriff was open too. Her bosom flexed as her arms moved, each breast a live thing straining at the halter. Her blonde hair was tied back, but several major strands had pulled away and now whipped across her face erratically.

Ah, she was lovely now—far more so than when she had affected nudity that one time just after they landed. Clothes made the woman, not the man, for they supported and concealed and enhanced and made mysteries where mysteries belonged. Not that she was unattractive, nude; oh no! But now—now he felt like charging through the water, sweeping her up entire, and—

And nothing. With Aquilon it had to be voluntary—even in his fancy. The mere touch of her fingers on his arm meant more than the definitive embrace of any woman he had known before. Her smile gave him a shortness of breath, though he had loved her long before he had seen her smile. Even that time on planet Nacre, when she had made that shocking expression, as though the muscles of her face were connected up the wrong way—even then, his horror had been because he *cared*. In fact, it hardly seemed that there could have been a time when—

The raft broke away from whatever submarine object

111

had held it, and Veg tumbled forward into deep water. He let go the rope and clamped his mouth and eyes shut as he hit. The warm bath tugged at his clothing, and trapped air hauled him immediately back to the surface before bursting out of his shirt in an embarrassing bubble.

For an instant his eyes opened under water. It was clear, here.

A gigantic fish was coming at him. It resembled a swordfish, but it had a fin on its back like that of a shark and its eyes were each as big as a human head. The creature was well over twenty feet long, sleek, swift, and strong.

Veg propelled himself out of the depths and onto the reef in a manner he could never afterward recall. He stood at the brink, dumbly pointing.

The fish broke surface and leaped partially into the air, its tremendous nose-spine opening to reveal many small teeth. Vapor spouted from a blowhole over the eyes.

"That's no porpoise!" Aquilon exclaimed, amazed.

Cal stood open-mouthed. Veg had never seen the little man so surprised.

The creature departed as rapidly as it had come, never bothering to attack. Veg's knees felt weak. That dinner-plate eye! "Never saw a fish like that before," he said shakily.

"Fish?" Cal was coming out of his daze.

"Didn't you see it? With the beak and the—"

"That was *Ichthyosaurus*!" Cal said, as though it were marvelously significant.

Now Aquilon began to react. "The reptile?"

"The reptile."

Veg decided there was something he was missing, but he waited until the *Nacre* had been reloaded and they were on their way again before challenging it.

The treacherous reefs enclosed a moderately shallow ocean basin about thirty miles across. Into this projected two large islands separated from each other by a one-mile channel. They were mountainous; ugly black cones rammed into the sky from each, and yellow-brown vapor trailed from one.

112

"Scylla and Charybdis," Aquilon murmured. "Let's go around."

Veg obligingly angled north so as to pass Scylla on the western shore, heading in toward land. His keel, replaced, was not properly firm, but the weather in this cove was gentle and he had no trouble. About three miles separated the island from land, and on both sides were small white beaches backed by tangled jungle. Nearest to the water were tall tree-ferns, but inland, up the mountain slopes, he could make out the solid green of stands of pine and fir. There was a light haze, and every so often he sneezed.

"Heavy pollen in the air," Cal explained.

"Now that we're on the subject," Veg said, "what's wrong with that fish being a reptile?"

Aquilon looked at Cal. "He just won that bet about the dinosaurs, though he doesn't know it!"

"I did?" Veg asked. "All I saw was a big-eyed fish, dark gray with a light-gray belly and a snout that almost rammed me. And you—"

Cal looked serious. "Nevertheless, its presence forces us into a considerable reappraisal."

"Funniest looking dino *I* ever saw! How long did you say they've been dead?"

Aquilon reached up to ruffle his matted hair. She, at least, was at ease. "Extinct is the word, not dead. And it's been about seventy million years, on Earth. The dinosaurs died out at the end of the Cretaceous."

"So they've been gone five million years, here—and we haven't seen one yet, and maybe we won't unless we go back into the Bodacious."

"Cretaceous," Cal said, missing the outlandish joke—another sign that the man had been badly shaken up. "The name comes from the Latin word *Creta*, meaning chalk. So it's the chalk age. Chalky limestones such as the White Cliffs of Dover—"

"So the dinosaurs were full of chalk," Veg said, wondering how far to take this game. "Used it in their big bones, I guess."

"I'm afraid that's not quite it. The chalk came from the compacted skeletons of billions of single-celled animals, the *Foraminifera*, who lived in the shallow seas. But such

113

animal chalk deposits are hardly more than an episode in the seventy-million-year period of the Cretaceous."

Veg remained solemn. "On Earth, maybe. But this isn't Earth."

"But it *is*," Aquilon murmured. "Paleocene Earth. Dawn of the age of mammals."

"I *know* what mammals are," he said, looking at her bosom.

"Mammaries," she said, correcting him without embarrassment. "Typical of the mammals."

"Whose distinguishing trait is—hair," Cal added, suppressing a smile.

Veg let that pass, seeing that Cal had gotten over his disturbance. "So if there are dinosaurs, this would be Creta instead of Paleo. Now how about this famous fish?"

"Cal just explained," Aquilon said. "It's *not* a fish. It's *Ichthyosaurus*—a swimming reptile. Its ancestors walked on land, and it breathes air."

"Same as a crocodile. What does that prove?"

Cal took over. "*Ichthyosaurus* is a member of class *Reptilia*, order *Ichthyosauria*—the swimming reptiles. It is not considered to be a dinosaur. The dinosaurs are actually a popular composite of two reptilian orders, the *Saurischia* and the *Ornithischia*, respectively 'lizard-hips' and 'bird-hips'. They were primarily land or swamp dwellers."

"Somewhere in there I think you brushed near my question. Icky is not a dinosaur, just as I thought. Good. So now tell me why you figure it's so significant, this fish-reptile. What's it got to do with dinosaurs?"

"He's got you there," Aquilon said to Cal.

"They were contemporaneous phenomena. The Cretaceous was the zenith of the reptilian radiation. Almost all the lines flourished then—and almost all died out before the Paleocene. The *Ichthyosaurus* passed before a number of the land-dwelling forms, so—"

"So if Icky's still here, so are the dinos," Veg said. "*Now* I make the connection. It *is* like a dinosaur poking his snout over the hill."

"Of course that doesn't necessarily follow—"

"Oh, no, I'm happy to have it follow. Serves you right."

"But you see, this *is* the Paleocene," Cal said. "The

114

ocean fauna, and everything we have observed on land—the evolution of the other species is cumulatively definitive. Dinosaurs have no place here, no place at all, unless—"

"Unless?" Veg and Aquilon were both curious.

"Unless there is an enclave. An isolated carryover of the Cretaceous fauna—doomed to extinction, but surviving the demise of its age by a few million years. Those sea reptiles that fed on fish or belemnites might endure, such as the particular ichthyosaur we encountered, but not those specializing in ammonites. Though why there should be no fossil record—"

"It *could* have happened on Earth," Aquilon said. "We might yet discover a submerged bed of fossils that proved—"

"Down!" Veg whispered ferociously.

They obeyed immediately, cutting off the conversation. In silence they followed his gaze.

They had been rounding the green bend of the island Scylla, Vog now poling the craft along. Standing, he had the best view, and so had seen it first—but it made them all flinch. In the silence one of the mantas poked around the shady side of the cabin: Hex, getting his own eyeful.

It was a tremendous serpentine neck, seeming at first to be truncated just short of the head. The column projected fifteen feet from the water and was barely a hundred feet from the raft. It was smooth and round and gently tapering—and as Veg examined it more closely, he found that it terminated in a head hardly larger than the neck's smallest diameter. An eye was half hidden under a kind of fleshy crest, and beyond that was a rounded, wrinkled snout. Despite the small appearance of the head, he judged that the jaw was a good two feet long. That creature could, Veg reflected, finish a man in just about three bites lengthwise.

Plumes of vapor formed above the crest, signifying the location of nostrils, and now Veg could hear its heavy-bellows breathing. There had to be a lot more body out of sight beneath the water, for he could make out no expansion and contraction of the visible portion as the air rushed in and out.

As they watched, the minuscule head dipped in toward the land, to take a swipe at floating foliage there. The teeth were pegs that clamped rather than cut or chewed. The creature either hadn't noticed them, or it considered them to be beneath notice.

Veg poled the *Nacre* quietly backward. Slowly they rounded the turn of Scylla, passing out of sight of the monster as it lifted its head high to swallow.

"That is the biggest snake I ever heard of," Veg announced when they had achieved the limited safety of distance.

"No snake could lift its head like that, that far," Aquilon said, obviously shaken. "Not unless it were over two hundred feet long—and that's unlikely. I think that's some other swimming reptile. There was one with a long neck, wasn't there, Cal?"

Cal smiled with some obscure satisfaction. "Yes there was, 'Quilon. Some types of plesiosaurus. But such a creature could hardly stand still in the water like that, and would not feed on watercress. This is a reptile of quite a different nature—a true dinosaur, in fact. We saw only a tiny portion of it."

Aquilon stood up straight. "Of course! The thunder lizard—*Brontosaurus!*"

"No. Not quite. The head does not conform. The brontosaur's nostrils were at the apex, and I doubt that many survived much beyond the Jurassic. This would be its later cousin, the largest of them all: *Brachiosaurus.*"

"Brach," Veg said, pinning down the name. "Sounds like some fantasy hero."

Aquilon merely shook her head, not recognizing the designation.

"*Brachiosaurus*—meaning 'arm-leg,' because its arms are longer than its legs, in a manner of speaking. *Brontosaurus* was the other way around, its hips being higher than its shoulders."

"I always thought Bronto was the largest dinosaur," Aquilon said.

"Bronto weighed as much as thirty-five tons. Brach may have gone up to fifty tons."

"Oh."

116

"Quite innocuous, except through accident. The sauropods are herbivorous, and would not become violent unless hard-pressed. But their size—"

"Vegetarians," Veg said. "Good guys. Let's get acquainted, then."

"With fifty tons of nearly mindless reptile?" But Aquilon shrugged. She, like Veg, seemed to have become inured to a certain extent to personal danger—and Paleo, so far, was as safe as Nacre had been.

They advanced again, cautiously. The head and neck remained, feeding as before, resembling a crane as it hoisted up and down, with visible bulges from the down-traveling boluses of greenery.

"Harmless, you said," Veg murmured, losing his bravado as he was forcefully reminded of the scope of this creature.

"Bear in mind that the sauropods are not very bright, as 'Quilon mentioned," Cal said. "And as *you* mentioned, big vegetarians—"

"Are good guys—but sometimes squish nasty little carnivores by accident," Veg said, smiling.

"The carnivores were not necessarily small, in the age of reptiles. But as I was explaining, this creature may run eighty feet in total length, and it takes time for the neural impulses to travel along its—"

"Yeah, I know about that." They were whispering now, subdued by the presence of the giant. "So if Brach thinks we're food, some kind of new turnip maybe, and wants to take a bite, it'll still be a while before he gets around to doing something about it."

Aquilon was now busily painting the portrait of the fleshy column. "By the same token, if it changes its mind and decides *not* to take a bite, we may be halfway down its gullet before it desists."

Cal smiled. "Actually, it could probably desist from *biting* quickly enough, since its brain is adjacent to its eyes and jaws. But larger motions—"

They were now quite close to the feeding head, lulled by its pacifistic and plodding manner. Down—bite—up—swallow, and repeat. Veg glanced into the cabin to see how the mantas were taking it, and discovered that only two remained. The others had evidently left during the excitement, perhaps taking advantage of the temporary overcast that now existed. But he couldn't spare the time to investigate; Brach was too important.

Closer yet, and an impressive view. The skin of the neck, rather than being smooth, was covered with wartlike tubercles, and on the head wrinkles overlay creases on bulges, the topology changing with every slow shift of the jaw. The mouth swept up leaves, stems, water, and mud from the bank, straining some of it back out in the haphazard process of mastication. Brach was either very old or very ugly. But the muddy water still concealed the rest of the reptile's body.

"I heard once that if a dinosaur were walking along," Aquilon remarked, "and discovered that it was about to step over a cliff, by the time it could make its legs halt it would have gone over. So its very size led to its extinction."

"Like much hearsay, not true," Cal said. "I suppose that if a creature the size of *Brachiosaurus* were proceeding on land at a full gallop, its mass could carry it over the cliff in such a situation. Fifty tons do not stop on a dollar. But Brach would never find himself in such a predicament."

"Why not?" Veg's own query, though he was hardly interested. This dialogue was merely a way of rationalizing the incredible and postponing healthy fear. They were talking too much. Yet the monster went on feeding.

"Because Brach would not be found innocently trotting along like that. Full-grown, he's far too heavy to walk on land with any comfort. He must stick to water, or at least swamp, so that his body is buoyed up."

"So I see," Aquilon said.

"Brach, much more than Bront, is adapted for deeper water," Cal continued. "Note the placement of the nostrils and the angle of the head. But his range is sharply limited to the coastal shallows. His presence here, rather than Bront's, is an indication that the flat swamps are less extensive than they were. And of course we've seen that directly. Evolution is never random."

"Perhaps we should get moving again, if we're going to," Aquilon said gently.

118

"But all we've seen is his head!" Veg protested face-tiously. Fifty tons was too large, even if all he could actually see were two or three tons; it alarmed him.

"That's all anyone usually observes," Cal said. "Assuming that anyone before us has had the opportunity. Better be satisfied."

Veg was willing to be convinced. He poled the craft into deeper water, and he and Aquilon took up the paddles. They passed about forty feet behind the busy head. He judged that Brach was standing in about twenty feet of water—and that implied much about its size.

His paddle struck something. "Obstruction!" he said. "Log, maybe, under the surface. Sheer off before we—"

Too late. The raft collided with the object, jarring them all. Veg felt the rending of the keel as it tore off. There would have to be substantial repairs.

"Reef?" Aquilon inquired, brushing back hair that had fallen across her face.

Veg probed with the pole. "Water's deep here. I can't find bottom." He angled the pole forward, searching for the obstruction.

Cal had been shaken harder by the bump, partly because he was less robust physically, and partly because he had not been anchored by a paddle. He must also, Veg thought, have been preoccupied. Veg himself was able to accept something like a dinosaur on Paleo, but the concept evidently came harder to Cal. The little man was sitting very still now, recovering his wind while the others assessed the situation.

"Move out—fast!" Cal snapped.

Again they responded to the need of the most urgent member. First it had been Veg, spotting Brach; now it was Cal, not as winded as he had appeared. They had worked together long enough on Nacre, and now on Paleo, to know almost intuitively when life depended on instant cooperation.

As the raft began to move, thanks to the strenuous efforts with the paddles, Cal explained: "That was no log or reef. That was the tail."

Aquilon looked at the troubled water behind. "The tail—of the dinosaur?"

119

But again events provided confirmation. From the water came the tip of a massive fleshy extremity, stirring up waves.

Veg peered across at the head. "It's still feeding. This can't be the same—"

Then the head stopped chewing and sifting. It lifted and rotated to face them, while the tail struck the water furiously.

". . . that slow reaction time," Aquilon murmured.

"Keep moving," Cal said urgently. "It's aware of us now, and that blow to the tail must have hurt. If it decides we're an enemy—"

"Harmless, you said," Veg repeated, with some irony.

"Oh, I'm fairly certain it won't attack. Its natural inclination would be to flee from danger. But—"

"We *did* bruise its tail," Aquilon said.

They could all see it now, as the tail lifted clear of the waves again. Diluted blood streamed off it. Their keel had cut a gash in the spongy flesh—not a serious injury to an animal of that size, but enough to color the surrounding water.

"Smarts, I'll bet," Veg agreed with some sympathy. A wound of that magnitude in a lesser creature would have been fatal. It was several feet long and inches deep.

Then the water churned in earnest. Brach had made its decision.

"Move!" Cal cried. "He's running!"

The two mantas remaining in the cabin popped out, though there was still direct sunlight. They sailed over the surface. Veg knew they couldn't keep it up long; the sun would burn them terribly and injure the eyes.

But the dinosaur was coming *toward* the *Nacre!* The tiny yet ponderous head looped about, gliding low over the water, and the neck threw up a white wake. The tail retreated, its tip skipping over the waves smartly. Between the two—a distance of about fifty feet—something like a whirlpool formed, and from it several tiny indentations spun off.

"Divert the head!" Cal called. "Don't attack! Herd it!" He was addressing the two mantas, who now circled the raft uncertainly. "Bluff it! Move it aside!"

120

Hex and Circe (Veg was sure he recognized them) seemed to understand. In turn they swooped at the head, banking with kitelike flares of their bodies. The head reacted fairly quickly, flinching away from them, but still approaching the raft. As Cal had explained, it took time to change the course of such a mountain.

Brachiosaurus came at the trio—but the head missed by twenty feet, the eyes not even focusing on them. Water surged aside, rocking the raft as though a huge mass trailed that wormlike forepart. In a momentary eddy they saw the speckled flank, and the muscular rhythm of it.

The body missed them by only ten feet, and that because the raft moved with the current of water thrust aside.

Then the main torso was beyond, and they balanced precariously on the swell, relieved. In that unguarded moment the tail struck. It was not the cutting whip of the manta, but its blind ponderosity was fully as devastating.

The tail rose from the water under the rear edge of the *Nacre* and flipped it over.

Aquilon dived away sidewise, hitting the water before the raft toppled. Veg hooked his right arm around Cal's midsection, lifted him as the *Nacre* came up, and shoved off to the left. The raft bobbled endwise, sinking into the water; then it rebounded and seemed to fling itself on over. Veg kicked his feet, keeping his arms wrapped around Cal, driving away from the splash.

The waves subsided. The dinosaur was gone, the raft inverted but steady, and already the two mantas perched on it. Aquilon waved, showing that she was all right. And, blessedly, a cloud dimmed the sun, giving the mantas relief.

Veg lifted up Cal, hoping the man had not taken in much water, but his concern was needless. Cal blew out the breath he had held during the upset, smiling. Veg kept forgetting that his friend had recovered considerably since Nacre. Cal remained small and light, but by no means infirm.

Veg let go, and together they swam back to the raft. Aquilon joined them there. They peered at one another over the shattered keel, and at the two mantas.

121

"Does this seem familiar to you?" Aquilon inquired with simulated brightness. Her hair was dark and lank, now that it was wet, and her eyes more gray than blue.

He knew what she meant. Back on Nacre, at once like yesterday and a decade past, they had begun the adventure that was to meld them into the trio. Beginning at the corpse of a tractor, and knowing that their journey back to the human camp would be a terrible one. Blood had been shared, literally.

He clung to the edge of the raft and looked about at the debris. A can of kerosene floated nearby, but there was no sign of the lantern it serviced. Beyond it was a wicker basket, empty of the food it had carried. Aquilon had found ways to occupy her nimble fingers during the long southward voyage, fashioning things from natural materials; it hurt him to see her handiwork adrift. Most of their equipment remained lashed to the raft, for the bindings were tight. It would be a tedious job getting it loose safely, but could be done.

Their radio set, so carefully conserved if used, had ripped away from its mooring, and now surely lay at the bottom of the channel. Their theoretical contact with civilization was gone.

Yes, it was like old times—and he wasn't sorry. They could stay lost forever here, and he'd be satisfied. A friend like Cal, a woman like Aquilon . . . and of course the mantas.

At least the paddles remained. One was broken, but could be mended or replaced: palm fronds were plentiful. The stout bamboo pole was undamaged.

It would be pointless to try to right the raft here. They would have to haul it onto land, then see what they could salvage. Most of their supplies could survive such a dunking.

Hex and Circe took off and pounded over the water. At once they circled back. "Oh-oh," Veg said. "Trouble?"

Two snaps, almost in unison: each manta agreeing. They seldom spoke at once like this.

"Predators!" Cal cried. "I should have thought! The wound—"

He meant the blood that still discolored the water

around them. Veg knew that Cal still did not like to say that word—blood. Of course the flavor would attract the vicious creatures of the sea. Brach must have bled gallons, kegs, barrels. . . .

"Sharks!" Aquilon exclaimed.

And the three human beings were out of the water and aboard the inverted raft. Veg was sure that neither of the others was aware of scrambling up, any more than he was. When one thought of sharks or crocodiles while swimming, one left the water in a hurry, that was all.

It was no mistake. There were sharks, invulnerable to the lash of the mantas' tails because they swam below the surface. Veg splashed with the good paddle—how had he brought that up with him?—and they retreated, but not far.

Cal's face was pinched. "The sharks won't come up after us," he said. "But the reptiles—if *Kronosaurus* ranges these waters—"

"Who?" Aquilon had the broken paddle, and was fishing with it for the floating pole. Veg let her fish; if he moved over to her side, the raft would tilt, and stability was suddenly very important.

"*Kronosaurus*—a short-necked plesiosaur. Fifty feet long, jaws twelve feet long, the size of a small whale—"

"I get the message," Veg interrupted. Prodded by this vision, he thought to pry his own paddle against his side of the raft, pushing forcefully outward so that the *Nacre* nudged toward the pole Aquilon wanted. She hooked it in, then went after the kerosene.

They conferred hurriedly and decided on the obvious: landfall at the nearest point. That way the *Nacre*'s beachhead could mark the spot where the lost radio lay on the ocean floor. Assuming recovery of it would do any good at this stage, since it hadn't been sealed against such total and prolonged immersion. He and Aquilon started paddling.

"Harmless, you said," Veg muttered, his spirits rising as they passed out of the pink water, spotting nothing but frustrated sharks. "Would run from danger, you said." But he was smiling.

"It *did* run, if you mean Brach," Cal replied. "But it ran to deeper water. Most of its enemies are land dwellers."

And they had been between the dinosaur and deeper water, and Brach was not very bright. It figured.

He still had not seen the creature. Only its head and tail, and a portion of its shoulder.

The sharks, apparently satisfied that no advantage remained in following the raft, disappeared. But no one offered to swim.

Laboriously they brought the raft to poling depth, and then shoved the ungainly monster up against the shore.

Fern trees leaned over the water, giant cousins of the plants Veg once had picked by hand near his cutting acreage on earth. A strange conifer rose above them, its needles bunched peculiarly. He saw no grass, no flowers. Half-floating water plants massed at the tideline.

"Cretaceous landscape," Cal murmured. "Astonishing." But he sounded awed rather than surprised.

There were, fortunately, no shore-dwelling predators in sight. Calf-deep in muck, Veg and Aquilon hefted the loaded raft up. But it was far too heavy to be righted this way. They would have to hold it while Cal braced it with sticks; in this marshy terrain there were no rocks to set under it, and no really solid footing. But first they had to slide it up beyond the level of high tide, so that it would not be carried away in the night. " 'Quilon, you steady it while I heave," Veg said.

They tried, but the *Nacre* lifted only inches while his feet skidded away in brown slime. "No use," he grunted. "We'll just have to take it apart and rebuild it right side up. Might as well make camp."

He was not unhappy at the prospect. Sailing, he decided, was not his forte; hiking and camping were better. It reminded him of their other hike together, on planet Nacre. Something had begun then between him and Aquilon. Something intriguing. More and more, his mind was coming to dwell on that.

His gaze met hers, over the raft. She realized it too. Their return to Earth had cut off what had been developing; she had wanted it that way for some reason. But

124

now—now there could be a middle and an end to that beginning.

No, he did not mind being stranded for a few days or weeks or longer. He did not mind danger or hardship. To be here in the ancient forestland with Aquilon, here for the second session. . . .

"Probably Brach wouldn't have been feeding here if it weren't fairly safe," Cal remarked. "A large land carnivore might bite off Brach's head, and that would be, eventually, fatal. Reptiles die very slowly. So while I couldn't call our encounter with the monster exactly fortunate, it does have its redeeming aspect. We can't tell what we might have met, farther in."

"Still, let's not try to camp right here," Aquilon said, looking down distastefully at the bubbling goo covering her feet. "Sleeping in a flooding cabin was bad enough, but this—"

There was something hilarious about it, and Veg laughed. Aquilon tried to glare at him, but looked at her mired ankles again and joined in.

Yes, it was good to be back. Earth was like a pressure cooker with the temperature rising and the escape valve blocked. They were better off here.

The two remaining mantas, Diam and Star, had rejoined them at some point, perhaps while he was preoccupied with the problem of landing the raft. Veg was sure they agreed. They hadn't been scouting this territory just for the fun of it.

Night found them camped under a large tree whose stout branches and small twigs gave it the aspect of a stiff-armed octopus. Each twig had a cleft, fan-shaped leaf, unlike the branching veined greenery of conventional trees. This was a ginkgo, and Cal seemed to feel it was something special, though he claimed they existed on contemporary Earth.

They were in a lean-to improvised from cycad barrels, palm fronds and fern leaf, on a rise overlooking the beachhead. Cal had designed it, showing more practical ability than Veg had expected. Veg had done the brute work, collecting the peculiar wood. Aquilon had plaited fibers to make the roof tight. Yes, they were a functioning team, a good one.

The finishing was a more tedious task than the designing or building, and Veg had time to loosen the nylon bindings of the *Nacre*, get the logs enough apart to free the supplies within the crushed cabin, and begin ferrying supplies to the camp. Cal and Aquilon remained cross-legged by the lean-to, weaving fern stems in and out.

Veg kept a sharp lookout for life, hostile or otherwise, though Hex was with him and made an effective bodyguard. He did not know much about dinosaurs except that they were big and dangerous—even the herbivorous ones, as the wrecked raft testified. Brach would not be wandering on land, however, if what Cal said was true—and of course it was. But other creatures might be found anywhere. Brach would not have been so ready to flee to deep water unless there were things on land it feared.

A creature that could frighten a fifty-ton dinosaur could hardly be ignored by a one-tenth-ton man.

Unfamiliar birds twittered in the tree-ferns, scouting for bugs. Small things scuttled in the brush. Fish swam in the water. There was plenty of life, but nothing to fear, yet.

He lifted the last of the cases they had decided to move, brought it to his shoulder, and tromped through the sludge. Yes, they all had to be alert here, on guard against unknown menaces. But the air was wet and warm, the biting insects had not yet discovered him, and he felt marvelously free. Perhaps he would die tomorrow in the jaws of some monster whose name he could not pronounce—but he would die a man, not a sardine.

Hex ranged ahead as they came out of the swamp and recovered firm footing. It was dusk, growing too dim for him to see clearly, but he liked the challenge. The manta drifted to one side and stopped beside a tree—a maidenhair, Aquilon called it, but it looked exactly like the ginkgo—and stood as a black blob. By tricks of vision—looking slantwise at specific objects, narrowing his eyes—Veg coud still make out good detail. What was Hex looking at?

He came up and peered. Was that a—?

It was.

Veg squatted down beside the manta, holding up the teetering carton with one hand while he cleared away obscuring foliage with the other.

It was the print, in hardening mud, of either a bipedal dinosaur or a very large bird. Three sturdy clawmarks, the points digging down and forward, no rear toe showing. Whether toothed or beaked, a land walker armed with effective talons that could gut a man in a hurry.

The creature was somewhere within range of their camp. Veg was glad the mantas would be mounting guard this night.

XI: ORN

The spoor was not fresh; only its protected location had preserved it. It could have been made a season ago, since the merest suggestion of odor remained. But it was sure, for his memory was strongest of all on such identification: a female of his species had roosted here.

Did she remain in the valley? Was she still alive? Could he locate her? These questions were vague and peripheral and largely beside the point. His mind grasped the fact that she existed, and his glands responded and ruled. The mating urge was upon him, no longer to be denied.

Orn spent the night under the waterfall. It was uncomfortable and tiring, on top of his preceding labors, but the discovery of a trace of his own kind prevented him from leaving. He had to begin here and follow the trail until it became fresh. Convenience was unimportant. If there were another male—but there was not; the trace was that of an unbred bird. Such things were specific, in his line.

In the morning he explored the neighboring terrain. She had been here; there had to be signs of her avenue of departure. He would discover them, however faint or fleeting.

It was not easy, but he was geared for this. He would not be able to perceive so old a trail at all, were it of any other creature. But his pumping glands sharpened his senses, and all his memories focused on this one task. His search pattern identified another trace, downstream, and a third, and he was on his way.

In two days he located fresher spoor, and in another day the roost she had used for a time. It was in the raised hollow of a rotting flat-leaf tree. Nose and eye and memory informed him that she had departed when a predatory rep had scouted the region. She had lost some feathers, but not her life.

She had fled into the mountain, perhaps as recently as Orn's meeting with the expanding sea on the other side of the continent. This season, certainly. Here the trail became exceedingly difficult, for she had passed over shuddering, heated rock in her effort to shake the pursuit. But Orn widened his search pattern and persevered, as he had to, and in time picked up the spoor again where she had descended to the valley.

Her prints and smell became mixed with those of many animals, as though she had frequented the haunts of a herd of Tricers. Again he had to cast a wider net, seeking a line of emergence, and again he succeeded, as he had to. Days old now, her trail stimulated him exquisitely. She was alone and nubile, and not very much older than he; she wanted a mate, but had found none. All this he read in her spoor, knowing the signals from millennia past, and his desire for her became savage.

But he did not find her. She found him.

She had come upon his own trail, in her roundabout rovings, and recognized it immediately. In less than a day she had caught up.

Orn looked up from the newly hatched brach he was feeding on, suddenly aware of her presence. Across the open space of the deserted Tricer stamping ground they peered at one another. His beak was smeared with the blood of the fleet young rep, his nose suffused with the fresh odors of its open carcass, and in this delicious and romantic moment he viewed the bird who was to be his mate.

128

Ornette: she was shorter than he by the width of one dry tail feather. Her beak was slender, a delicate brown matching the scales of her muscular thighs. Her eyes were large and round, half shuttered by the gray nictitating membranes. The white neck feathers were sleek and bright, merging gracefully into the gray breast area. Her body plumage fluffed out slightly, lighter on the underside, for she had been moving through high brush. Her wings were well kept and handsome, looking larger than they were because of the unusual, almost regressive length of their primaries. Her tail, too, had sizable retrices, and the coverts displayed the grandeur of the nuptial plumage. Even the claws of her feet glistened with natural oil. From her drifted the perfume of the distaff, at once exciting and maddening to the male. She was beautiful and wholly desirable.

Then she was away, whirling her shapely sternum about and running from him; and he was running after her with all his strength, his meal forgotten. She disappeared into high palmetto brush, outdistancing him; but it was a chase he was certain to win, for his thews were heavier, his masculine endurance greater. This was the way it was meant to be, and had been, throughout the existence of the species.

She fled toward the swamp, passing into the territory of the Struth, that zealous rep so like Orn himself. That surely meant trouble, but there was nothing Orn could do about it. If he tried to circle to head her off, he would only lose distance, for she was for the moment as fleet as he.

She dodged around a giant fir, sending green sprigs flying, and sheered away before encountering the Struth. She knew! She bore north, much to his relief, though that was territory he had not scouted. Her pace slowed as the ground became marshy—but so did his own. It would be a long time before he caught her, this way. This, too, was as nature had decreed.

She ran north for a time, then veered west, toward the mountains. Soon they were ascending, leaving the steamy valley below. Flying aves scattered from their path and grazing young reps scooted away. A wounded adult

129

Tricer, come this far to die, looked up startled. Through increasingly leafy trees they went, where mams twittered in the branches, and on into the grassy elevation where arths swarmed in sunlight, but Ornette did not slacken her pace, running up until the air became cool; on until the snows began. But Orn did not feel the cold. Slowly he gained on her.

She changed course at last, running north along the fringe of white while the sun dropped toward the mountain crest. Then down again, into the valley, into the thickest greenery, spreading her wings to aid control in that precipitous descent. She gained on him again, utilizing those longer feathers, but on the level bottom where the reps roamed he got it back. And up again, almost to the snow, and still Orn gained on her, though he had never run so long without resting.

The second time they came down at the northern apex of the great valley, beyond the swamp. Here there was a higher plain, too dry and cold for the comfort of most reps though the little mams were plentiful. And here, abruptly, the light of the sun was cut off by the mountain range. It was early dusk.

Ornette stopped, panting. Orn, hardly two wingspans behind, stopped also. The chase had to halt when the sun dropped, to resume in place when it rose again. The night was for feeding and resting and ... courtship. Thousands of generations before them had determined this, and the pattern was not to be broken now.

The swamp spread out below from a comparatively tiny tributary stream here, and there were fish in it and mams in burrows adjacent and arths available for the scratching. They hunted separately, and fed separately. Then, as full darkness overtook them, they began the dance.

Ornette crossed the plain, away from him, until she was a female silence in the distance. Orn stood, beak elevated, waiting. There was a period of stillness.

Then Orn stepped forward, spreading his wings and holding them there to catch the gentle evening breeze. He gave one piercing, lust-charged call. She answered, demurely; then silence.

Orn moved toward her, and she toward him, each

130

watching, listening, sniffing for the other. Slowly they came together, until he saw the white of her spread wings. The remiges, the rowing feathers, were slightly phosphorescent when exposed in this fashion, slick with the oils of courtship exercise; and so she was a winged outline, lovely. He, too, to her.

In the sight of each other, they strutted, he with the male gait, she the female. They approached, circled, retreated, their feet striking the ground in unison, wings always spread. Then Orn faced her and closed his wings, becoming invisible, and she performed her solo dance.

Wings open; wings closed. On and off she flashed, a diffuse firefly, her feet beating the intricate courtship meter, now steady, now irregular, always compelling. Far back into her ancestry the females had done this series for waiting males, taunting them with the nuptial ritual.

Then her dance halted, and the plain was quiet again. Orn's turn. He spread, commenced the beat, closed, whirled, jumped, spread, and instinct carried him on irreversibly. Tat-tap-tap against the turf, the flapping of wings measured by that cadence but not matching it. A faster, fiercer dance than hers, domineering, forceful, signifying what male expression in any species signified, but artistically, and not without gentle undertones. Forward, back, around; one wing flashing, then the other, as though he were jumping back and forth. But silent, except for the feet; a pulsing ghost. Finally an accelerated beat, wings and feet together, climbing as though into takeoff—and silence.

The dance was done. Orn rested, alone in the dark, letting his heart subside. It had been a good effort, following a good chase—but better things awaited the morning. He made his way to the roost he had selected while foraging. Ornette, out of his sight as the ritual dictated, did the same.

A quick meal at daybreak. Then, as the sun struggled over the eastern pass, the chase resumed. She was fresh again, recovering better than he, and she was familiar with this terrain, and he lost ground. Up the face of the northern range, across a low, hidden pass leading into another rich valley—but she turned back into their own, south. Even to the verge of the swamp she ran, passing briars, moss, and fungus that wrenched feathers from him or powdered him with spores as he charged carelessly through. At one point she intersected the spoor of a giant rep predator, and reversed her field hurriedly. It would not do to have trouble of that nature on this romantic occasion!

Up to the snows again, across a hot stream that melted its own channel through ice, down . . . and before noon Orn was gaining on her again. She was tired; her feathers no longer glistened sleekly, her beak was no longer held high. She made to ascend once more, but he shortened the distance between them so rapidly that she desisted, staying on the contour. They were near the southeast corner of the valley now, separated from his original entry by swamp and bay.

Orn approached within a wingspan, no longer straining. She was so worn he could keep the pace easily; his season's travel had conditioned him for this, and he had recovered his strength during his days in the valley. And—he was male. But the time to catch her was not quite yet, and he dallied.

Aware of her defeat, Ornette stumbled and hardly caught herself in time. In desperation she waded out into the shallow water of the bay, toward a nearby island, but she was so gaunt and tired that this was even worse, and she had to turn back.

Orn was waiting for her, victorious. As she climbed slowly to the bank he pounced on her and buried his beak amid the tender down feathers of her neck, but did not bite. She hardly resisted; she had been conquered. She dropped to the ground and lay there at his mercy.

Orn shook her once, not hard, and let her go. He trotted to a nearby bed of moss. He gathered a succulent beakful and brought it to her as a counteroffering. She sniffed it weakly, looked at him through the nictitating lid, and accepted.

With these first tokens of submission and of the nest they were to build and share, their courtship was done. They had found each other fitting; soon they would mate and settle, uniting their memories in their offspring.

Another morning—the first of their new life. They scouted the vicinity and decided to cross to the island Ornette had not been able to reach before. This was thickly wooded with firs, and seemed to represent a suitable haven from most carnivores. The big land walkers would have difficulty crossing to it, while the sea dwellers would be unlikely to venture among trees of such size, even if they were able to leave the water.

The two waded in and paddled with their abbreviated wings, entering the water while the chill remained in the air. The sea itself was warm, and they would be vulnerable to submerged predators. But the reps of the surface or shore would still be torpid, and so less dangerous than usual. Morning was the best time to forage when such creatures were near.

Not a ripple disturbed the sea, apart from those of their own motions. They crossed quickly and safely—but this was not a risk they would take again soon.

The island ground was spongy but not soggy; the matted fir droppings made an excellent fundament. Though the island was small, it was not flat. The trees ascended a mound in the center. Orn perceived it for what it was: the tip of a submerged mountain. Once it might have stood as tall and cold as the peaks of the ranges enclosing this warm valley, but its understratum had given way and allowed the bay to encroach. Its original formation had been volcanically inspired. None of that animation remained to it now, or Orn would not have stayed.

Near the water were thick stands of club moss, the tops of the plants as high as his head. Once this species had been a giant many times that height, but somehow it had diminished to this innocuous status, and was still shrinking elsewhere on the continent. Horsetail rushes were also abundant, though similarly restricted in size.

At the fringe of a twisting inlet they discovered the ideal nesting site: a mossy peninsula sheltered within a northern baylet. It was protected from the harsher waves of the ocean, and from the openness of the main island. The bridge to the site was narrow, so that a single bird could defend it, and the bay itself was deep enough to discourage wading. Yet the mouth of the inlet was toothed by jagged rocks, preventing access by most large sea creatures. A stand of several pines served as a breaker against offshore wind, and the main body of the island guarded against the sea wind. The soil was rich with grubs, and small fish teemed in the inlet, and clams in the gravel below it.

Ornette was pleased, already casting about for the specific spot for the nest. But Orn was more cautious. The experience of his ancestry told him that seemingly ideal locations generally appealed to more than one individual or species. Sometimes a flawed site was actually superior, because of this competitive factor. And he was directly aware of the fate of his parents, who had nested on another apparently ideal island. Orn did not want his own chicks to be orphaned as they hatched.

The smell of rep was strong here, and there were many droppings. Something used this peninsula regularly, but he was unable to identify the particular creature before actually seeing it.

Ornette, female, had few such compunctions. Defense of the nest was not her primary responsibility; filling it was. She scratched the earth in several areas and fluttered for his attention. This spot? This? Or nearer the water?

Unable to subdue her enthusiasm without unreasonable gruffness, Orn approved a site beside the inlet. This was atop a large elevated stone, concave above, that he deemed secure from both flood tide and the intrusion of egg-sucking reps and landbound arths. A wingspan across and half that high, it was large enough for a proper nest yet had a sharply defined perimeter. The eggs would be as safe there as anywhere in the open, and of course they would never be left unattended.

If only he knew what manner of rep frequented this locale. It might be innocuous.

All afternoon they worked on the nest, foraging amid the pines for needles and cones, and fetching moss for spongy lining. Ornette wove the long stems of shore plants into a great circular pattern and calked the interstices with the clay Orn scooped up from beneath the water. The nest would have to bake for a day in the sun before the padding was installed, and if it rained they would have to repeat the calking and wait again. Orn hoped that such delay would not happen. The nest had to be complete before mating occurred.

As the sun touched the bright crest of the mountain wall, shapes appeared in the sky. They were the huge gliding forms of the ptera, largest of the flying reps. Orn recognized the creature now, as the visual trigger activated his memory. The trees, the droppings, the odor— this was a nesting site for the enormous gliders.

The shapes came in, drifting on the rising currents in the atmosphere but steadily approaching the island. Orn stood in the center of the peninsula beside the stoutest tree and made ready for the confrontation that had to come. Ptera generally did not get along well with true birds.

Three spiraled toward him. Their wings were monstrous: four times Orn's own span. Their heads were large, with long toothless beaks and crests of bone that extended back as a counterbalance. A flap of skin stretched from the crest back above the body, serving as a rudder that oriented each creature into the wind. Their bodies had neither hair nor feathers, but scales as fragile as natal down and hardly more protective.

Orn continued to watch, remembering more. The ptera, like the other larger flyers among the reps, had tiny legs to which the rear of the wings attached. The tail was so small as to be useless. The forelimbs that braced the wings were many times the size of the hind limbs, and the fourth phalange extended half the length of each wing. Ptera, able to glide all day without respite, could not walk on land. There was nothing to fear from this particular species; any individual who tried to attack him in the air would be at a severe disadvantage because Orn could knock it down and kill it while it flopped helplessly on the ground. A ptera could not fly from ground level.

Orn dropped his fighting stance, though he kept close watch on the visitors. One could never be certain what a rep would do, though the ptera were not notably foolish.

The three circled overhead, then evidently decided that he was not a threat and swooped at one of the pines leaning over the water. Each passed over a horizontal

135

branch high on the trunk, let down its little legs, caught hold with marvelous accuracy and spun around.

Then the wings folded and they hung inverted, three suddenly smaller bodies wrapped in folded leather, the downy scales outward. They were well beyond Orn's reach and he, effectively, was beyond theirs. Friends the two species were not, but coexistence was feasible.

The mystery of the rep inhabitant had been alleviated. The three ptera combined would mass no more than Orn alone, for they were insubstantial things despite their monstrous wingspan. And if they nighted safely here, so could he.

Ornette was unconcernedly scooping small fish from the water. She had known it all along.

They fed together and slept that night beside the half-constructed nest, the head of each tucked under the wing of the other, sharing warmth and love. It rained, forcing them to scramble to shelter the nest with their spread wings; but it was a good night.

The ptera were not early risers. Long after the birds had foraged for their morning meal, the three reps hung from their branches tightly cloaked. Only when the sun itself touched their bodies did they move, and then stiffly. The scant chill of this valley night was enough to incapacitate these creatures who lacked internal control of their body temperatures. Even the hairy mams were better off than that.

The nest was baking. For the present, the birds had nothing constructive to do, so they explored the peninsula thoroughly, searching out the best fishing area and the richest infestations of edible arths—and watched the reps.

The three began to stir more actively as the sunlight heated them. Their heads rotated and the small claws at the break of their wings flexed. They began to flutter gently, opening their membranes to the warmth. Those tremendous wings could trap a large expanse of sunlight, heating the entire system.

Then, one by one, the reps dropped. The first fell almost to the water before leveling out, then swooped perilously close to the surface. Its wings stretched out so thinly that the sunlight made them translucent, the veins

136

showing dark like the webwork of deciduous leaves. The ptera flapped clumsily, its very bones bending in the desperate effort to gain altitude, and Orn felt a surge of longing. Once his own line had flown, and takeoff had resembled this. He knew the rep had to reach an updraft quickly, for its reserve of energy was small and a descent into the cool water would be fatal.

It found a favorable air current and fought its way to a safe height. The second ptera dropped, following a similar course. But the third, the largest, did not. The wind had shifted, and that particular corridor to the sky was closed. Anxiously it maneuvered from side to side, but remained too low. The tip of one wing as it banked touched a wave, jerking the creature about. It righted itself, but now was too low even to flap without disaster.

The drama was not over. Carefully the ptera circled, coasting closer and closer to destruction but never quite touching the sea. It came in toward the island, toward Orn's nest.

Alarmed, Orn ran to protect their property. But the ptera was only trying to reach land before falling that last bit. It did not succeed. With a sick splash it struck the water, so close to the nest that Orn spread his wings quickly to intercept the flying droplets before they wet the clay and forced a postponement of his nuptial.

The ptera had reached the shallows, however, swimming ineffectively but determinedly, and was able to struggle the small remaining distance to the shore. Dripping and bedraggled, it climbed to land and lay there for a moment, watching Orn.

The creature was exhausted, cold and helpless now; it would be easy to kill. It had very nearly killed itself, bouncing over the rocky barrier to the inlet. But Orn, imbued with the romance of his newly completed courtship and sympathetic to a certain extent to the rep's plight, did not attack. Anyway, there was very little good meat on it, and he was not hungry at the moment. Had such a creature fallen near him as he struggled through the desert, it would have been a different matter.

After a while the ptera pulled itself away from the bank, scraping along on bedraggled, wet, folded wings and weak legs. It was unable to stand or walk, but it could crawl. It seemed surprised that no attack had come, but was not remaining to contemplate the matter. Indeed, Orn was not certain he had done the right thing; it went against his nature.

The ptera scrambled awkwardly to its tree, then hooked its wing claws into the bark. Laboriously it climbed, clinging to the trunk with its wings draped down from the bend, a dripping cape. Only when it reached its branch did it rest again, flopped halfway over the wood with its long heavy head hanging in fatigue.

At last it assumed the sleeping position, but did not sleep. It walked out from the trunk, sidestepping upside down, until it had good clearance. It spread its wings so that the sun caught them and warmed them and made it entirely dry. Then it dropped again.

This time it completed the maneuver successfully, and disappeared proudly into the sky.

That day they watched the pteras feeding by swooping low over the waves and scooping small fish into their long bills. Because they did this at high speed and always facing the wind, they were able to touch the water and recover elevation without being immersed and trapped, and the massive rearward bones of their heads balanced the weight of the solid morsels they lifted. It was a graceful operation.

Orn hardly cared about the life and fate of any given rep, yet in some fashion his act of mercy enhanced his relationship with Ornette. Together they gathered the last of the supplies they required. All day the sun shone without remittance—unusual, for this valley—and by late afternoon they decided the clay was firm enough. They packed in the lining layers and made the nest smooth and comfortable.

That night they occupied their nest for the first time, snuggled pleasantly together within its bowl. And Ornette presented, and they mated at last, while the three ptera hung silent.

138

XII: AQUILON

She had slept in close proximity to these two men before, both on the planet Nacre and the raft *Nacre*. She knew them well and loved them both. But now she felt an increasing discomfort, a sense of impropriety. She had almost decided to leave them rather than continue to come between them, back when they had orbited Earth in the quarantine capsule. Events had prevented that, but did not really dispel the mood that had precipitated the decision. For surely she *would* come between them, and be the cause of sorrow and misfortune, if she remained a member of the party. She felt the female urges within her, compelling her to—

She peered at the roof of the lean-to, invisible in the darkness but present to her mind's eye, for she had spent hours plaiting it. Yes, she felt compelled—but to *what*?

To choose.

Aquilon was a woman. She had breasts and they were not simply for appearances; she had thighs and not entirely for walking. She was long past adolescence. But she had not felt the need of the physical male until—that agent Subble had aroused her, somehow, back in her tight Earth apartment, and turned her down. She had never realized before that a man could do that to her, and it had been a shock. When she had had no smile to show the world, she had bypassed social life, of course; but that new smile had seemed to open all the world to her, to lay waste all prior mysteries. Subble had routed that euphoria.

She had not loved him, those few hours they conversed, but she had felt his controlled masculinity tangibly. He had made her realize that the love she professed for Veg and Cal was an intellectual thing possessing no physical substance; a sympathetic resonance of the love they professed for her. She had never actually imagined herself undertaking a sexual relation with either.

Subble had been an agent, in more senses than one. He could move with seemingly irresistible speed and force and accuracy, yet hold a difficult pose indefinitely without sagging. He could talk philosophy and he could kill without compunction. He was handsome, yet ruthless even in his kindnesses. He was a body like Veg's, a mind like Cal's. He had understood her.

Subble had died, making any consummation with him, however theoretical, a waste of emotional effort. Of course there were hundreds, perhaps thousands, of agents virtually identical to him, and, designed to be exactly that, computerized. But it had not been the assembly-line physique and mind that made the connection between him and her; it had been their mutual experience. *The* Subble was gone forever; the close resemblance of other agents was irrelevant.

That threw her back into the trio—with a difference. It had taken her this long to realize it.

But what to do about it?

She fell asleep without an answer. Her dreams, however, were not of love; they were of *Brachiosaurus*.

The explorations of the next week banished any doubt they might have entertained about the nature of this region. They had struck paleontologic gold. This was a thorough Cretaceous enclave in the Paleocene world. The full spectrum of the golden age of reptiles was present—a vast pyramid of ecology, with inordinately plentiful small forms, largely mammalian, and lesser numbers of larger, dominant reptiles. Here, in fact, there were dinosaurs.

Ten miles up the shore, northwest from their camp ("There's nothing so permanent as a temporary camp," Cal remarked, and smiled for some obscure reason), the ocean inlet became the delta of a southbound river. It was evident that the towering mountain chain had once enclosed a salt-water bay some forty miles across and sixty miles long, but almost all of it had been filled in by the rich silt and debris of the river to form a tremendous warm swamp. Its center was a freshwater lake, swollen daily by ungentle rain, overgrown by soft vegetation, while its fringe rose up into the foothills of the giants. All of it was tropically warm, near sea level, the nights dropping down to a temperature ot aout 65° F., the days rising to—85° F., with the predominating level toward the higher end of that scale.

In the direct sun it was much hotter, of course. At midday hardly a reptile moved. They were all hiding in whatever shade was available, predator and prey together. Aquilon had forgotten how much reptiles liked to rest.

The corner of the delta nearest them was the sporting place of several families of duckbill dinosaurs. Cal insisted on using the proper classification terms—the "family" being ranked below "order" and above "genus"—and of course the reptiles did not have families in the social sense. But they did associate in small or large groups, except for the carnivores, and Aquilon preferred to anthropomorphize to that extent.

In the liquid portion of the swamp a lone *Brachiosaurus* browsed, perhaps the same one they had encountered so awkwardly upon their arrival. It consumed anything soft that grew within range of its neck, and once she saw it scoop up a fair-sized rock. Cal had abated her astonishment: it developed that such reptiles normally swallowed rocks to aid in their digestion of sturdier morsels. Long periods of stasis were required while the voluminous and tough material being processed was crushed and gradually assimilated; this was one reason, he explained, why mammals and birds were far more mobile than reptiles on a twenty-four-hour basis. Superior digestion eliminated that torpor. She decided that she'd feel torpid too if she had to let rocks roll around in her stomach.

Sometimes the sauropod disappeared entirely, and she presumed it was taking a nap under the surface. It was an air breather, but probably it could hold its breath for a long time without particular discomfort, much as a whale did—or would do, tens of millions of years hence.

Across the bay near the eastern mountains were more duckbills, these ones grotesquely crested; she meant to have a closer look at them in due course. And in the plainlike reaches between slush and mountain, where fern

141

trees and cycads were particularly lush, were herds of *Triceratops*, plus scattered *Ankylosauruses*, both armored reptiles of considerable mass. Truly, it was a paradise of paleontology.

And Cal, the paleontologist, was becoming more and more depressed. She found this hard to understand. Cal had a pessimistic view of life, but there was always sound reason behind his attitudes. If only he would explain what was bothering him!

Meanwhile, she drew a map and filled in all the details observed and conjectured to date. She put in the volcanic mountains, and Scylla and Charybdis, and their camping place. She marked a dotted line to show their route of entry. Perhaps this could serve as an adjunct to Cal's eventual report.

They found a better location about twenty-five miles north and made a second, more permanent camp beside a streamlet coursing down from the western range. She updated her map accordingly. There was a pleasant waterfall nearby, and hilly ground that seemed to be secure from the plains-dwelling armored dinosaurs, and the air was cooler here. She liked it very well. Veg, exploring indefatigably, said there was a snowy pass through the range at the head of the stream, and some hot areas of ground: even the silent volcanoes were far from defunct.

There was danger here, certainly; there were savage predators larger than any existing on Earth before or after, though she had seen only their tracks so far. But danger was not objectionable per se, so long as one did not push one's luck. This was a visit in history, in historical geology, an experience like none possible to any homebound person. So very like Earth. . . .

Like Earth? It *was* Earth, according to Cal, though he hadn't spoken on that topic in the past month. She kept forgetting that. Perhaps it was because she thought of Paleo as a world in its own right; or maybe she simply could not assimilate the notion that something she might do here could change her own world, perhaps even eliminate the human species and extinguish her too. Then she could *not* come here, because she didn't exist, so no change would be made after all. . . .

No, it made no sense, and this was Paleo, and she refused to be ruled by fears of paradox.

But there were mundane problems. The insects were fierce, after they had zeroed in on the new arrivals, and all three of the humans, and for all she knew the mantas too, had welts from nocturnal bites. Someone had to keep watch part of the night, because they had agreed that it wasn't fair to make the mantas assume the whole task. That meant that one of the three was generally short of sleep and temper. It was surprising how quickly a nagging itch and insufficient rest could flare into personal unpleasantness. And the food—

Her hands were raw and her nails cracked from scraping in the dirt for edible tubers. Veg ate no meat at all, and she had stopped doing it the past few months, but now the thought of roasted fish was tempting indeed. Coconut was fine, and so were the few small berries growing on the mountainside, and she had pounded nutlike fruits down into powder for something vaguely like bread, baking it laboriously over the kerosene burner. But the lush greenery of the waterside was tough and stringy and internally gritty even when thoroughly cooked, and tasted of creosote. It made her appreciate why Brach needed rocks in his belly to grind it up; he couldn't stand to keep it in his mouth long enough to chew it! The Tricers didn't bother; she had seen them biting off entire fern trees, and chewing up the trunks, their beaks and phenomenal back teeth like sawmills. Cal had explained that too: the Tricers had multiple rows of teeth set one on top of the other, the worn ones being replaced automatically with new. And the upper jaw did not meet the lower directly; the teeth slid past each other in a sheering action controlled by jaw muscles a yard long. To think that some researchers had theorized that the dinosaurs died out because they could not chew the flowering plants!

For the supposedly superior dentition of the human beings, the softer tubers were better—but some made her sick, and she could not be sure, yet, which. The effect seemed to be delayed and inconsistent. Cal did eat fish, and also cooked fat lizards without compunction, and had no trouble. By unspoken agreement he did it alone; none

143

of them were sure to what extent their dietary differences were idealogical or physical, but no one criticized another in this one area, even when tempers were shortest.

She saw it coming: in time she would change over again. On Earth she had been appalled at the way animals were raised in cruel captivity for slaughter, but here the animals were wild and free and able to look out for themselves, and it was the natural order that the weak or slow or stupid become food for the strong and swift and clever.

But mainly she was hungry, and her tastes were falling into line. What held her back was the fear that the moment she reneged on vegetarianism, Veg would turn from her, and thus she would have made her choice of men involuntarily. Perhaps Cal, with his brilliant mind and strength of will, would be the one anyway—but she wanted to make the decision freely, not via her intestines.

Meanwhile, too, there was considerable drudgery in paradise.

She broke from her task—picking over a basket of objects resembling beechnuts Veg had gathered from somewhere, to eliminate the green or rotten or wormy ones (about half the total!)—and picked up her sketch pad. At least she still had that: her painting. She headed downriver, in the direction of chopping noises.

Veg was hacking down selected hardwood saplings, comparatively rare in this valley, and skinning them. He had a row lying nude in the sun, each about six feet long and one to two inches in diameter, depending on the end. He was using his hefty scout knife, rather than attempting to harvest the slender trees by axe, and his large arm muscles bunched handsomely as he worked.

Yes, she thought, he was a powerful man, if not really a handsome one. Hardly the kind she would have taken for a vegetarian, a hater of killing. A strong, strange man, for all his simplicity.

"What are you making?" she inquired at last.

"Quarterstaffs," he grunted.

"Quarterstaff? Isn't that a weapon?"

"Yeah. We lost our steam rifle in the turnover, and

there are animals here even that wouldn't faze. Got to have something. Staffs are defensive, but effective."

"But a weapon—"

"Defensive, I said!" Last night had been his turn on watch, the human half, and he had whistled cheerfully. But now he was feeling it. She knew what four hours of sleep felt like, but still didn't appreciate his tone.

She kept her voice level. "You mean against a dinosaur?"

"I figure you could jam it down his throat, or maybe stop his jaws from closing on you, or just bop him on the nose. Lot better'n bare hands."

She eyed the slender poles dubiously. "I wouldn't care to try it on *Triceratops*. He'd bite it right—"

"Nobody's making you!" he snapped.

Affronted, she walked away. She was disgusted with herself for reacting emotionally, but she was angry at him too. He didn't have to yell.

She found Cal farther downhill, north of camp, observing a small tame dinosaur. She had seen quite a number of these innocuous, almost friendly little reptiles about, for they usually grazed in herds of a dozen or more. This one was about five feet tall with a head of considerable volume compared to the average species of reptile. Brightly colored tissue surrounded its face, red and green and yellow; it circled all the way around its head and rose above in a spongy dome. Aquilon had no idea what such a display did for its possessor, but remembered that evolution always had realistic purpose.

The creature was nibbling bracken, and though it looked up as she approached, it returned to its meal when she halted. Harmless, certainly; had it been a predator, it would have attacked or retreated immediately. Aside from that she could tell by its tooth structure that it was herbivorous.

She came to stand behind Cal, knowing the sound of her voice would spook the beast. She opened her sketch pad and painted the dinosaur's portrait, not one to miss the opportunity. Her paper, fortunately, had been salvaged from the raft wreck, though each page was discolored around the rim. Perhaps it was not as valuable materially

145

as the radio equipment, but she was much happier to have it.

She was intrigued by this reptile. It looked defenseless, and its head was so large and tall! Did it have a brain capacity rivaling that of man? Could it be intelligent, in human terms? Its actions suggested nothing of the kind, but—

When she finished, Cal handed her a sheet of his notes. Usually he employed the voicetyper, but this time he had been doing it by hand, to preserve silence. She looked at the crude writing: *"TRÖODON,* 'bonehead' ornithischian. Solid bone skull, small brain."

Solid *bone*? That skull she had thought to contain a massive brain . . . What a waste of space!

There was more, but she looked up to see one of the mantas approaching. The little dinosaur took alarm and bounded away like a huge rabbit, keeping its head erect.

"Why all bone?" she demanded, free to speak now. "Doesn't it just slow it up, when there is danger?"

"That has bothered paleontologists for some time," Cal admitted. "I'd very much like to see Tröodon in a situation of hazard, and make notes. At present I can only conjecture. A large carnosaur would ordinarily bite the head off one that size, as the best way to kill the creature rapidly. The body would still cast about a bit, but the predator would be able to hold it down and feed on the carcass at leisure. But if it sank its teeth into Tröodon's soft-seeming skull. . . ."

Aquilon laughed. "No teeth! It wouldn't try *that* again!"

"Not exactly. There are several inches of fleshy padding around the bone, that would cushion the impact. And the carnosaur would soon learn to take in the entire head, not part of it, and so succeed. But this would still be a respectable mouthful, perhaps quite tasty—yet unchewable. I think that by the time the meat were off the bone, the others in the herd would long since have taken advantage of the carnivore's preoccupation to get away. So it would be an indirect measure, protecting the herd more than the individual."

"That's a grisly mechanism!"

"Yet it would seem to limit herd liability, and perhaps

discourage careless predators entirely. We do observe a thriving population of this species, at any rate."

The manta had arrived and settled into its lumplike posture. "What is it, Circe," she inquired, knowing that there would be valid reason for such an interruption. More and more, the mantas were keeping to themselves, associating only loosely with the human party. One always showed up for watch at night, and they certainly were not hiding; but they seemed to prefer their own company. Communications were adequate; she could understand Circe quite well now.

STRANGE—IMPORTANT, the manta signaled with that combination of gesture and tail snaps they had gradually worked out as their code.

"Dangerous?" She remembered how well Circe's warning had served the first time, when the tsunami came.

NO. But the denial lacked full force, showing probability rather than certainty. THIS. And Circe snapped her tail in the dirt four times, leaving a mark like a footprint.

"The bird!" Cal exclaimed. "The bird that made those tremendous prints we saw at Camp One!"

YES. TWO, Circe indicated.

"What's so distinctive about a large bird, here in the land of giants?" Aquilon asked Cal.

"It may be our substantial evidence that this is a discrete world."

"Discreet? Oh, you mean 'e-t-e'—discrete, *separate?*"

"*Alternate.* A world parallel to our own in virtually every detail, but distinct. The concept is certainly more sensible than that of temporal displacement."

"Temporal—? Time travel? Changing the past? Paradox?" As though she hadn't worried about it too!

"Something like that. The resemblance of Paleo to Earth is far too close to be coincidental. The size of it, the gravity, atmosphere, every matching species—but we've discussed this before. I've been assigning Earthly nomenclature because it fits, but I simply can not credit time travel. There has to be another explanation, and the alternate-worlds framework can be made to fit."

"Back where we started from," she murmured. "But Earth didn't have dinosaurs during the Paleocene."

147

"We can't be sure of that, 'Quilon. This is an enclave, isolated rather stringently from the rest of the continent. It could have happened on Earth, and have been entirely destroyed, so that no fossils remained as evidence—or merely be buried so deeply that we haven't discovered them yet. This location, particularly, would be subject to such an upheaval. I'll certainly check that out when ..." He paused, and she knew he was remembering their banishment. They could not return to Earth soon, if ever, even if they wanted to. "It *could* have happened, and I rather think it did. The San Andreas Fault of our time is the landward extension of a Pacific oceanic rift. The continent has overridden it, burying enormous amounts of undersea landscape. This valley could be part of that vanished structure, the mountains a reaction to the extreme turbulence of the area. There is nothing here inherently incompatible with what we know of our own world."

"I'm not sure I follow all that," she said, wondering which of them he was straining to convince, and why the point was suddenly so important. "But I gather that Paleo either is or is not Earth."

He smiled momentarily. "That would seem to cover it. This *could* be Earth—except for that pair of birds Circe reports. Everything else fits, except the chronology of some of the reptiles, such as the pteranodons. They should have become extinct before—"

"But a big bird *doesn't* fit? I'd think that two birds would be easier to explain than a whole enclave of anachronistic dinosaurs."

"Not so. The enclave is merely a remaining pocket, a brief, geologically speaking, carryover. The bird—one of this nature, this early—would have had to evolve over the course of millions of years, and it would have ranged widely. There would have been fossils, other evidences of its presence."

"Cal, that sounds thin to me. There are so many giant gaps in the fossil record—"

" 'Quilon, we are faced with drastic alternatives. If this *is* Earth, we are faced with paradox. Paradox can't exist in practice; nature will resolve it somehow, and we might

148

not like the manner of that resolution. Not at all. Principle of the monkey's paw."

"The what?"

He didn't seem to hear her. "But if this is *not* Earth, the implications are equivalently awkward. It is necessary to know."

"But it's ridiculous to claim that one bird—I mean *two* birds—that we haven't even seen—" She stopped. She had just left an argument with Veg, and now was provoking one with Cal. Whatever the geological, ecological, paleontological, philosophical implications, their discussion would not affect the truth, and it was silly to let it prejudice their personal relations. Cal obviously had something more than a mere bird on his mind; that was a pretext to cover what he refused to discuss. Otherwise he would surely have seen his own illogic.

It was her place to smooth things over, not to aggravate them. "Let's go see!" she said.

Cal nodded.

They rejoined Veg, who seemed to be in better spirit now that his self-appointed task was done. Aquilon didn't mention their prior exchange.

"How far?" was all Veg asked.

Circe explained: twenty miles across the water.

They used the raft, rather than make the dangerous trip around and through the unexplored swamp. They backtracked to Camp One, rebound the *Nacre*, and poled as far as the remaining day permitted.

It was good to be afloat again, Aquilon thought, as she lay wedged between the two men in the cabin. Somehow, aboard the raft at anchor, decisions were not so urgent, and she appreciated the fact that the security of their position allowed all three to sleep at once. It would otherwise have been her night to stand guard. . . .

They had merely to pull together as a team of three, while the mantas relaxed, wherever it was that the four were spending this night. Let the theoretical questions settle themselves. Here it was nice.

"Oh!" She jumped as a cold wash of water slid over the cabin floor, soaking her derrière. She had forgotten

149

about that hazard. Tomorrow she would set about recalking the *Nacre*. . . .

Next day they beached the *Nacre* on the south shore of the small island Circe indicated and proceeded forward overland. They were quiet and cautious, so as not to frighten the anticipated birds. Each carried one of Veg's new quarterstaffs, just in case.

There was no excitement. The island was nothing more than the long-eroded peak of an ancient volcano, covered with firs and pines and surrounded by deep water. No large reptiles were in evidence, though there were some duckbill footprints. The human party crossed without event to the north side and discovered a tiny peninsula-and-inlet complex.

A bird five feet tall stood guard at the neck of the peninsula. Veg marched at it, poking with the end of his quarterstaff. "Shoo!" he said.

The bird did not squawk and flutter away in the manner Veg evidently expected. It spread its wings, which were quite small for its size, and struck at the pole with its great curved beak. As Veg drew back, surprised, the bird raised one powerful leg high in the air.

"Careful, Veg," Cal called in a low tone. "That's the one we're looking for, and it's dangerous. It's a predator— a killer. Look at that beak, those talons, those muscles. It could disembowel a man with one stroke of that foot."

Veg had come to the same conclusion. He brought the quarterstaff around sharply, striking the bird midway down its long neck. The bird fell back a pace, hurt.

"Oh," Aquilon exclaimed, putting her hand to her own neck. She didn't want the bird to be injured, particularly if it were as rare and significant as Cal intimated. It wasn't, of course; it could not be. But it was a remarkable specimen in its own right.

She looked beyond it and spied the second bird, perched on a rock near the water. Worse and worse—that would be the standing one's mate, sitting on her nest. She would have moved by this time, either to come to the aid of the male or to join him in flight, if she were free to do so. The

150

fact that she stayed put meant that she had eggs to protect and warm.

The humans were intruders on a nesting site, trouble-makers.

But Veg had now seen this too. Embarrassed, he retreated. "Sorry, pal," he said. "Didn't know it was your home. Thought you were just getting in the way. Sorry."

The bird watched him, standing unsteadily, neck crooked where it had been struck. The second bird watched also, from the nest.

Veg, backing away, had forgotten where he was. He stepped off the narrow bank and toppled beautifully as his foot came down on water. The quarterstaff flew up as he went over, flailing. There was a tremendous splash.

Aquilon couldn't help laughing. The change from crisis to ignominy had been so sudden. Then, to cover up, she trotted to the bank to see what help she could offer.

Circe stood a few yards away, watching but not partici-pating. What had passed through the manta's mind as she watched this farce?

The male bird peered at the scene but did not move either. As Veg staggered out, dripping, and Aquilon as-sisted him, it unkinked its neck and reached down to peck exploratively at the forgotten quarterstaff.

The human contingent withdrew. The manta observer disappeared. The bird remained at the neck of the penin-sula until contact was broken. Aquilon held back just long enough to sketch its proud portrait.

They camped on the (calked) raft again, anchored south of the island. They consumed their respective suppers with-out conversation, and lay down together in the cabin when it became dark.

"That bird is intelligent," Cal said. "I suspected as much from its foraging habits. Did you observe the way it reacted? None of the blind animal instincts. It was study-ing us as carefully as we were studying it."

"I wish you'd told me that was the bird we were looking for," Veg complained. "Here I was, trying to scare it away—I thought you wanted some giant!"

Aquilon stifled her laugh. The unforeseen problems of

communication! Veg must have imagined a bird proportioned on the scale of *Brachiosaurus!* The fabled roc. . . .

Then she thought of something else. "How did you know how it foraged?" she demanded of Cal.

"I followed its tracks, naturally." She heard Veg stifling his own laugh, at her expense. She had overlooked the obvious, much as he had.

"I lost the trail in the marsh," Cal continued, "but I learned enough to convince me that the originator resembled class *Aves* about as man resembles class *Mammalia.* That was significant. So I asked the mantas to watch for it."

"Now he tells me," Aquilon muttered chagrined. Of course a really intelligent bird would be a different matter. She, like Veg, had been thinking only in terms of size, and probably it hadn't occurred to Cal that either had misunderstood him.

"Now that I have seen it directly, I'm almost certain," Cal said enthusiastically. "No such creature walked our Earth in Mesozoic or even Cenozoic eras. This is Earth—but a parallel Earth, not our own. Very similar, but with certain definitive differences developing. And there is a displacement in time, so that this world runs about seventy million years behind our own, geologically. Perhaps there are an infinite number of alternates, each displaced by an instant of time instead of by physical distance. Our connection happened to be to this particular alternate, Paleo—a purely random selection. We could as easily have landed on a world removed by a single year, or by five billion years."

"Or one ahead of ours, instead of behind," Aquilon murmured. Cal had not been joking about the implications being as severe as time travel. What Pandora's box was opening up for mankind with this discovery?

"It may be possible to trace the entire history of our own Earth, simply by observing the progressive alternates, once the key to their controlled discovery is perfected. But in the interim we are free to manipulate this specific world to our advantage, knowing paradox is not involved."

There was something about that phrasing Aquilon didn't like.

"I don't know what you mean, friend, but it doesn't sound good," Veg said. "What do you want to do with Paleo?"

"Why, open it for human colonization, of course. It is ideal for Earth's population overflow. Same gravity, good climate, superior atmosphere, untapped natural resources, few enemies—apart from certain reptiles of this one enclave, and perhaps scattered others. This could be preserved as a zoo; it will be invaluable for research."

"Colonize?" Aquilon didn't like the sound of this any better than Veg did. "This is an independent world. Who are we to take it over for our convenience?"

"We are men, generically. We must consider the needs of men. To do otherwise would be unrealistic."

"Now let me get this straight," Veg said in his play-dumb fashion. She could feel the tenseness of his body as he lay beside her. "You say we should turn in a report saying that *Paleo* is A-O.K. for people to come in and settle, and make it just like Earth. And if a few birds or lizards get in the way it's their tough luck?"

"Well, provision should be made for the fauna. I would not condone genocide, particularly in so fine a paleontological laboratory as this. But apart from that your summary is essentially correct. This is a wilderness area, and Earth needs it desperately; it would be a crime against our species to let it lie fallow."

"But the bird," Aquilon protested, her heart beating too strongly. "You said it's intelligent. That means Paleo is technically inhabited—"

"Intelligent for *Aves*: birds. That can't approach human capability. But yes, it is most important that this—this *Ornisapiens* be preserved and studied. It—"

"Orn," Veg said, simplifying again. "In a zoo."

"No!" Aquilon cried. "That isn't what I meant. That would kill it. We should be *helping* it, not—"

"Or at least leaving it alone," Veg said. "It's a decent bird; it didn't jump me when it had the chance, and after I'd hit it with the staff, too. We don't need to lock it up *or* help it, just let it be. Let them all be. That's the way."

"We appear," Cal remarked, "to have a multiple difference of opinion. Veg feels that man can not sit in judg-

153

ment over the species of Paleo, either to assist or to exterminate."

"That's what I feel," Veg agreed.

" 'Quilon feels that the bird, Orn, deserves assistance, because of its apparently unique development as a creature distinct from Earthly genera. Obviously Orn is not common here, and may be in danger of extinction."

"Mmmm," Aquilon agreed. Cal was that most dangerous of opponents: the one who took pains to comprehend the position of his adversary.

"While *I* feel that the needs of our own species must take precedence. It is nature's decree that the fittest survive in competition, and if Man *can* control this world operating from a tiny beachhead in the Pacific, he deserves to and is required to. The fact that the animals here resemble those of our own past is irrelevant; our species must have room to expand."

"*Lebensraum*," Aquilon whispered tersely.

"Adolf Hitler's term," Cal said, picking up the allusion immediately, as she had known he would. "But he used it as a poor pretext for conquest."

"Aren't *we*?"

Cal shrugged in the dark.

She felt herself getting flushed. "Suppose some other species—maybe an advanced version of Orn—had felt that way about our own Earth?" she demanded. "Suppose they had come when we were apelike primates, and used advanced technology to push us out?"

"We'd have deserved it. We're *still* apelike primates."

"Maybe we should vote," Veg said.

"No problem," Cal said. "Are you ready, mantas?"

From the roof came a tap—the contact of a manta's tail on the wood. Aquilon was startled, though she should not have been. They had probably come after dark and viewed the leaking sound waves, thus picking up the entire conversation. Cal had certainly been aware of the audience, and he seemed to have confidence in the outcome. Why?

Veg was silent also, probably wrestling with similar concerns. How, she wondered hurriedly, would the manta mind view this crisis? They saw things in terms of their

154

own Nacre framework, manta framework—carnivore, omnivore, and herbivore—with rights and wrongs being interpreted through this. Veg's vegetarianism had been the original key to contact with these creatures, since they had seen him as theoretically in need of protection from the omnivore of the party: her. It wasn't as simple as that, Cal had maintained; but as an analogy it would do. Of course she had shifted from omnivore type to herbivore type, while Cal had gone from carnivore to omnivore; apparently the mantas were now wise enough to the ways of man to accept these changes. All human beings were true omnivores, regardless of their diets of the moment; man's brutal nature defined him.

"What do birds eat?" Veg inquired.

It was a stupid question and no one replied. Veg knew what birds ate; he was a veteran birdwatcher. Funny, she realized now, that he had treated the Orn so brusquely. Perhaps he only identified with small birds, the seed-eating, fly-chasing kind. As a species, of course, birds were omnivorous.

Omnivorous.

The question had not been stupid at all. Suddenly she knew which way the manta vote would go. "No," she said, trying to control the tremor in her breast. "Don't vote."

"Why not?" Cal asked her. He knew his advantage, and was pressing it ruthlessly despite the mild words. In body he was small, in mind a giant—and that went for discipline as well as intelligence.

"It's too important," she said, dissembling, knowing she could not prevail against him, and that Veg would be even less effective than she. Cal had the brain and the votes. "Before, it was only where we wanted to go as a group, not a really critical decision. This time it's the fate of an entire world. *Our* world, or one very like it. This isn't the manta's business."

She saw the teeth of the trap and scrambled to avoid them. "Colonization would destroy Paleo as it is, you know that. They'd decide the dinosaurs were a menace to tourists or navigation or something, and wipe them out. So we can't decide a question like this by ourselves."

"I was hardly suggesting that we should," Cal replied

155

calmly. "We have merely to make an honest report to the authorities on Earth, and let *them* decide."

"But they're omnivores!" she cried, knowing this implied that she endorsed a dishonest report. Omnivore—she meant it as a description of character, not diet. The omnivores of the planet Nacre were utterly savage, with virtually no redeeming qualities, in her terms. This was in contrast with the innocuous herbivores and deadly but disciplined carnivores. The term "omnivore" had come, for her, to represent all that was despicable in life. Man *was* an omnivore, and had already demonstrated his affinity to the Nacre breed. That ruthless action on Earth itself to eradicate potentially dangerous fungus spores—

"So is Orn," Cal said.

"That isn't what I meant!" she exclaimed, defensively angry.

"You're being emotional rather than rational."

"I'm a woman!"

There was a freighted silence.

Cal was right, but she knew he was wrong, ethically. Cal had decided against Paleo the moment he was assured that it was safe to do so. The mantas wouldn't care. The Earth authorities would be concerned only with exploitation of natural resources and the temporary relief of population pressure. They would much prefer to devastate another world, rather than to abate the mismanagement of the first. There was no one she could appeal to.

"I can't participate in this," she said at last. She got to hands and knees and crawled out of the cabin, leaving the men lying there separated by a woman-sized gap. She was dressed; the niceties of contemporary convention were ludicrous here.

She stood aboard the raft in the gentle night wind, looking across the moonlit water toward the island. Large flying insects hovered about her head and tried to settle on her. She jerked her hood up and fastened the mesh over her face, batting it against the sides of her head to clear it of trapped arthropodic life. Then she drew on her gloves, so that no portion of her skin was exposed. The night was warm, and this confinement made her hot, but it was better than submitting to the appetites of the winged ones.

It was stupid, it was cruel—but it would be worse to go along with this genocidal majority. She had witnessed the ways of man on Earth, and could not bear the thought of the rape of Paleo that was surely in the making. So—she had to go her own way, whatever that might mean.

She looked over the black water. She would have to swim. At least that would cool her off! The chances were that no large marine predators were near. The reptiles didn't seem to be active at night, generally, and their size kept their numbers down. Still, she hesitated, sadly confused inside. She tried to tell herself it was because she knew *Ichthyosaurus was* a night hunter, because of those pumpkin-sized eyes . . . but it was the separation from those she had thought lifetime friends that really dismayed her. How could she return, once she made this break?

There was the scuffle of another person breaking through the cabin net, and Veg stood up beside her. "Better your way than his," he said.

She experienced a choking surge of gratitude toward him. She had made her decision on her own, not presuming his. The ties between the two men were strong, however different their temperaments and physiques might be. She had not even thought what she might do, by herself, or how she would live. Now she was immensely relieved to know that she would not be alone.

"We'll have to swim," he said, echoing her own thought. "You were headed for the birds, weren't you?"

She hadn't planned that far ahead, but it seemed to fit. The schism had started with the birds, really.

She touched his arm, not wanting to speak within the hearing of Cal, or even to gesture, knowing the mantas were watching. Cal was the weakest member of the group (physically!) and the raft required muscle to operate. Muscle the mantas could not supply. By leaving him, they were marooning him.

"I'll check back in the morning," Veg said. "We'll work it out." He dived into the water, making a phosphorescent splash.

Relieved, she followed him.

XIII: ORN

Well after dusk Orn lifted his head, disturbed. Beyond the normal noises of the night he perceived a differing manifestation, and in a moment placed it: the awkward progress of the monstrous mams.

The confrontation of the day still distressed him. The really strange or inexplicable or completely unremembered bothered him because he did not know how to deal with it, and this recent encounter had been all of that. Mams themselves were familiar enough; they were everywhere, more plentiful by far than the reps even here in the heart of this enclave. Elsewhere on the continent they were larger and bolder and farther developed than were the primitive samples here. But nowhere did they approach the size of either Orn himself or any of the larger reps, except perhaps for their largest and stupidest herbivores. He had adapted to the changed situation in the world and learned to cope with the new creatures, before settling into this more familiar valley. But to be so abruptly confronted by bipedal mams larger than himself!

That shock had very nearly cost him his life. He had stood bemused by the appalling gap in his memory, trying to fathom the life history of the species so that he might know how to deal with it. Size was only one feature of many; these mams were *different*. Their myriad peculiarities had rendered them nearly invisible to him at first. Only his prior practice in visualizing unfamiliar creatures in terms of familiar ones had enabled him to grasp their nature at all.

Meanwhile, one of the creatures had approached and made contact. Orn, mindful of Ornette and their two precious eggs, had had to act to repel the intrusion.

The mam had struck him with an inanimate object, another astonishment. Orn had never realized that such a thing was possible. Inanimate things could be used for roosting or nest-building, or even riding across rough water, but never for the work of claw or beak. Hitherto. What could it mean?

And the final fluke: the mam, having by its alchemism rendered him vulnerable, had failed to kill him. The creature had instead plunged into the water and retreated, and the others with it. If they had come to fight and feed, this was nonsensical.

He remembered the way he had spared the ptera, that first day of their nesting. It was possible to abstain from easy victory, in the absence of hunger. Yet that offered no comprehensible clue to the behavior of the big mams.

Orn ruffled his wings restlessly. He was not equipped to think things out; his memory ordinarily made such effort unnecessary. But now that huge mam was coming again, in the night. Orn had to react, and to protect himself and their nest more effectively than he had before. No ancestor had faced this particular problem.

At least this night attack was in character. The mams, like the aves, were able to move about as readily by night as by day, and a number preferred the cover of dark for their foraging. Indeed, many would not survive long in this homeland of the reps otherwise, for there were many empty bellies and sharp teeth on patrol by day, and mams were tasty morsels. Only by occupying regions too cold for the reps and by feeding at night had the mams prospered.

But these were so clumsy! If the creatures—only two were coming this time—were hunting, they would never overtake their game so loudly. If they thought they were hiding, they were disastrously inept. Was it that they were so large for their type that they were stupid, like the brach swamp dweller whose plentiful young were such ready prey? But even the mam amblys were more careful of their own well-being than that!

Yes, they were coming here. Orn raised himself from the nest and Ornette moved over to cover the eggs fully. One of them had to warm and guard the eggs at all times, and Ornette, gravid with the third, did not forage at all now. Three times they had made connection, and two of the eggs were incubating. The final one was due tonight, and a disturbance would be harmful. He had to guard the nest from every threat.

He strode to the isthmus and waited for the two lumbering mams. Male and female, both grotesque in their inept giantism. What their mission was he could not know, for they lacked the furtive manner of egg stealers. But he would turn them back. There was a bruise under the feathers of his neck, from the previous encounter, and the muscles there were sore, but it had been an important lesson. He would not let such an object strike him again, not stand dazed. He would kill the first mam immediately and be ready for the second.

They arrived. Orn waited, standing just behind the narrowest section of the isthmus so that they would have to approach singly. Perhaps they were egg stealers after all, depending on brute strength rather than stealth. He twitched the claws of one foot in the turf, ready to lift and slash ferociously. The eggs must not be imperiled!

"He's there." It was the male, making some kind of hissing growl that still did not quite resemble a challenge to battle.

"Veg, he thinks you're after the eggs. Don't go near him." That was the female, her growl more sustained and variegated. It was as though she were cautioning her mate about the coming encounter.

The male halted in bright moonlight about four wing-spans from Orn. He held a length of tree in his paws—the same object that had surprised Orn before. It was in fact a substitute beak or claw, for the mam had no effective armament of its own. Orn visualized it as the latter, for it attached to the limbs. He would have to strike around it, diving for the open throat or gut.

But the mam did not make an overture for combat. He stood for an interminable period, while the female stroked a twig against a flat object. Orn comprehended neither the action of the female nor the inaction on the male.

"I've painted his portrait. We'd better leave him alone." Noises from the female again, as she concealed her twig and tucked the flat thing under one forelimb.

As though that senseless series of female squawks were

160

a signal, the male dropped his length of barkless tree and took a step forward.

"Veg!"

There was no mistaking that cry of alarm. She understood, at least, that the male was on the verge of an encounter likely to end in disembowelment. Orn would not permit it near the nest.

Still the creature approached, taking great slow steps, pausing between each. Now it had its fleshy forelimbs behind it, exposing his entire torso. It was only two wingspans distant, entirely unarmed and vulnerable; Orn could leap across that space and stab the large mam heart he sensed, then retreat to the superior position on the isthmus. But he held back, leery of attacking when he did not comprehend the meaning of the mam's actions and could not interpret them in terms of any similar creature. It could easily be a death trap for himself.

Another step, and now he was aware of the tension in the mam. It was afraid yet determined, not in a kill fury. Did it want to die? Certainly it did not want to fight! It had made itself entirely vulnerable to Orn's beak or talon, while its mate whimpered behind.

Then everything fell into place. These huge, awkward, bumbling things—they didn't know *how* to fight. They could strike out with pieces of tree, but were unable to follow up any advantage gained. Both would soon become prey to a predator rep unless they found sanctuary somewhere. So they had come to this isolated island, and, still afraid, had sought Orn's protection.

He would ordinarily have killed it anyway, or at least wounded it sufficiently to drive it off, this alien male. He was not hungry for the meat. But the very nest that made him stand his ground against an unremembered antagonist also made him disinclined to kill unnecessarily. His being was suffused with the juices of cohabitation and protectiveness; he had his own mate to comfort and eggs to warm, and bloodshed made a poor nesting mood.

The mam kept coming. Orn had either to kill him or let him pass, thereby extending his protection to the strange pair.

He heard Ornette pant with the first laying pangs.

Orn stood aside.

The female crossed then, and the two mams joined appendages and skirted the opposite shore of the peninsula. Orn stepped backward toward the nest, anxious to be with Ornette in her time of pain, but compelled to watch the mams lest they make some hostile move. He was profoundly uncertain, more so than he had been when he spared the ptera, but at least he had avoided battle and killing.

He came at last to the nest, and stood beside it for some time, listening to the mams while one wing touched Ornette's back. The creatures were behind the clustered pines, scraping the ground with their soft digits and uttering their ugly, drawn-out cries, but never coming toward him. They seemed to know that they lived on sufferance, and that the vicinity of the nest was forbidden. He would have to kill them if they came near Ornette or the eggs, particularly tonight.

Finally they settled down, and only their vocal noises persisted. That was their oddest trait: the perpetual and irrelevant sounds they made in their throats and mouths.

"I wish there were some other solution." The female making tones of disturbance. "I hate to leave him alone like that."

"He's got a lot of know-how." Now the male was replying with assurance. Their moods were not so different from those Orn shared with Ornette; only their vocalizing differed substantially. They employed drawn-out, modulated chains of sound in lieu of simple pitched honks. Apart from the clumsiness of the mode, it served. Everything about these ungainly mams was like that, however. Even their fur was matted and creased as though it had been baked in mud until it hung in chafing sheets. Nets of hair had fallen over their heads as well, obscuring their vision and smell perceptions and surely interfering with feeding.

"He'll know better than to try to go anywhere." The female was uttering modulations of self-reassurance now. "The mantas will protect him."

"Yeah."

One thing about their continuing utterances: it enabled

Orn to keep track of them without leaving the nest or straining his perceptions. He settled down beside Ornette, who was relaxing for the moment, and listened.

"I wish we could get dry." Female. "I know it isn't really cold, but with this soaking and the sea breeze—I'm shivering."

"I brought a tarp in my pack." Male. "Make a passable blanket, if that helps. It's watertight."

"You're thoughtful, Veg. But the wet clothing is right next to my skin, and the tarpaulin would prevent it from evaporating. I'll have to take my things off."

"I'll set up shop in the next gully."

"But you're cold too, Veg. You're just as wet as I am, and there's only one tarpaulin."

"I've roughed it before, 'Quilon. Don't worry about me."

They were doing something. Orn heard the rustle of something he could not identify. Not leaves, not bark, not tangled fur. Concerned, he stood up quietly and moved to where he could oversee the mam camp.

The male was drawing flexible material from a rock-shaped object. It was as though a giant clamshell contained matted ferns. He spread it out, a single sheet, so that it settled over the female.

It was all right. They were merely spreading bedding.

"Veg—"

" 's okay. The tarp's dry. I had it sealed in. Got a dry T-shirt for you, too. Wrap it tight to keep the bugs out though."

"Veg, you're not very bright sometimes."

"I know. I should've thought of dry clothing before diving in. In the morning I'll go back and pick up some. Now you fix yourself up, and I'll go down a ways and—"

"Veg, if we sleep apart we'll *both* be cold."

"I know, but no sense getting everything wet again with my sopping rags. You're better off by yourself."

Orn realized that they were disagreeing with each other in some awkward mam way. The female wanted something but the male didn't understand.

"Veg, remember when I spoke about making a choice?"

"Yeah, 'Quilon. Back when we broke it up on Earth. I never forget things like that."

"I made it."

The mams were silent for a moment, but Orn, watching and listening and sniffing, was aware of a continuing tension between them. Some kind of understanding was incipient. He flexed his claws, ready to move if the creatures attempted to make a night raid on the nest.

"Yeah, I'm not very bright." Male sound again: comprehension and triumph.

Then the male put his soft mam digits to his own fur and ripped it apart. It fell from his body in wet lumps, leaving him plucked. The female stood up and did the same. Orn was amazed; he could never have removed his own feathers like that, or have endured the pain.

The mams got down together and wrapped the big sheet around them, as though they were two hairless worms in a single cocoon.

Orn listened for a while longer. Then he realized the significance of their actions. *They were nesting!* What had passed before was their odd mam courtship, and now they were ready to copulate.

Relieved, he returned to his own nest. At last he understood the complete motive of this pair of intruders. They had sought a safe place to reside during their mating and confinement, and so had chosen to make common cause with his own family.

The big mams were not as stupid as he had supposed, merely strange.

That night, while the mams embraced cumbersomely and made sounds reflecting labors of universal significance, and while the three ptera hung in cold silence from their branches, Ornette gave birth to the final egg.

Peace and joy were upon the peninsula.

The mams woke in the morning but remained in their bundle for a time, waiting for the sun to strike away the chill. As the ptera began to stir, the mams unwound, attended to their special toilettes, and climbed back into their ugly fur. They ate from a cake of scorched, impacted plant stuff and drank copious quantities of water from a strange container. Like all mams, they imbibed and ejected an appalling amount of liquid.

"Look at the pteranodons!" The female was making her excited noises again. Orn, initially irritated by this constant and useless chatter, was becoming used to it. He accepted every creature for what it was, and it seemed the giant mams were noisemakers.

Then a trach crossed the water from the mainland and sported about the peninsula, browsing for shore herbage. This rep fed mainly on pine needles and cones, grinding them up with its flat bill full of little teeth. Though it was large, standing four times Orn's height and possessing a flat, sleek muscular tail, it was harmless unless provoked. It needed its full height to reach the succulent (to it) needles growing from the lower branches of the tall trees. It was related to the para Orn had first seen dead beyond the mountain range, but lacked the elaborate bonework on the head. A para could thus outrun a trach, because it ran cooler; but the trach was of sturdier construction.

Orn stood by the nest and let the rep graze as it would, leaving its webbed prints in the muck. That was why the island location was so good: most large reps that were able to reach it and climb on land were those that ate neither flesh nor eggs, and so were reasonably safe. Like this good-natured trach.

The mams also watched, but with greater caution. Their exclamations suggested that they were not accustomed to such proximity to the trach. Soon they relaxed, however, watching the rep's easy motions.

"I better check on Cal." And with that utterance the male was off, charging through the brush like a small tricer. The female remained to watch the trach play and feed.

Ornette rose from the nest, and Orn covered the three living eggs while she exercised her legs and wings and cleaned herself off at the edge of the water. She had had a hard night, and was not entirely easy about the presence of the mams or the trach, but deferred to his judgment.

Orn watched the female mam speculatively. Most mams did not lay eggs, of course; they gave live birth, like the ichthy rep of the sea. After the authority of the mating

165

ritual of the night just passed, this process was surely commencing within this female. Would the two mams remain on the island for the denouement? Perhaps the mam litter would grow up with Orn's own in compatible proximity. This would be a curious phenomenon, but not objectionable, so long as there was no strife between them concerning tasty grubs and such. His ancestors had nested upon occasion in harmony beside tróös and even ankys, though the parent reps never went near their eggs once they had been deposited. Rep nests were far more transient than those of aves, so it didn't matter. But his species had never shared territory with struths or tyranns or crocs of any age; indeed, Orn would smash and consume any eggs he found of these creatures. It depended on the type of rep.

It depended on the type of mam, too. He would just have to be alert.

It was during this contemplative interlude that the first tremor struck.

XIV: CAL

It hurt Cal, this schism; he could not deny it. The group had come upon it almost incidentally, yet he had known it was brewing, and it had bothered him increasingly. They had been fortunate that it had not occurred on Nacre. Veg believed in life, however naïvely; Cal believed in death. Aquilon fell between, vacillating, but tended toward life. This was not so simple a concept as good and evil; both qualities were represented on either side of this issue. It was primarily a question of what was necessary.

The four mantas understood that much, as they had demonstrated by their action at the orbiting station. Their view of man's endeavors was dispassionate, as was their view of the entire animal kingdom, since they were not of it. They remained with him because they knew that his approach to the problem of Paleo was realistic rather than emotional. Had it been otherwise—

He sighed. Had it been otherwise, he would have relegated all Earth to limbo, for the mere love of Aquilon. He acted as he had to, but this did not alter his love for her. Nor did her figurative elopement with Veg affect this; he was aware that the simmering chemistry of heterosexual existence had to boil over at some point. They loved life, and this was the essence of life; the fact that Cal had increasing yearnings of his own of that nature could not change his overall orientation. They were his friends, and he had more pressing responsibilities; he could not begrudge them their joy.

Meanwhile, he had a job to do. Paleo was suitable for colonization by Earth, and no report he could make could conceal that. In fact, it was vital that he make the matter entirely clear, though this would sacrifice this beautiful world, for there were larger concerns. If the rape of Paleo diverted mankind long enough to allow information to circulate to those who could and would be stimulated to ensure proper protection for the other worlds of the alternate framework—the positive backlash—the end did in this case justify the means. Whatever Aquilon might think. This would necessarily entail the retirement of certain native fauna, and was certainly regrettable; but nature's way, properly guided, was best. No species could prevail by holding back. That was the way of self-extinction. The philosophy that saw virtue in the preservation of species and systems unfit to survive competitively—that philosophy was quaint but futile. Nature had no such sentiments.

Cal studied the raft in the morning light. He would have to arrange to sail it back across the bay by himself, then make the trek overland to Camp Two for supplies. Then a longer sea voyage back to their Paleocene camp, where the one remaining functional radio was located. After that it would be merely a matter of waiting. Earth would decide.

It was not an easy journey he contemplated. Veg could have done it, but Cal was a far cry from that! Still, his philosophy accounted for this. He would make the at-

167

tempt. If he failed, the report would not be made, and perhaps Veg and Aquilon would have their way. If he failed, he deserved to fail.

His strength was not great, but it was more than it had been. He could rig the sail, tie it in place, and handle the rudder provided the winds were moderate and favorable. He would have to be alert for large reptiles and stormy weather, assuming that either could be avoided. How he would navigate the barrier reefs he did not know; possibly he could map a channel through them at low tide, then follow that course at high tide. He judged that the odds were against his completing the trip, but with proper application and caution he hoped to make a worthy run for it.

"Ahoy!"

It was Veg hailing him from the island. Cal waved.

"How're you doing?" Veg called. Then, not waiting for an answer, the big man dived into the water and stroked for the raft.

"I'm going back to the Paleocene camp," Cal said as Veg clambered aboard. "The radio is there, and I believe the winds are shifting enough to make it feasible."

"Feasible, hell. You can't make it by yourself. Why don't you talk to 'Quilon again? We shouldn't split like this."

"Three, as the saying goes, is a crowd."

Veg covered up his embarrassment by going to the tied mound of supplies. Most of their equipment remained at Camp Two, but they had come prepared for several days. "She needs some dry clothing, okay?"

"She is welcome. Take some bread, too. She made it, after all. I'll be moving the *Nacre* out soon." There had not been any official division of spoils, but it was tacit: Veg had the woman, Cal the raft. And the mantas.

"You'll kill yourself."

Cal shrugged. "Death is no specter to me."

"Here." Veg busied himself with the sail, hauling it into position and tying it securely. "If you get in trouble, send a manta."

They shook hands awkwardly and parted. Already the *Nacre* was tugging at the anchor.

The wind was fair and gentle, the sky overcast, and progress was satisfactory. The mantas sailed out over the water, stunning fish with their tails. Cal scooped them in with the net and piled them aboard the raft so that the mantas could feed at leisure.

It was interesting that the sea here was completely Paleocene. No ammonites, no rudists. Would Aquilon have dreamed about the rudist bivalve if he had described it to her as another typically Cretaceous sea creature? Only the reptiles had retained their hold on the sea, as part of the enclave. What did this signify about the relation of land and sea forms? There had to be some continuing link between the reptiles of land, sea, and air, so that they became extinct almost together. . . .

The island was a mile astern when the tremor came. The water danced as though rain were hitting the surface, but there was no rain. The mantas, disgruntled, closed hastily on the raft and boarded. Debris sifted down from the trees visible along the shore, and dust came up in peripheral sections of the valley.

A tremor—no more than fifteen seconds in duration, not really severe. Cal did not react with unreasoning dread. Perhaps this little shake signified nothing—but it could be the prelude to a far more violent siege.

Veg and Aquilon were on the island, stranded there until they could construct a second raft. Certainly they would not attempt to swim to the mainland during the heat of the day; the carnivores of water and shore forbade it. But of course there was no security from an earthquake. They were as safe on the island as anywhere. Perhaps safer, when the great land predators, surely roused into anger by the shake, were taken into account.

He could return, but it would not resolve their interpersonal dilemma. The arguments had been made, the positions clarified. Best to continue as he had planned.

In the distance, in the strait between the islands Aquilon had dubbed Scylla and Charybdis, he made out animate activity. The water dwellers had indeed been shaken up by the tremor, and were casting about, trying to flee or attack but finding no way to isolate the cause. Cal decided to steer well clear of them. Most were far smaller than

169

Brachiosaurus, but many were more predacious, and even a herbivorous dinosaur was dangerous when alarmed, as the battered craft testified.

Tremendous pteranodons sailed in the sky, the only creatures unaffected. No—as he watched, the winged reptiles changed course en masse. The wind had shifted, as though blunted by the tremor.

That meant trouble for him too. He had traveled under fair auspices so far, but any change in the wind would be the worse for him.

He untied the sail and began to haul it down. Now his lack of strength was critical, for what Veg made seem easy was a tremendous strain on his own resources. The sail, under tension, resisted his efforts.

Then the wind shift caught up. The sail fluttered violently as it was struck almost at right angles, and the raft began turning. Cal knew how to adjust the sail and use the rudder so as to tack into the wind, but he also knew that he had neither the agility nor the strength to perform the coordinated tasks required. Sailing a clumsy raft was at best a two-man job, and tacking took muscle.

He did the next best thing. He steered the *Nacre* around forty-five degrees, heading northwest instead of west. This would bring him to land too soon, but seemed to be his safest course.

The mantas perched on the cabin roof, unable either to assist or to offer advice.

All too rapidly the *Nacre* came at the shore. This was the swampy region where certain tribes of duckbills foraged, but none were in evidence at the moment. Just as well. They were not inimical to man, but would have reacted unpredictably to a charging raft.

Now was the time to drop the sail, but the line was still jammed. The *Nacre* was driving relentlessly for the bank of land, carving a ragged course through the water plants.

The mantas dived for the sides. So did Cal.

He hit a cushion of soft plants and took in a mouthful of warm, slimy, but not salty, water before finding the mucky bottom with feet and hands. The depth here was about a yard.

The *Nacre* ploughed on, slowed by the thickening

growths. Then the keel scraped into something more solid than the bottom mud, and the whole thing crunched to a halt, upright and listing only momentarily. The jammed rope let go, and the sail dropped resoundingly to the deck, releasing the raft from the urging of the wind.

Cal had taken his plunge for nothing.

He waded up and sought the crude anchor. This might not hold against a determined offshore wind, but again there was nothing better he could do. He would have to leave the *Nacre* and hope it remained secure for a day or two, until he could return. He was, at least, on the right side of the river.

He donned a small pack, taking only enough baked fish to last him a day, since he hoped to pick up supplies at Camp Two. He would be foolish to wear himself out prematurely, on this easiest leg of his journey.

As an afterthought, he took his quarterstaff too.

It was now early afternoon, and he knew he could not make the twenty miles the compass indicated before dark. He would have to husband his strength and do the job in stages. Time was as critical as survival.

He trekked through the slough all afternoon, resting more frequently than he needed to. His strength was for the moment his most precious commodity, and he guarded it jealously. The mantas stayed with him though they would have been happier on their own; they were evidently concerned for his safety. By dusk he had achieved higher ground. He threw himself down, eyes closed, not bothering at first with any formal bedding.

Veg could have made this distance in an hour, he knew. But to Cal it was a victory, for a year ago he could not have made a tenth of it. He was tougher than he had been in a decade, and he took an unobjective pride in it.

But he still assessed his chances of success at less than even.

He ate a salted fish for breakfast and moved out. His legs were stiff, but he felt stronger than ever. This was the first time in many years he had traveled by himself, and he was pleased to discover how well it was going. He was making much better time on this firm terrain.

There were more deciduous, broad-leafed trees than he had supposed at first. Counting them idly, he found that fully a third of the substantial growths were familiar hardwoods—beech, birch, maple, ash, elm, and so on. Though the typically Cretaceous flora predominated, the balance was even now shifting to these newer types. The land, like the ocean, was advancing relentlessly into the Cenozoic Era. Only the reptiles lingered.

By noon he was within five miles of the camp. The intricate distance-gauging compass assured him of that, since it had been keyed to Camp Two. He stopped to eat the last fish and sup water up from a small rain-formed pond, and the mantas ranged out to bring down their meals too. He was not worried about nourishment; the mantas would gladly kill for him if that became necessary, and show him the way to fresh water. He would spend the night in the lean-to, then attempt to make the return trip in one more day. There would have to be many such journeys, of course, for he could not carry much at a time—but the exercise over a familiar trail should toughen him up for the major journey ahead. Perhaps he could fashion a harness-drag, and transport a greater weight at one time. He felt better able to cope than ever before.

Hex came in, tail snapping. Trouble!

A predator dinosaur had come across his trail and was pursuing him. The mantas had tried to distract it harmlessly, but it was intent on one scent. This was what they had been alert against. A big one, Hex clarified: *Tyrannosaurus Rex*, king of the carnosaurs.

The creature could be stopped, of course. The mantas could harass it and probably blind it. *Tyrannosaurus* was far larger than the omnivore of Nacre, but no more dangerous to the swift manta. Four against one—

"Do not attack it," Cal said.

Hex didn't understand.

"This creature's world is on trial. If I get to the radio and send my report, my people will come and exterminate the biological system that now obtains. Not all at once, but over the years, the centuries, until the only dinosaurs remaining are caged in zoos, and the same for most of the primitive Paleocene fauna. Modern mammals will be introduced that will compete aggressively with the less sophisticated natives, and the trees will be cut for timber and pulp and the rocks mined for precious minerals. So *Tyrannosaurus* is fighting for his world, though he doesn't see it that way. If the reptile brings me down, the report will not be made, and man will not come here—at least, not quite so soon. If I escape the reptile, I will have vindicated my right, according to the implacable laws of nature, to supersede it on *Paleo*. It is a contest between us, and the prize is this world."

He had issued a statement whose entirety they could hardly be expected to grasp, but it seemed better not to confuse things by attempting to simplify a difficult concept. The mantas should understand that he did not want them to intercede on his behalf, and that he had reasons that were sufficient for his own mind. That should be enough.

The other mantas came up, and an eye-to-eye dialogue followed. Would they acquiesce?

"Let me meet Tyrann alone," he repeated. "You watch, but do not interfere. Mammal against reptile, the chosen champions, one to one."

Hex snapped once. Yes, they accepted it. The mantas understood the rite of personal combat.

The four spread out to the sides and disappeared amid the cycads. Cal was on his own.

But not for long. A mile back, the giant was coming, crashing through the brush horrendously.

It had been easy to commit himself, for that was necessary by his definitions. It would not be as easy to survive the consequence of that decision. He was hardly the best representative of his species or class for such an encounter. But that was the way circumstance had offered, and he was ready to abide by nature's verdict. He had never been one to avoid confrontation with death.

Cal waited where he was. He wanted to face his opponent. It would be no good for him to sneak away, even if that should fool the reptile. He had to stand up to Tyrann, let the thing know he was challenging it. Then he could make his escape, if it was in him to accomplish it.

The ground shuddered, and not from any geologic tremor. *Tyrannosaurus* was closing in, unsubtly. Every step rocked the land, and the crashing of saplings became loud. This was the pinnacle of reptilian predatory development; no more massive carnivore had ever walked the earth.

The slender fern trees swayed aside, as though reaching to the ginkgo for comfort. A terrified bird flew up. Through the palm fronds poked a gaping set of jaws— fifteen feet above the ground. Then the whole of it came into view: seemingly all teeth and legs, so tall that a man could pass upright under its thighs and tail without stooping. A roar like none ever to emanate from a mammalian throat shook the air, and the tiny cruel eyes peered down.

Tyrann had arrived.

XV: AQUILON

"He's sailing the *Nacre*," Veg said as he reappeared. "Going back to the radio and send the message." He threw down the pack of supplies he had brought from the raft.

Aquilon was appalled. "He can't possibly do it by himself!"

He shrugged. "Can't stop him from trying." But his jaw was tight.

He knew the mantas represented a formidable bodyguard, but there were things they could not protect Cal from. Drowning, physical injury, heatstroke—

Still, Veg was right. If Cal insisted on attempting a suicidal journey, that was his concern. At least, so long as the break between them continued.

If only it were something other than the future of a world at stake! She would gladly have gone along with Cal for the sake of unity on any lesser matter. But his report to Earth would damn Paleo by its praise, and she could not go along with that. It would violate all her most cherished, if uncertain, principles. The wolf should not be loosed at the lamb, not this way.

She felt guilt for either outcome: Cal's success or his failure. She knew he would not change his mind. If he lived, Paleo would die.

Now, too, she felt uneasy about her night of love with Veg. She had made her choice—but she had done it because of the convenience of the moment, and that was not far clear of prostitution, in retrospect. And she suspected from Veg's silence on that score that he felt the same. They had wronged Cal, whatever the merit of their respective positions.

The Orn birds went about their business, first one sitting on the nest, then the other, but usually the female. There were eggs, naturally; she had not glimpsed them, for the birds were sensitive about any human approach to the nest. But nothing else would account for such care.

The first day passed in beauty. She watched the *Trachydon*, the large duckbilled dinosaur, feeding among the pine trees. It was sleek in the water, with webbed feet and a tail flattened like that of a crocodile. When it stood on land it was fifteen feet tall, resembling an outsize kangaroo, and the hind feet were revealed as possessing tripartite hoofs. Duck*billed*—but not duck*like*!

Trachydon spent most of its time chewing, as though its digestion not only began in the mouth but ended there. Its hide was pebbled, without scales or other armor, and the play of the creature's musculature was quite clear underneath the skin. Its underside was whitish, reminding her of a snake. Its sheer size fazed her at first, but Trach was really quite likable when familiar. It almost seemed to pose for her, remaining impossibly still except for its jaws, and she painted many portraits. She was sorry to see Trach go, once its belly was full of pine.

At night the pteranodons returned to their bough to sleep, and that was another impressive spectacle. She had somehow imagined all dinosaurs to be ravening monsters or dim-witted behemoths, before coming to Paleo; this day on the island, watching *Trachydon* and pteranodon in life, banished that prejudice forever. These reptiles had

175

individual personalities and problems, and were bright enough about the latter.

She also saw, that first day, the raft sailing before the wind, angling in toward the mainland, and finally anchoring there. She knew why: the wind had shifted after the tremor, and Cal had been unable to sail directly back to Camp One. At least he had made it safely to shore.

The second night she and Veg slept under the tarpaulin but did not make love.

Two nights and a day on an isle very like paradise—but the tension was cruel. What was Cal doing? He was so small, so weak; he could be lying exhausted in the swamp. . . .

No. The mantas would come back and report. He must be all right.

Still—

"One's coming!" Veg called, looking up from the new raft he was building.

She ran to his side to see. A lone manta was speeding across the water toward the island. Circe!

The story did not take long: a tyrannosaur was after Cal. He had forbidden the mantas to help. Circe departed.

"The crazy fool!" Veg cried. "He's suiciding again!"

But it was not that simple. Cal *wanted* to fight the dinosaur, according to Circe. Ritual combat.

"I know how he thinks!" Veg said. "He wants to prove he can do it by himself. And he can't."

"You mean, prove he's better physically than a dinosaur? That doesn't sound like the kind of thing—"

"That he can get through and send his message, no matter what. Our leaving him didn't stop him, Tyrann won't stop him. That makes it right, he figures."

Suddenly she saw it. The mammals against the reptiles, each represented by its most advanced stage, one individual meeting the other on the field of honor. The decisive combat. The carnosaur had size and power; the man had brain. It *was* a fair compromise, a way to settle an otherwise insoluble dilemma. If Cal won, he would send his message and be justified in the spoils; if he lost—well, it was an answer, and he had chosen the way to come by it.

"I'm going over there," Veg said.

"Veg—"

"I'll have to swim to the mainland and run along the shore. Cross the river up where it's narrower, nearer Camp Two. Hope I can pick up his trail, or maybe a manta'll show me. Fastest way. Might make it in time to haul him out of there alive." He was fastening his clothing for swimming as he spoke.

"Veg, I think we should let him do it his way. On his own. That's the way he wants it."

"He'll get killed!"

She hesitated. "Maybe—that's best."

Veg stiffened. Then, so suddenly that she did not realize what had happened at first, he hit her. His arm came back in a hard swing that caught her across the side of the head and sent her reeling to the ground.

By the time she righted herself, he was in the water, well on his way. She must have blacked out momentarily, for she had not seen him go.

Her hand lifted to touch the stinging, swelling side of her face gingerly. His wrist had struck against her cheekbone; there was no blood. Veg had not even paused to see whether she was hurt. Thus eloquently had she been advised of his first loyalty.

Had she worried about coming between these men? She should have known there was no danger of that!

Yet is still seemed to her that Cal was not only courageous, but right. She could abide by the decision, made that way. Veg, long as he had known Cal, loyal as he was, did not understand. Nothing would be settled if he got there "in time."

She turned to find Orn—yes, that was the name that fit—standing behind her. He was close and quite formidable, suddenly, with myriad tiny scars showing on his legs and beak, and some feathers not completely grown out to replace lost ones. He could have struck her down easily while she stood bemused, but she sensed no hostility in him.

Hesitantly she reached toward him, experiencing an overwhelming need for companionship of any type. She was alone now, on a strange world, without any genuine

177

hope of seeing either man again. Cal's mission was suicidal—but so was Veg's. It might be that the only company she would know henceforth would be that of the big birds.

Orn opened his mighty beak and caught her hand within it—and did not bite. She felt the knife edges of his jaw and knew that her fingers could be severed cleanly by its vicelike compression. But the touch was token.

Then Orn dropped her hand and returned to his nest. It was as though he had touched her in comfort, but not remained to make an issue of it. She was deeply grateful for the gesture.

She roused herself after a time and foraged for edible roots on the main body of the island, since her supplies would not last indefinitely. Her heart was not in it, but she did have to eat. She found a lone banana plant, but the fruit was not ripe. It was afternoon, and she knew nothing of the progress of the two men. She might have expected Circe to stay with her, but the manta was away on some other business. The rapport she had thought she had with the creature of Nacre was fading. . . .

A second tremor came—a stronger one. The ground did not shudder, it rocked. It was as though the soil had turned liquid, and she was riding the waves. She kept her feet with difficulty.

She had a sudden and ugly premonition of what such a quake would do to a nest built on a rock, and to the fragile eggs within that nest. She ran swiftly back to the peninsula as the motion of the ground subsided.

The site of the nest was chaotic. Both birds were standing beside the rock, fluttering their vestigial wings. The worst had happened.

They did not challenge her as she approached, too upset, she realized, to maintain their guard. The nest was damaged but largely intact. The eggs—

Fragments of thick shell projected up, and white and yellow jelly filled the base of the main cavity. The eggs had been shattered by the quake. The birds seemed stunned by the calamity. She visualized the mutilated corpses of human babies in place of the smashed eggs, and thought she understood how the Orns felt.

But one shell appeared to be intact. Aquilon touched it hesitantly with a finger and found it warm and firm. It was eight or nine inches long and slender in proportion, the surface rough. She reached both hands around it and lifted the object out, careful not to let it slip in the slick fluid around it.

Both birds were still, watching her helplessly. "This one's all right," she said.

From somewhere in their throats came an incredulous, hope-dawning cooing.

She carried the egg to a dry hollow and set it down. "Keep it warm," she said. "You can make another nest." She backed away.

After a moment the female—Aquilon thought of her as Ornette—came over and studied it. Then, in a kind of nervous collapse, she sat on it.

But one crisis had passed only to lead to another. The odor of the broken eggs had attracted a predator. Sleek and very long in the water it came—a giant crocodilian reptile, not closely related to the modern crocodiles of Earth but similar externally and every bit as dangerous. Twenty feet from snout to tail, it hauled itself out of the water at the rocky mouth of the inlet and scrambled overland toward the nest.

Orn charged it, squawking loudly and beating the air with his wings, but the armored reptile only snapped sidelong at him and continued without pause. Nothing Orn's size could hurt it seriously; that was obvious.

Would it stop with the nest? Aquilon knew it would not. It must have swum over from the main swamp, for she had seen nothing like this near the island before. The duckbill would hardly have been so casual, either, had it sniffed this predator. Perhaps the quake had jolted it from its accustomed beat. It was hardly in a mood to be reasonable by any mammalian or avian definition. Now that it was here, it would pursue all food available—and that meant the third egg, and the bird protecting it, and probably the stranded bipedal mammal, herself, as well.

Aquilon fetched her quarterstaff. She held it by one end and ran at the crocodilian as though she carried a lance. The forward end struck the creature's leather-tough neck

179

and bounced off, denting it only slightly but delivering a severe jar to her.

The long head swung about, jaws gaping. Aquilon braced herself and swung the pole like a club, striking that snout resoundingly. Unhurt but annoyed, the reptile charged her, its horrendous teeth leading.

Fighting instinctively, she drove the quarterstaff lengthwise into its mouth. To her horror, the entire pole disappeared into that orifice, and the snapping jaws barely missed her hands. She scrambled back.

But it was enough. The crocodilian coughed and shook its head, pained by the object in its throat. Unable for the moment either to swallow it or spit it out, the monster abruptly plunged into the water. It swam to the rocky inlet mouth, jammed itself between the stones so violently that it left scrapings of flesh, and departed. As it passed from view, she heard its teeth clashing together as it sought vainly to bite down on the obstruction anchored neatly between the dental rows.

Aquilon sat down hard, discovering herself panting desperately. She had expended more energy than she realized during the excitement, and was nearly exhausted. But she had won! Her omnivore heritage had come to her rescue and she had driven off the predator.

At the cost of the only weapon she had. Well, she could make another.

Was this the type of creature she was striving to protect from Earth's ravages? A twenty-foot, merciless egg-eating carnivore?

With this in the water, and others like it—had Veg even made it to the shore?

Dusk was coming—where had the day vanished!—and with it the pteranodons. Aquilon got up, still too tense to eat, and began to walk to the tarpaulin on the other side of the peninsula.

Orn blocked her way. She stared at him blankly, then tried to step around. He blocked her again, herding her back by spreading his wings. They were larger than she had thought; their total span, tip to tip, was about five feet. Far too small to enable him ever to fly, but handsome in their own right. The under surfaces seemed almost to glow. Some of the feathers had been freshly broken off, courtesy of the crocodilian. But Orn's manner was not threatening.

She turned and walked toward the makeshift nest, now buttressed by bits of moss Ornette had found within reach. Orn followed. She got to her hands and knees beside Ornette, then curled up and lay beside the huge bird. Orn settled down at her exposed side, spreading one wing to partially cover her body. It was like a thick, warm blanket—and yes, it made her feel immeasurably safer.

No—*this* was what she was fighting to save! This unique, intelligent family, related to her only in spirit.

Comfortable and secure between the two great warm bodies, she slept.

XVI: CAL

It was mind against matter. The mind of man against the matter of reptile. One would prove itself superior in this contest, and to that one would go this world. That was the way it had to be. Except for one small factor—

Tyrannosaurus rex—the tyrant lizard king—charged down on him, banishing that speculation. Yet in this moment of confrontation he had an aberrant vision of Aquilon, so lovely she blinded even his mind's eye. She would have understood this, had she known of it, and perhaps she also would have approved. Had he known this opportunity would arise, he could have arranged to avoid the schism in the human party.

But Veg would not have gone along. The big man tended to overlook the nuances of interspecies morality, and so relied on conformance to a simplistic code. Thou Shalt Not Kill—except when threatened. And who could say what constituted a legitimate threat? The corollary was taken as Thou Shalt Not Eat the Flesh of Any Member of the Animal Kingdom—forgetting that man

181

was a natural predator, owing much of his progress to his diet. So how could such a code solve or even ameliorate the myriad problems of the species? No matter; conform.

All this, in fragments, while Tyrann crashed toward him, head swaying from side to side for balance, eyes fixed on target. The reptile was now within a hundred feet: twice its own body length, five times its height. It was moving forward in a roughly straight line at some twenty miles per hour, ten tons of malevolence. Perhaps it was disappointed in the size of its quarry, hardly worth the effort—but this did not slow it.

No, Veg would not have understood. So it had to be this way: a battle without witnesses, except for the alien mantas. If he lost, his friends would assume he had been suicidally foolish. If he won, lucky. But *he* knew, and that was what counted.

Time to stop reminiscing and start competing.

Cal waited until Tyrann was within a single body length, calculating the time factor. Fifty feet at twenty miles an hour would be about a second and a half until contact—too brief for fine adjustments on its part. The maneuverative advantage did not lie with size. At that critical point—fifty feet—Cal dodged to the side.

His velocity from a standing start was slower than that continuing motion of the dinosaur, but he had a smaller distance to go. He covered only fifteen feet before the six-inch teeth clashed where he had been, and another ten by the time the tremendous thigh and foot rocked the ground behind him. But the margin had been sufficient.

Tyrann, discommoded by the miss, drove his nose into the dirt and came to a roaring halt. He lifted his mottled head, dewlap stretching, small eyes peering balefully about while leaves and twigs tumbled wetly from his jaws. It took him a moment to realize what had happened, but not a long moment. He was a predator, and few of that ilk were stupid or slow when hungry. He had been fooled once by a seemingly petrified morsel, but now he knew it for one of the quick-footed mammals, and he would not underestimate its agility again.

Cal, meanwhile, had made it to the nearest large palm tree, holding his quarterstaff aloft. He had won the first pass by utilizing his advantage of mobility. His shorter neural chains permitted faster responses; the distance from his brain to his feet was a fraction of the corresponding connection in the dinosaur. But the overall advantage remained with Tyrann, who could outrun him on the straightaway and catch him when the dodging slowed.

Of course even that was not clear-cut. Tyrann had a great deal more mass to sling about, and a sprint would wear him out rapidly and overheat his tissues. Cal could probably outrun him in the long run, if he survived the short run.

The reptile sniffed the air and oriented on Cal's tree. There, too, was a weapon: the predator's well-developed nose. There was room in that huge head for capacious nasal chambers, and though the gleaming teeth were superficially impressive, they were dependent on the functioning of that nose. The eyes and ears were less important, since Tyrann was not a sneaker. He required one sure way to locate his prey, and the nose was it.

Fortunately for Cal, the sense of smell was ineffective as a guide to the whereabouts of a fast-maneuvering creature. Cal could not hope to hide long or steal away any great distance, but right now he could force the carnosaur to use his less effective senses. That was the function of his brain: to divert the contest to his opponent's weaknesses, his own strengths, and thus prevail.

Maybe.

Tyrann charged the tree. It seemed ludicrous to imagine weakness in connection with twenty thousand pounds of predator, or of strength in his own hundred pounds. But— that was the thesis he intended to prove.

Tyrann knew about trees. He did not bite the palm or crash into it. His forelimbs, smaller than his own great toes, were useless; they were hardly more than toothpicks projecting from the neck. Literally: Tyrann cleaned his teeth with those vestigial, two-clawed arms, though even that made him contort his neck to make the connection. So it seemed that he could not get at Cal, so long as the man kept the broad trunk between them.

Not at all. The dinosaur turned and swept his massive tail against the trunk. The tree vibrated; loose fronds dropped, forcing Cal to cower. A spearlike dry seedpod plunged into the ground next to his head: the thing was a yard long and well pointed. He jumped away from the tree, realizing how hazardous its cover was—but stopped, realizing that that was what Tyrann intended.

The tail itself whipped around, a scarred column of flesh, and caught him smartly on the hip as he was trying to get back to the palm. Its force had been broken by the trunk, and its vertebrae did not permit much flexibility, but the residual nudge was enough to send him lurching away from his cover again. His quarterstaff was jolted wide, and he had no chance to recover it. Now he lacked even token armament.

And of course Tyrann was ready. He pounced.

Cal ducked under the dinosaur, avoiding the gaping jaws again by the surprise of his motion. Tyrann had anticipated flight *away* from him, and had compensated accordingly. Cal bounced off the hanging skin of the reptile's neck, scraping his arm against the horny creases, and jumped for the tree again, panting.

He was thankful he hadn't tried to escape by climbing the palm. He would have been an easy target for that tail. Tyrann could not use it to reach or clutch or coil, but that brute banging against the base of the tree would have shaken almost anything loose.

Tyrann swung around again, watching Cal with one eye. The tail lifted, swung.

Cal didn't wait for it this time. He sprinted away from the trunk, eyes open. As the tail struck and whipped over, he threw himself down flat and let the tip pass over him. Immediately he was up again and running for the next tree, legs and lungs straining.

Tyrann let forth a bellow that sounded like gravel being dumped on a metal roof. He followed. Cal didn't stop at the tree; he passed it and angled for a small forest of firs he saw a few hundred feet ahead. His breath rasped in his throat, saliva streamed back across his cheek, and a pain in his side blossomed into a square foot of agony, but he could not stop.

The dinosaur was impeded by the trees, since he had to circle them with wider clearance, but still was making

184

better speed. His two feet came down like pile drivers, shaking the earth with an oddly measured beat.

Cal's heart was pumping harshly, and now his entire chest was aflame. He saw that he could not make it to the pines, the spruce. Tyrann should be getting winded himself by this time—but it seemed that the dinosaur's strides were so long that this pace represented walking, not running, and so was not tiring. Cal dived behind a leaning oak and propped himself against it, too fatigued to do more than watch Tyrann.

But here he had a fortunate break. The small-brained reptile had forgotten his quarry's predilection for changing direction, and charged on by the tree. Then, realizing the error, Tyrann cast about, but could not immediately recover contact. The smell of the mammal was stronger behind than ahead, and that did not make immediate sense to the reptile.

Cal slid around the tree, aware that the accidental respite had probably saved his life. But he knew very well that the war was not over; this was only an intermission, and a momentary one.

Tyrann got his bearings and approached the tree. This time he waited to see which way Cal would bolt, not aware that the man had scant energy left to move at all. Yes, the dinosaur learned by experience—but not quickly enough, in this case. He lunged ahead when caution was best, and practiced caution when the direct approach would nab the prize. But that was his handicap: he was bright enough for a reptile, but hardly in the intellectual league with a man.

The truth was that Tyrann would be better off giving up on Cal and looking for some careless upland-dwelling baby *Brachiosaurus*; those young did not reside in the water until their developing mass required it, and by then their numbers had been thinned to the verge of extinction. The adult female Brachs made annual pilgrimages upland to lay their eggs, and they too would be easy harvest for Tyrann. But this dinosaur had determination; he had settled on Cal as prey for the day, and would not give up. Cal respected that; this was a worthy opponent, over whom a victory would be meaningful.

185

By the time Tyrann decided that the prey was not going to move, Cal had recovered the better part of his wind, and the pain in his bowels had abated. Oddly, he felt stronger than ever, as though tempered, as though his exertions had been pouring energy into him rather than drawing it out. This was possible: his weakness had been a symptom of an Earth-nurtured psychological syndrome, rather than anything initially physical. At Nacre he had tasted his first hint of freedom from it, aboard that sparsely populated world and with staunch companions. On Paleo he had his second experience—and though there were elements of disharmony, the overall effect was beneficial. And by this very chase he was resolving the last of that internal conflict. The long agony of indecision was over; he would prove himself—and his species, and his genus, family, order, and class—or die. He did not need to cripple himself any longer.

So now, perhaps, the bodily resources that had been so long suppressed were reappearing, and he was ready for the dinosaur. It was a good feeling.

Tyrann lunged at the tree, but this time did not swing about to threaten with his tail. He put his head beyond the slanted trunk and stopped.

Cal scooted a quarter of the way around, but halted when he saw that his opponent was there too. One giant leg came down beside the tree, while the nightmarish head descended from the opposite side. Tyrann *could* close the circle, when he happened across the right technique!

But with difficulty. This was an unusual maneuver, and the dinosaur's reflexes were geared more for crashing through than for curling around. The closure occurred slowly, and the tail could not make it at all. The highly flexible neck was the principle instrument, coming to meet the tremendous thigh—Cal between.

Saliva dripped from the grinning mouth, spilling over the double-edged teeth. The stench of reptile was oppressive. Cal peered into the near eye, just a yard away and huge from this vantage. The lower jaw widened just below it, making anchorage for bulging facial muscles. The skin was rough, covered irregularly with tubercles, puckered in the region of the ear hole, and hung below the chin in a kind of extended wattle: the dewlap. Oh for the lost quarterstaff now! He could have used it to poke out that eye!

He glanced down, seeking some weapon, but there was only loam and acorns. A handful of coarse gravel hurled into that eye might start the job; but *acorns*?

Slowly the jaws parted, the lipless skin peeling back from every dagger-jagged tooth, and sliding across the muscle-filled fenestrae, the windows in the skull. The alien reptilian breath blasted out, hot, not cold. It was a misnomer to describe reptiles as cold-blooded; their body temperatures were variable, determined by external conditions and exertion. In this warm valley, the reptile ran about as hot as the mammal and functioned about as well.

The stunted forelimbs turned out to be as large as Cal's own arms, their claws long and sharp. Useful for holding the slowly dying meat firmly against the mouth, certainly: much as a busy executive might hold the telephone receiver against his ear by hunching his shoulder, aided by a little harness. Hardly essential, but useful upon occasion.

One tooth was broken, leaving a gap, and the gum there was black. Tyrann's temper could hardly have been improved by that recent accident! But already the replacement tooth was pushing up.

This was a strange situation: he was about to be bitten in half, in slow motion! If he ran for it, Tyrann would catch him; he could see the tension on the ponderous leg muscles, ready for that forward thrust around the tree. But if he remained—

Closer. Tyrann's nostril, inconspicuous from a distance, now seemed large enough for Cal to put his fist into. But the eye, though within reach, was guarded by a heavy overhanging ridge of bone and skin; he was sure that if he struck at it the eye would blink shut, and he would smash his hand against that protection painfully. The ear indentation did not even penetrate the head; skin covered the canal just inside the depression. Yes, the dinosaur was well protected.

Still, Tyrann could hear well enough. Cal leaned toward the head until only inches separated his face from the skin of the monster. The rank odor made him want to gag, and he could see body parasites in the folds.

"Boo!" he yelled.

The dinosaur jumped.

Cal was off and away, sprinting again for the copse of assorted firs. Tyrann recovered in a moment, merely startled by the unexpected noise, but too late. A jump reaction, in a creature of that size, was a matter of seconds from start to finish. The prey had won another round.

The firs were not large, but were close together and thickly spoked. The proximity of the trees served to break off useless lower limbs—but many of the stubs were jammed into neighboring trunks, forming rungs. Cal scraped himself getting through them, but was grateful for their protection. Tyrann had to crash through headlong, and that was noisy, painful and time-consuming. Cal was able to catch his breath again as he slowed to a walk and scramble, threading past the worst of the maze.

But it was another brief respite. Tyrann could knock aside those slender trees and bulldoze them down, and was doing so. The stand was not as extensive as Cal had hoped; a few minutes would see little besides cordwood here. And the dinosaur, stung by repeated jabs of fir spokes, was beginning to grow perturbed.

Beyond this was palm-dotted prairie. That was sure victory for Tyrann.

Except—there was a herd of *Triceratops* in sight, lazing in the shadow of the trees and browsing on the fronds. If he were able to play one species off against the other—

Cal ran out toward the herd. A bull winded him and looked up, a morsel of palm stalk projecting from his tremendous beak. Then the Tricer spotted the carnosaur behind. Why the herd hadn't noticed the intrusion before, Cal could not say. Perhaps they had been aware of Tyrann right along, but had known he was after other prey and therefore no immediate threat to the herd. That, combined with the discomfort of having to walk through the sun to find other shade, must have kept them where they were. It was a complacency that armored brutes of this magnitude could afford—but no lesser creatures!

By running at the herd, however, Cal was luring Tyrann

too close. The bull gave out an oddly regressive hiss, and suddenly there was motion elsewhere. The adult Tricers bullied their young into a confined area adjacent to the trunk of the largest palm, then turned about and formed a ring outside, just at the fringe of the shade, armored heads pointing out. It was a formidable phalanx, executed with military dispatch.

Cal was daunted himself. These were tremendous animals, and dangerous. Those beaks, intended for slicing through palm wood, could as readily amputate his limbs; and as for the horns. . . ! But he had no choice. Tyrann was closing the gap again, and there was no other cover. He ran at the defensive circle of behemoths.

The nearest bull didn't like it. He hissed his challenge again and charged out of the pack. Sunlight glinted from his polished horns. The adjacent bulls rocked over to fill the gap, keeping the circle tight.

Cal, perforce, brought up short. No living animal ever resembled a tank more than *Triceratops*. Then he used the trick applied earlier to Tyrann, and jumped to the side.

Almost eight tons of armored flesh thudded by. The Tricer was not as large as Tyrann, but was more solidly built. Its body, exclusive of the tail, was twenty feet long, the head taking up about a third of it. Two devastating horns jutted above the eyes and a third, shorter but thicker, perched on the broad beak. Behind the head was a tremendous bony shield large enough for a man to ride on. The astonishing jaw muscles anchored to this, making even Tyrann's face seem flabby in comparison. There was more bone and muscle on Tricer's head than in the entire body of most other creatures. The skin of the rest of the torso, though technically unarmored, was ribbed like the hide of a crocodile, and Cal was sure it was just as tough.

Now Tricer confronted Tyrann—a situation neither had sought. Tyrann tried to skirt around the bull to get at Cal, but Tricer would not permit an approach near the herd. To it, the small mammal was an annoyance—but the carnosaur was a threat.

And so they came to unwilling battle, these two giants of the age of reptiles. The one would not relinquish his chase; the other would not permit passage.

Tyrann, goaded to fury by the unreasonable interference of the bull, roared and gestured: an impressive spectacle. Tricer merely waited, the three fierce horns focused on the enemy. Tyrann skittered to the side, seeking a vulnerable point beyond horn and shield. Tricer whirled with surprising finesse, the neck muscles flexing hugely, and gored him in the thigh.

Tyrann screamed and bit at the briefly exposed rump. The teeth sank in, but Tricer whirled again, the three horns swinging about like the machine-gun turret of the tank he resembled, and the hold was broken. Cal observed that the broad bony shield did double duty: the neck musculature also anchored to it. Just as a flying bird needed a strong keelbone to brace the flying muscles, so Tricer needed that shield to whip his massive head about. What an engine of defense!

Blood speckled each combatant, but inhibited neither. Tyrann did not take lightly to being balked, but Tricer would not give way.

Then a second bull came out, and Tyrann backed off hastily. *Two* trios of horns could destroy him. But this one was after Cal, and the man had to flee even more precipitously. Apparently the herbivores had decided that he was too much trouble to entertain. Or they had realized that Tyrann would not leave until the mammal did.

The two bulls were between Cal and Tyrann, each herding its object before it. Cal was amenable; this allowed him to increase his distance from the carnosaur. He spied an inlet of water and headed for it, congratulating himself for a winning tactic.

Tyrann finally freed himself from the harrassment of the bulls and charged in Cal's direction. Cal threw himself down a short steep bank and into the bay.

It was shallow. He had succeeded in covering himself with muck, but knew that two feet of water would hardly balk Tyrann for long. The carnosaur probably chased after water reptiles to depths of ten feet or so. He had made a tactical error.

Tyrann splashed down, sending muck flying. And sank in to *his* tall knees. Instead of firm bottom, it was ooze bottom, and the dinosaur's much greater weight put him as deep, proportionately, as the much smaller man. They were even. Cal chided himself for not realizing that beforehand. So far, he had prevailed more by chance than by application of brain, and that was not as it should be, if he were to prove anything.

Again in grotesque slow motion, man and reptile staggered through the swamp. But again the pursuer was gaining. Cal had supposed that Tyrann was basically a hide-and-pounce hunter, or a take-from-other-hunter bully: neither occupation requiring much stamina. But this chase had passed beyond that stage.

Cal looked for deeper water, hoping to lure Tyrann out beyond his safe depth. He was sure the dinosaur could not swim. Both of them would risk attack by swimming predators, but Tyrann would be the prime target there.

This, however, turned out to be a slender ribbon of swamp, extending like a tongue into higher ground. Deep water was too far away. He would have to slough along for a mile or more, and that was out of the question.

He heard Tyrann panting behind him. At least this was taking as much out of the carnosaur as the man. The creature had a lot more mass to haul around, and his energy requirements right now must be phenomenal.

Cal angled to the far bank and scrambled up. He gained distance as he hit the firmer footing. With another belated inspiration he ran along the bank instead of away from the water, tempting the dinosaur to chase directly after him. Tyrann did not understand about vectors; to him the direct route was the fastest and surest, whatever the terrain. So he waded after Cal rather than cutting to the bank and gaining high ground first. Cal's lead increased dramatically.

Tyrann was almost out of sight behind when the terrain shifted to favor him again. Nature played no favorites! Cal had been running downhill, toward the main swamp, and the land was becoming generally lower and flatter. Soon he would have no firm footing remaining, and would have to wade or swim again. That might get him away from Tyrann—but without that close pursuit, there would be nothing to distract the attention of the water predators from him. They were as dangerous in their medium as

191

Tyrann was on his—and Cal's contest was with *this* reptile, not some aquatic monster. If he had to be eaten, it was only proper that Tyrann be allowed the honors. He had already earned this meal!

Cal reversed his field and ran headlong the way he had come, ducking down to avoid Tyrann's sight. It worked; the dinosaur continued sloshing downstream. By the time Tyrann realized what had happened, Cal had a lead of half a mile.

He needed it, in order to cross the plain and achieve new cover. Tyrann came into sight again, making excellent time, probably spurred by increasing appetite. Nothing like a walk before dinner! But the reptile's persistence was amazing. The chase had lasted a couple of hours now, and was far from over.

Yet this, of course, was the way Tyrann obtained his meals. He was not a swift runner compared to *Struthiomimus*, the "ostrich dinosaur," or an agile hunter compared to even primitive mammalian carnivores. He was limited largely to land, which meant that he seldom dined on *Brachiosaurus* in quantity. The young Brachs were of course available—but swift and small, and the fleet amphibious duckbills were similarly elusive. Stealth was not, as it turned out, Tyrann's way, nor was he particularly clever. Probably he dined on carrion as often as not, sniffing out the rotting carcasses of creatures who had perished by other means, then driving off other predators. But this would be an uncertain living at best, and live meat was a treat worth striving for.

No—*Tyrannosaurus* succeeded largely by determination. Once he fixed on his prey, living or dead, he never relented. Other things might intersperse themselves, such as the fir grove, a *Triceratops* herd, and swamp channel, but Tyrann would keep after his original objective until he ran it down. That way his meal was certain, eventually. And his meager intellect was not strained, and his energies not wastefully dissipated in fruitless asides. Even the fleetest prey must succumb in time.

It had become a contest of endurance. Though the carnosaur was wounded—Cal could see the blood along the thigh where the bull had gored—he still had substantial physical resources. But the prey, in this case, had equivalent *mental* resources. Which would prevail—muscle or mind?

Cal headed uphill. Right now he'd be happy to trade a few points I.Q. for a few pounds of striated tissue in the legs and torso. The vagaries of the chase had caused him to bypass Camp Two, and he was ascending the mountain face beyond it. The climate was changing rapidly, both because of the waning of the day and increasing elevation. This had to shift the balance somewhat in his favor, because he was a controlled-temperature creature while Tyrann was not. He could function efficiently regardless of the external temperature, theoretically. A reptile in the cold was a reptile helpless.

Yet Tyrann continued to close the gap, and once more was within a hundred feet. Now Cal had to dodge around trees and rocks, lest he be overrun. Damn that giant stride of the dinosaur! This should have been superior terrain for the mammal, with its myriad crevices, but none were secure for any extended stay. He had to keep moving.

He was tired. He was in excellent condition, considering his past history, but a pressing chase of several hours was more than his body had been geared for. Tyrann, on the other hand, seemed to have most of his original vigor about him. Endurance: yes. Or merely pacing.

Cal fell. At first he thought that fatigue had brought him low; then he realized that the mountain had thrown him down. The earth was rocking violently, and Tyrann was screaming with cantankerous surprise. It was an earthquake—far more severe than the tremor he had observed while on the raft yesterday.

Cal was small, light, and lucky. Tyrann was none of these. The dinosaur was upended and rolled several hundred feet downhill to crash into the brush. Nature had played favorites this time.

Cal needed the reprieve, but he resented it. He wanted to win by his own abilities, nothing else. He sat down after the earth was still and waited for Tyrann to resume the chase.

The dinosaur was slow in doing so. A roughing of that nature was hard on him, because of his size. A mouse might fall a hundred feet straight down and survive nicely; an elephant might fall its own height and be killed on the spot, because of the problems its magnified mass brought. Tyrann had merely rolled—but that probably represented the most brutal punishment he had ever had. Internal organs could have been ruptured, bones splintered. . . .

But no. Tyrann got up and resumed his ascent—but with only a fraction of his previous vigor. Now Cal could stay ahead without panting.

So it continued, slower. The air became cool and more than cool as dusk and height came together. Even through his exertions, Cal felt it; his clothing had dried on his body and was fairly good insulation, but still he was not dressed for freezing weather. Yet Tyrann continued, bruised and scarred and shaken in more than the thigh, but seemingly unaffected by the temperature.

Of course! The dinosaur had considerable mass, and so was slow to cool. And his giant muscles would generate a large amount of heat, keeping him going longer. Tyrann could probably keep up the chase as long as Cal could, even into the snows of the upper mountain.

Unless Cal could trick him into remaining stationary for a few hours. . . .

Meanwhile, he would have to drop down into the warmer region. He was quite tired now, and the buoyancy of the chase was giving out. If he rested in hiding, the cold would get him. And he couldn't hide anyway, even in the dark, because Tyrann would locate him by smell.

Yes, it was brains against brawn—but in what manner could brains mitigate the cold? If only he had warm clothing! Then he could ascend into the very snows, while the dinosaur slowly capitulated to nature. The mammalian form *was* superior; a hairy animal could have lost Tyrann easily here, or even turned and challenged him. A woolly elephant—

Cal stumbled, pushing himself up with difficulty. Why dream? It was his own body he had to make do with, and his own brain he meant to apply. Tyrann was still hardly more than fifty feet behind, but Cal had become used to that distance. They both knew that the chase had come down to its essential: the first to give way to exposure and exhaustion would forfeit the game. The sudden charges and matching dodges were over, as were the peek-a-boo games around trees. The rules were set, and the mammal could afford to stumble so long as he got up promptly.

Still he hesitated—and Tyrann hesitated also, as though waiting for him to proceed. They had become accustomed to each other, the tiny man and the giant reptile. They had been over much territory together, shared many experiences—even an earthquake. There was a camaraderie of a sort in experience and fatigue.

But he knew the dinosaur would gobble him up when that phase ended. Camaraderie did not presume amity. It was merely a kind of appreciation in adversity. He hesitated not from any sense of safety, but because something was trying to impress itself on his cold-dulled sensitivities. Something—warm.

Warm. The ground was wet and the wetness was soaking through his footwear and in that moisture was heat, as though he had stepped in the drain chute of an outdoor bathtub. But the temperature of the air was near the freezing point of water. What was this—a hallucination brought about by his deteriorating condition? Was he about to imagine himself falling into a lush warm paradise, a tropical garden near the snowline where rapture abounded . . . while in reality his feet froze and the jaws of the carnosaur crushed out his life?

Tyrann approached at last, and Cal moved—uphill. His feet sloshed in the drainage and absorbed heat. The dinosaur's feet also sloshed, and he paused to sniff the ground suspiciously. No hallucination.

A quarter mile higher it was warmer than ever, the air and earth as well as the trickling water. They were in a high valley, a kind of cleft in the mountain; not far away Cal could make out light snow, still bright in the fading day. But within this deepening hollow it was beginning to be comfortable. Ferns spread richly at the bottom, and toadstools and moss, and tiny salamanders scuttled out of his way.

Cal recovered energy as his surroundings became conducive, but Tyrann remained slow. One advantage of smaller mass was a faster response to changed circumstances. Conditions were improving; he knew it, but Tyrann did not yet. But in this narrow chasm he would hardly be able to lose his pursuer, and there were no hiding places. It was risky comfort, this winding summer crevice.

Unbidden, the explanation came to him. Volcanism! This was an overflow of a hot spring, the water emerging from conduits passing near the perpetual furnace of the volcanic mountain. The gully owed its warmth to the same force that heated this entire Cretaceous valley. No mystery at all, but something he should have anticipated. And that very realization, even so late, gave him the clue to victory!

The vegetation diminished as the temperature continued to rise, and he knew he was approaching the outlet of the flowing water. If it were a bubbling spring, he was in trouble; but if—

He came into the presence of the upper end of the cleft abruptly. This *was* a drainage ditch, formed by erosion, and above the emergence of the water the normal contours of the mountain resumed. The outlet pipe was a cavern, as he had hoped.

Sweating now, Cal plunged in. The river here was too hot to touch for any length of time—perhaps 130° F.—but there was clearance at the brim. The opening was large: large enough for Tyrann. But still it meant mammalian victory.

He moved ahead, unable to see anything inside. Tyrann's outline showed against the faint light of the entrance, but Cal knew the dinosaur would not follow.

The key was this: while cold was inconvenient for the great reptiles, and slowly fatal in the regions of its intensity, heat was more critical. A reptile's peak efficiency was at a body temperature of from 95° to 100° F.—about the same as for mammals and birds. But above that, the reptile would succumb more quickly than a mammal, because it lacked any internal heat-control mechanisms other than inaction. Cal could survive for a reasonable period in an environment of 115° F. or more; a reptile in the same situation would cook, literally.

If Tyrann were to enter this cave and remain for any length of time, he would die. Dinosaurs could not sweat.

On the other hand, Tyrann would soon grow hungry waiting outside. Indeed, he must be ravenous already. There was no food nearby. Cal would suffer too, of course—but he could rest in warm comfort, and drink water to ease the pangs.

He heard a funny lapping sound and peeked out. Tyrann was hunched before the cave licking his wounds. There was blood on his body in many places besides the Tricer's gore wound. That earthquake had really battered him! No wonder he had settled for a relaxed pace at the end. The wounds that didn't show, the internal ones, must be even worse.

Cal found himself a comfortable ledge, sprawled out, and fell into a perspiring stupor. It occured to him that one of the duckbilled dinosaurs, such as *Parasaurolophus*, might have entered this cave safely. That creature's nasal passages traversed the entire length of its enormous crest. This would make for super-efficient smelling ability—but probably also provided efficient cooling of the blood by evaporation from those passages. Perhaps more than one duckbill had escaped Tyrann by entering such a cave. However, hunger and the rising heat inside the mountain would have killed any creature venturing too deep, too long. Perhaps there were mysteriously defunct bodies washed out in the lower subterranean rivers every so often. . . .

He slept.

XVII: ORN

"*Tyrannosaurus rex* was galloping after Cal, those awful double-edged half-foot teeth snapping inches short of his frail palpitating body, the feet coming down on him like twin avalanches. Snap! and the rag-doll form was flung high into the air, striped grisly red, and that color reflected in the malignant eyes of the carnivore. One giant claw toe came at that torn form where it landed, crushing it into the ground; the jaws closed, ripped off an arm. Cal's tiny head lolled back from a broken neck, the dead eyes staring at me not with accusation but with understanding, and I screamed and woke."

Orn saw that the mam female was troubled. She had slept restlessly and awakened noisily, and now was in a continuing state of agitation.

"How close to reality was that dream? How great is my guilt? Cal wouldn't have gotten into that thing, if I hadn't forced the issue. If he's dead—I'm afraid to think of it—it's my fault."

Orn stood up and stretched his wings. There did not seem to be anything he could do for her. Her mate had deserted her.

"And Veg—I dreamed of him too. It wasn't love, it was sex, and ugly. I tried to split their friendship, and now they're both—gone. I should never have come with them to Paleo."

Ornette still slept, fluffed out over the single egg. It was the youngest and fairest of the three, and now it was everything. Orn had picked the site for the nest, and he had erred; now two of his three chicks were gone. He could not mourn specifically, but he felt keenly that he should not have come to this island.

"But it wouldn't make sense for me to chase after them. I couldn't do anything, even if it weren't already way too late. All I can do now is hope. Hope that the two men I love are still alive, and that this strange but beautiful world can live as well."

Orn intended to guard that last egg more carefully. The mating cycle was over. There would be no new eggs until next season. This egg had been shaken by the earth one day, and almost smashed the next; another siege could occur at any time. Could he protect the egg against that? He felt the need, but could not formulate a resolution.

"I know what's bothering you, Orn. That egg's in a precarious spot. I'll move it for you, if we can find a better place. I might as well help *someone*. Maybe the worst is over. . . ."

The sun was lifting, a bubble of light behind flashing mountain silhouettes. Soon it would touch the hanging pteras and animate them. Daybreak was such a struggle for that type!

The mam got up and crossed to the main island. Orn knew she had to attend to her eliminations and did not wish to soil the nest area. Not all mams were that considerate.

He looked about. Several of the pines had been overturned in the quake, and the configuration of the peninsula had changed. Now a second bridge of land joined it to the island. That was not good; it would be harder to safeguard now. Another shaking like the last and there might be no peninsula at all! He had seen what the ground could do on the island of his own hatching.

The mam returned and began to forage for edible roots. She had what smelled like food in her nestlike container, but appeared to be storing that. She found nuts from two varieties of flat-leaved trees and seemed to have enough to sustain her, though Orn could tell she was not fully satisfied. He, meanwhile, had hooked some fat fish out of the inlet and gutted them with beak and talon, offering the delectable innards to Ornette first. He wasn't certain whether this mam ate fish also. He offered her one but received an indefinable response.

"I think the main island is better for the egg." She had started with her noises again. "It's less likely to sink under the wave." She was trying to convey something to him, and he had an idea what. He could feel the continuing tension in the rocks, the distant motions increasing local stress. The earth would twitch its tail again, soon. His memory informed him that changes normally requiring millions of years could occur in an instant, when the ground got restless.

"I'll scout for the best place, Orn." For a moment something like the innocent levity of a hatchling chick lifted her. "And you can call me 'Quilon, since we're on a first-name basis now. Short for Aquilon, the northwest wind. 'Quilon."

She tapped her own body as she repeated a certain sound, as though identifying her species. Of course such sounds were meaningless, but he would now think of her as the quilon giant mam

She departed again, questing for something. He watched her thoughtfully as she retreated. Yesterday he had extended his tolerance to this quilon whose mate had deserted her (no bird would do that!). Then the earth had moved and slaughtered two of his chicks and put the third in peril, and the quilon had helped him save the last. But for that, the problems of his own hatching might have been repeated here: one egg surviving, both parents dead fighting a crock. Now his egg would have a better chance, for there were three to guard it, counting the quilon. Perhaps it was her blunted nesting instinct: she guarded his egg because she had none of her own.

Mams were not notably trustworthy around eggs, but the circumstance was special. This was a strange, huge, clumsy, yet brave and loyal mam, with surprising comprehension despite her annoying noisemaking. It was almost as though she had her own type of memory, so readily did she grasp things. And she had saved the egg. She deserved his companionship.

The egg had to be moved. It was not safe here; a single tilt of the land could roll it into the sea, where the penetrating chill of the water would quickly extinguish it. But he could not move it; only the quilon could do that. Fortunately she was warm; that was a trait the mams had acquired even earlier than the aves. She could touch the egg without hurting it, and her digits, because they were soft, could lift it. He had no memory of any creature with this ability to turn seemingly useless appendages to such direct purpose. Limbs were generally adapted to running or foraging or fighting, while these unspecialized mam limbs turned out to be adapted for carrying a single egg!

But all this thinking and reasoning was hard. His brain had not been evolved for this, and only his solitary life and the radical change of the world had prompted this quality in him. Ornette depended on her memories far more than he did. It was as though his mind had mutated into something else in a jump like that of the strained earth—something unique and unnatural.

Then he felt it: the earth was beginning to break. He ran toward Ornette and the egg, but there was nothing he could do except settle down next to them and try to shield it with his body. If the ground jumped again, even this would not save it from cracking, for there was no proper padding beneath the egg.

The quilon ran after him. She scooped up the egg as Ornette jumped nervously aside, and held it cushioned in those almost hairless fleshy forelimbs.

Then the land broke apart. Orn was hurled into the water, to scramble back dripping; Ornette fell in the opposite direction, flapping her wings. Only the quilon remained upright, flexing her tremendous legs and leaning over the egg, protecting it.

The motion changed. Orn felt it: somewhere deep below a support had snapped. The land on which they huddled was sliding down, away from the island, becoming an island of its own. The water surged around it. The shudders continued, rocking the diminishing perch farther. The pines were standing in water now, and falling as the land slowly tilted.

There was nothing in his memory to account for this particular sequence, and he could tell that Ornette was as mystified as he. The quilon just stood with the egg, looking about. There was nothing any of them could do.

It occurred to him that the reason he had no memory of such an event—a fragmenting, slowly sinking island—was that no potential ancestor had survived the experience.

The last of the pines crashed down, tumbling over its fallen neighbors and splashing into the water. Orn thought of using it to float to safety, but realized that the quilon could not do this while carrying the egg. Without that egg, and within it the nascent memory and experience of all his ancestry and Ornette's, there was no point in escape.

At last the motion stopped. Their new island was separated from the larger one by the length of a full-grown brach rep, and it was only slightly greater than the length of yesterday's croc in its diameter. They stood on its highest point: a terrace near the original site of the nest bounded by an escarpment leading into the water where the isthmus had been before; the land had actually risen slightly here. But on the opposite side the surface tilted down more gradually. Had the trees remained standing they would have been at an angle.

Where would the ptera sleep now? They would perish in the night unless they found new roosting.

The quilon settled down, supporting the egg on her thighs. She leaned over it, keeping it warm with her body and forelimbs. Ornette looked, but did not challenge; it was safest where it was, and this entire sequence had left her confused. It was hard to accept, this control of the egg by the mam, but it seemed to be necessary.

How were they going to get away from here? This was no longer a suitable nesting site, yet even the short distance to the larger section of the island was dangerous for the egg. Unless the new bay were shallow. . . .

"We might build another raft. Maybe the one Veg started is around, or pieces of it." The quilon was beginning to make sounds again, which meant she was returning to normal.

Orn stepped into the water, testing the depth. The footing was treacherous; he slipped and took a dunking. It *was* too deep, and far too chancy for the awkward mam. They would have to remain here at least until the chick hatched. They could forage on the island, swimming across individually. It would be an uncomfortable existence, but was feasible.

He sniffed. Rep, gross. Trouble!

As he scrambled back on land, he saw it: the towering head of an elas, the great shallow-water paddler. The quilon uttered a cry: "A plesiosaur!"

Orn had few direct memories of this creature, because its sphere of operations seldom overlapped that of his own species. He was aware of its gradual evolution from minor landbound forms struggling to come even with the large amphibs, finally returning entirely to the sea—and then a memory gap broken only by glimpses of the larger sizes, some with lengthening necks and others with shortening necks, until this line attained its present configura-

202

tion: eight full wingspans from snout to tail, the neck making up half of that. It was primarily a fish-eater, but it would consume carrion or land life if available. Orn would not care to swim while an Elas was near, but had no particular awe of it while he stood on land.

The rep came closer, its tiny head carried high. It smelled them, and it was hungry.

"The quake shook it up. It's crazed. It's coming after us!"

Orn would have preferred that the quilon not choose this moment to make her meaningless noises. Now the Elas was certain there was a meal here. The length of its neck was more than half the breadth of the island fragment. There was no section it could not reach from one side or the other, if it were determined. It could not leave the water, for that would destroy the mobility it required for balance—but they were vulnerable despite being on land.

They would have to fight it off, if that were possible. The ground and sea motion must have crazed the rep, so that it was not aware that it was fishing on land instead of in water. It was not particularly bright, but *was* dangerous.

The head hovered above the island, twice Orn's height. The neck curved back from it, then forward, in the manner of a wind-twisted rush. The alert rep eye fixed on Orn.

He leaped aside as the Elas struck. Like a plunging coconut the head came down, jaws gaping. The flat-flippered body lunged out of the water with the force of that thrust, and the jaws snapped within a beak-length of Orn's tail feathers.

This much his memory had warned him of: the Elas fed by paddling behind a fish and flinging its head forward suddenly, to grasp the prey before it could escape. Had Orn not jumped when the motion began, he would have been lost. Too quick a jump would also have been fatal, for the Elas could crook its neck about in a double spiral, and small corrections were routine for it.

But now the rep was in trouble. Used to dunking its head under the surface in the process of catching fish, it had not considered that land was different. It had bashed its snout hard against the ground. The jaws had actually snapped at the level of Orn's body, but reflex and follow-through had carried head and neck on down. Now its neck was spread full-length on the dirt and its mouth was bleeding where its teeth had crushed against stone and earth. Yes, it was crazed; it would ordinarily have been more cautious this near land.

Orn whirled and struck at the exposed neck near its joining with the torso. The creature was vulnerable now but would be deadly in its rage once it got reoriented. He dug his talons into the glistening, smooth-skinned column and probed with his beak for some vital or crippling spot. But the mass of flesh was too great and strange; he did not know where the key tendons were, and claws and beak were lost amidst its layer of blubber.

Elas emitted a high-pitched squeal and hauled its neck up in a magnificent undulation. The head looped back to come at Orn from the side, and he was unable to break loose immediately because his members were mired. He was lifted helplessly into the air, dangling by both feet.

Ornette leaped to help him. She aimed her beak at the rep's eye, but the Elas turned on her quickly and met her with wide-open mouth. She squawked once, pitifully, as the pointed teeth closed on her wing and breast; then she was carried upward.

Orn fought loose and fell into the water a wingspan from the rep's front flipper. He tried to attack again, but the Elas was already paddling away, Ornette dangling.

Pursuit was useless. Orn could neither catch the Elas nor harm it, and Ornette was already dead.

Orn climbed back on the island, blood-tainted and disconsolate. It was not exactly grief he felt, but a terrible regret. Ornette had died defending him, as he would have died defending her, and both defending their lone egg. Now her companionship had been severed and he was alone again.

Except for the egg! The most important part had been salvaged.

The quilon still warmed it. She had not moved during the struggle, and this was right. Ornette would not have attacked the Elas had the egg not been secure without her protection. Nothing took precedence over that egg.

Again the oddness ...ne to him: stranded on an exposed island, he without his mate, the mam without hers, the two of them guarding the egg neither had laid.

What was there to do but go on?

XVIII: VEG

Veg recovered consciousness painfully. He was lying on a hard beach, his face against a wet rock, his feet in water, and he was hot. He did not know where he was or how he had come there. His head was aching, his innards soggy, and the rest of him was hardly robust.

He sat up carefully and waited for the resultant dizziness to pass. The beach was scant, hardly more than a hesitancy between land and sea, and the land itself was brief. In fact, it was no more than a pylon of rock jutting up from the waves, with a single ledge he perched upon. Similar to the jigsaw reefs separating this section from the main ocean, really—not that that improved his position.

He had lost his quarterstaff, but retained his knife. The quarterstaff idea hadn't turned out very well; nobody had gotten any good use from the weapons. Well, next time he wouldn't bother. His clothing was torn, and his neck was welted with insect bites where it had been exposed. He wished he could puke up some of the muddy water he must have swallowed—but then he would probably feel hungry.

Strength seeped back unwillingly, and with it some spongy memories. He had fought a government agent— no, that was back on Earth, too long ago, and the man had turned out pretty decent in the end. Veg had been arrested and put into orbit with Cal and 'Quilon and the eight, no seven, mantas. Then—here to Paleo, with four mantas, and a trip on the ocean. And a bash with Brach, the arm-leg lizard ten times life size. And a bird, and—

He had made love to Aquilon! 'Quilon!

After that it became fuzzy. Her soft thighs, and Cal in trouble, and guilt and a swim and a run through the swamp and—

And here he was, tossed on a rock by himself. No friend, no manta, no woman, no bird. Time had passed; now he had a memory of shivering in the night and fading out again.

Why had he done it? After all this time, on three worlds—why had he taken her? It had not been a physical thing between them, only a promise. Now that promise was gone.

Then he remembered the rest of it. Cal—they had broken with Cal! The tyrant lizard was after his friend, while Veg had been mucking about with Aquilon. Too late he had remembered his loyalty and tried to get there. On the way there had been another quake that threw him into the water, and he had swum blindly, trying to get out of it.

He had been lucky he had not drowned. The waves had been bad enough, and any of the great sea animals could have gobbled him en route. Unless those swimmers were as shaken by it all as he.

He peered over the level water. They would not be shaken now—and the tide was rising. He had perhaps another hour before his island disappeared entirely.

Well, better get on with it. Maybe Cal was dead, and Aquilon too. But maybe they were just waiting for him to find them. He'd save his regrets for the facts.

He faced toward land and dived in, the splash a mark of defiance. The impact of the water against his skin invigorated him, and he stroked strongly for the shore. There were scratches on his back, and the salt sting did its part to spur him along.

Salt? He had thought this area was fresh water, from the stream and swamp. But maybe that was only when the tide was out, or in the river channel itself.

Something moved in the ocean. A snout broke the surface—a mighty beak. Veg saw it coming toward him.

A swimming Tricer?

It was a huge sea turtle, attracted by the splashing. Veg had little concern for turtles ordinarily, but this was hardly the kind he was accustomed to. It was twice as long as he was, with a heavy leathery skin instead of a true shell, and its beak was horrendous. Its two front flippers were roundly muscled paddles, propelling it rapidly forward. This was the beast that Cal had termed *Archelon*, when they had observed it from the raft. The only reason Veg remembered the name was its resemblance to Aquilon. Arky, he had dubbed it, and forgotten the matter; but it didn't seem quaint or funny now. The head alone must weigh as much as Veg did!

He treaded water, uncertain how to react. He didn't *think* turtles ate people. . . .

Arky glided up, sleek and swift in its element. Veg realized that he had been foolish to judge its capabilities by those of its cousins he had observed on land. This was a mighty creature, capable of wiping him out casually. He gripped his tiny-seeming knife. Would it even pierce that skin?

The turtle sniffed him. Veg wasn't sure that was possible with its head under water, but it remained the best description. Then it decided he was not edible, and nudged away, its ballroom carapace brushing his legs. He felt giddy with relief—a sensation rather strange to him. Obviously he wasn't as much recovered as he had thought. The cuts on his back smarted again.

Arky lifted its head above the water. Veg followed its seeming glance—and spied a ripple coming in from the open sea. It was another creature.

And—he saw the disk of a manta, also coming toward him. That was immensely reassuring. Hex, probably, on the lookout for the lost party. Now he could get in touch again, and find the others.

Provided they still lived. That quake had been rough.

Hex arrived before the sea creature, but not by much. The turtle floated just under the surface, twenty feet away, facing the swimming newcomer. Veg, now assured of his safety, stroked once more for shore.

He heard the thing come up behind him, splashing softly,

207

and had to look. It was a mosasaur—the most vicious reptile of the sea. Thirty feet long, the torso highly flexible, the tail splayed vertically and quite powerful enough, and four paddle-shaped limbs. The head was narrow, the nose pointed, but the jaws were lined with ample sharp recurved teeth. A kind of crest or ridge commenced at the neck and trailed all the way back into the tail, and this waved ominously just above the water as the creature swam. It was as though the worst features of crocodile, turtle, and shark had been combined and magnified—and Veg was frankly terrified.

Suddenly Hex's protection seemed scarcely sufficient. Mosa was too big, too ugly—and most of its body was shielded by water. It could come at him from below, and the manta would be unable to strike.

Mosa circled both him and the turtle, as though considering which one to attack first. Arky, fully alert to the danger, rotated in place, always facing the predator lizard. Evidently the turtle did not trust its armor to withstand Mosa's teeth, though possibly it was only the turtle flippers, which could not be withdrawn into the body, that it was concerned about. If *Arky* were worried, how should *Veg* feel?

The shore was far too far away; he could never make it now. The diminishing rock he had nighted on was still fairly close, thanks to his dawdling—but he couldn't get there either while Mosa was watching.

Hex paced above the water, making a tight circle inside that of the mosasaur. The reptile was aware of the manta, but not particularly concerned. Probably it thought Hex was a pteradactyl, waiting for the remnants.

Veg was pretty sure Mosa would decide on the warm, unarmored appetizer: himself. Then, invigorated by the morsel, it could tackle the tougher turtle at leisure. No particular genius was required to select the easy prey.

Mosa decided. It angled smoothly in toward Veg.

Hex struck out the exposed eye.

The reptile didn't seem to realize what had happened, immediately. It continued its charge, drifting in the direction favored by the remaining eye, its teeth snapping.

Veg started to swim for the rock. Mosa spotted the

motion and came at him again, jaws wide. By accident or design, its good eye was under the water, safe from Hex's lash.

Veg had an inspiration. He launched himself at the big turtle.

Mosa sheered off, momentarily confused by the combination of objects: two together in the water, a third in the air. Veg remembered something Cal had said once, about animals becoming confused by more than two objects; they could not count. Arky was also confused, unable to concentrate on Veg while the dangerous lizard was so close behind. It was also annoyed by the manta.

Veg bypassed the beak and touched the smooth hull. It might not *look* like a turtleshell, but it seemed rock-hard. He got behind it and stayed close. There wasn't anything much to hang on to. Mosa made a feint, and Arky forgot about Veg as it braced against the greater menace. Hex continued to pace the surface. It was an impasse of a kind.

Mosa circled, adapting to its limited vision. It had no intention of giving up the chase; in fact, the taste of its own blood might well be stimulating it to some berserker effort. And it seemed to Veg that mosa did have the physical wherewithal to prevail, for it outmassed man, manta, and turtle combined and was fully adapted to combat in the ocean. Even completely blind (Hex might yet get the other eye) it could probably sniff him out and finish him off. Arky was only a temporary cover; once the turtle decided to depart, mosa would pounce on the mouthful remaining, shrugging off the superficial lacerations Hex might inflict.

It was death in the making for him. A kind of checkmate demise, as one piece after another was nullified, but inevitable. Somehow the end no longer frightened him the way he thought it should. Had there been an element of chance about it, he might have been eager and nervous. As it was—

Chance struck. A school of sharks converged on the scene, slim sleek missiles of appetite. In a moment mosa, the wounded one, was the center of attention.

Suddenly Veg understood what had happened. He had

209

dived off his rock, originally, making a splash that attracted the turtle. But meanwhile his scratched-up back had
been bleeding into the water, and mosa had smelled it.
Then the commotion and mosa's own injury had alerted
the sharks. . . .

Chance? Maybe less than he had supposed.

But very soon those killer fish would come after *him*.

Mosa was now in a fight for its life. No single shark
approached the reptile in size, but there were as many as
a score of them, some as long as fifteen feet, all maddened
by the blood. Already they had torn great gashes in mosa's
hide. Several of their own number were dead, for mosa as
an individual was more savage than they—but now the
checkmate had been reversed.

Arky, no dumb bunny, took this opportunity to dive for
safer territory. Its mighty flippers clove the water, creating
a turbulence that jounced Veg around and towed him
under. Then the turtle was gone, moving more rapidly
than he could follow.

Veg struck for the rock. Two sharks detached themselves from the main platoon as though central command
had allocated them, and cruised after him. Hex sliced up
their projecting fins and set them to fighting one another.
This diversion was sufficient. He made it to safety.

He stood ankle-deep on his isle and wondered what he
would do when the tide made him available to the sharks
again. Hex could not divert them indefinitely. Veg could
not expect luck to save him again. He was not, in sober
analysis, one of those hero types who won out no matter
what the odds against success. He felt empty without Cal,
and deep remorse for the split that had overtaken them. It
hadn't really been Aquilon's fault, either; she hadn't meant
to make trouble like that.

How easy, now, to pass judgments on his prior conduct.

Hex perched on the highest point of the rock, his foot
splaying out to grip it clumsily. It was a sitting and
pushing type of foot, rather than a grasping member, and
the posture had to be uncomfortable—but Hex appeared
to be staying until the end. There was no use in Veg
himself trying to climb that point; it was too small and

steep for anything but a perpetual balancing act, and this would only postpone the finish, not change it.

Where was Cal now? The manta Circe had said the tyrant lizard was after him, alone. That was sure death for the little man. But Cal was funny about that sort of thing. He might have found a way to—

Impossible. What could a man, any man, do against Tyrann? Cal was digested by now.

No, he couldn't be. Not his friend!

Veg realized that he had only to ask Hex. The manta would surely know. A snap of the tail would tell him Cal lived; two snaps—

He choked on the question. It would not come out. He was afraid of the answer.

The water was at his knees. Already a small shark was circling the rock, waiting.

Should he die without knowing?

Maybe this was his punishment for despoiling Aquilon.

Veg looked across the water, at the savage valley, the snow-topped mountains, the islands reaching into the sea, the level horizon showing beyond the channel between the large harbor islands, Silly and Cheryb-dis. He looked, expecting nothing.

And saw a ship.

XIX: CAL

Tyrann's bulk almost blocked the opening. The carnosaur was sleeping, his body spread out along the stream bed to capture every vestige of warmth therein. The hot water from the cavern puddled at his nose and coursed along his neck—the only thing, in this snow-line dawn chill, that was keeping him reasonably functional. The flesh was discolored where the hottest water touched, but evidently the reptile had elected some heat discomfort in spots instead of the lethargy of cold all over. Probably it inhaled warmth this way. This was courage of a kind.

Cal stood just within the cave mouth, where a refreshingly cool circulation occurred, and surveyed the situation. It was possible that Tyrann was playing possum, waiting for the prey to come out—but Cal doubted that the reptile was capable of such subtlety. It was not an art large predators usually needed for survival. Tyrann would normally sleep until the heat of the day raised his body temperature to a suitable level. In the valley this would be a simple matter—but the chill of this upper region was apt to make it a long sleep indeed. It had been a mistake for Tyrann to settle down here, for without continuous muscular exertion to maintain his body heat, he could not survive.

Probably Cal could climb right over the ugly jaws and be on his way with impunity. Victor in their contest, he could make his way along the shore to the Paleocene camp. It might take him several months to make it, and there would be other hazards—but *if* he made it to that radio, his course was justified. To the victor belonged the spoils—the spoils of a world.

Yet he hesitated, looking down at the great prone reptile. He was not afraid of Tyrann—indeed, had never been—for he understood the creature's needs and motives. They were the same as his own: survival. Tyrann accomplished his purpose by size, power, and determination. Cal used his intelligence—and determination. The fact that he had won did not mean that his cause was morally superior. It meant simply that he had demonstrated a greater capability for survival, in this instance.

If he summoned the forces of Earth (for casuistry aside, that was surely the gist of his report), he would be pitting an advanced world against a primitive one. That would not be a fair contest. Very soon the dinosaurs would be extinct again, and Paleo would be just like Earth: crowded with neurotic humans, its natural resources depleted. . . .

Veg and Aquilon were right. His alternate universe framework was theoretical. Each world was a separate case, and the means did not justify the end, particularly

212

when it meant the destruction of a known world for the sake of unknown ones ... that might in time be ravaged anyway. Man did not have the esthetic authority to do such a thing to *any* world, and Cal had to judge by the case before him. He could not throw Paleo to the omnivore.

Studying Tyrann, Cal knew himself to be a hypocrite. The truth was that he had expected to lose, and thus preserve this world a moment longer. He couldn't accept victory, and had never intended to. He had argued the ugly cause merely to put both sides on record. That would be important, in the Earth-sponsored court-martial that would follow the abrogation of their assigned mission. That could protect the trio to some extent, and the mantas. Selfish motive!

Tyrann was too noble a brute to be arbitrarily extinguished at man's convenience. Let Paleo remain unspoiled a moment, geologically speaking, longer. Let the dinosaur find his own destiny. Let the king of the reptiles rule today, even if extinction was inevitable tomorrow.

But Tyrann would die today, in effect, if he remained before the cave. He had cooled off during the night, since the tremendous muscular dynamo of his body had cut down into torpidity. A lot of heat would be required to revive him, and it might never get warm enough long enough here in these mountain reaches to do the job. Tyrann could sleep himself into starvation.

The hot water, at least, would have slowed the process, and in any event it would take some time for ten tons of flesh to cool completely. If Tyrann were brought to consciousness before any further heat loss occurred, and while his considerable bodily energy resources remained. . . .

Cal stepped out of the cave, feeling the chill immediately. He kicked the yard-long snout where the water made it tender. "Wake up, lazybones!" he yelled.

An eye flicked open, but Tyrann did not stir. That insidious cold remaining in his flesh immobilized him, though the sun was now hot upon his flank and the water softened his belly. The mighty reptile had a mighty chill; he could not leap to full awareness and performance the way a mammal or bird could.

213

Cal put a foot on Tyrann's nearest tooth, slung his knee against the nose, mounted to the top of the head and tromped about. "Get on the ball, sleepy! I don't have all day!"

A hiss of annoyance issued from the tremendous, flaccid throat. The muscles of the bulging neck tensed and Cal slid off, caution not entirely forgotten. The skin was hardly sleek, this close; it hung in elephantine folds, mottled and blistered, and infested with insectlike parasites. Tyrann, he thought, probably itched hugely in his off moments.

Cal scrambled around the looming shoulder, avoiding the clenching, almost-human extremity below it, and trotted to the side of the gully. "Can't catch me!" he shouted. He pried a fragment of rock out of the rubble and lobbed it toward the head. It missed, but the second had better aim.

Tyrann bestirred himself. Water gushed down the channel as the ponderous body elevated. Stones splashed into it, dislodged by the hulking, careering shoulders. Clumsily, laboriously, Tyrann stood up and turned about.

Cal danced along the gully, skirting the hips and tail barely in time. He paused only long enough to be certain the reptile was on his trail again. Then he plunged downhill, following the warm channel. He wasn't worried—yet!—about being caught. It should be at least an hour before Tyrann was really alert. By then—

By then, perhaps, they would be well into the warm valley and he could slip away, leaving the monster frustrated but alive. Cal had won his victory; all he wanted now was to return Tyrann to his habitat. After that—well, he no longer had need of the journey up-coast, since he was not going to make the report. He'd just have to hope he had misjudged the intent of the Earth authorities.

Progress was faster than that. In ten minutes they were out of the snow region. In twenty, the air was appreciably warmer, almost comfortable. In thirty, away from the opening gully—

"Veg!" he cried. But it wasn't Veg.

The man nodded briefly, hands on his steam rifle. "Dr. Potter, I presume."

214

The exchange had taken five seconds. It was enough of a pause to bring Tyrann into sight. Still clumsy but recovering nicely, the dinosaur bellowed and charged down at them.

Almost casually the stranger aimed his weapon and fired. A hiss as the steam boosted away the shell and dissipated; a clap of noise as the projectile exploded. As Cal turned, Tyrann began to fall. His head was a red mass.

"Just about in time for you," the man remarked. "Where are your companions?"

Tyrann was dead. The great body still twitched and quivered, and would continue to cast about for some time, but the head had been blown apart by the explosion. The shell must have scored directly inside the mouth: an expert shot. It was a cruel demise for the carnosaur, and an unnecessary one; at this stage as horrifying as the murder of a friend. Cal's reaction of grief and outrage, rather than grateful relief, was evidently noted by the stranger, for one of his eyebrows rose in mild puzzlement.

Cal identified the stranger now: an Earth-government agent, similar to the one he had known as "Subble." There were many of them, all basically similar to each other, differing only in superficial respects. This was deliberate. They were, in a manner of speaking, made that way. This one was dark-haired and heavy-featured—but the body was that of a superman, and the mind, Cal knew, was abridged but very sharp. This man would be able to quote all the Bible and much of Shakespeare, but would not have studied either creatively. He would have no truly individual personality. His past was a prepared memory, his present a specific mission, and his future irrelevant.

The question was, why was he here? Here on Paleo, the world of the paleontological past. Here in the reptile enclave. There should be no human beings here, apart from the trio.

The only sensible answer was that the trio had been followed. That suggested that Cal's worst fears had been realized. Their debate about the nature of his report on Paleo had after all been academic.

"Come with me," the man said gently.

Cal offered no resistance. He knew the agent could kill him or severely incapacitate him in a single second or an hour, whichever combination he chose. And would, if the occasion warranted. Obviously this encounter had been no accident.

"I am Taler," the agent said as they walked south.

So he was of the generation after Subble: the T's. Agents tended to go by three-letter codes, modified for pronunciation. Each generation (speaking mechanically, not biologically) was uniform. A given individual would react to a given situation in a manner so similar to that of his pseudo-brothers that the coordinating computer could accept his report without modification for individual bias. This was said to facilitate law enforcement immensely, in its various and often obscure ramifications on violent Earth.

But why had an agent been dispatched at all? This was supposed to have been a civilian mission.

He was pestering his own mind with rhetorical questions. The answers were all there, if he cared to bring them forth. Why an agent? Because the civilians were no longer needed. Earth had already made its decision with regard to the disposition of Paleo.

Cal had not made any specific reports, but had been aware that the radios maintained a carrier signal, pinpointing their geographic whereabouts at all times. The one in the Paleocene camp was probably still broadcasting. The other must have stopped when the raft had been upset by *Brachiosaurus*, drowning the equipment. This could have looked very much like sabotage.

All he had promised had been an eventual technical report: itemization of flora and fauna, climate and geography. He had planned to deliver his conjectures on the nature of the planet itself—the alternate-world framework. That would have been food for thought, for it suggested that there was not merely one world available, but an infinite number, if only connections to them could be established. Paleo, instead of representing merely a regressed Earth, implied a new universe, some of whose worlds could be very close in nature to the modern Earth.

But the short-thinking authorities had not waited. They

had evidently concluded that if a party of three could survive this long on Paleo, it was habitable and safe, and therefore wide open for exploitation. No doubt many corporations were eager to make their investments and begin profiting. So a more substantial investigation had been organized—in fact, it had probably been in the making before the trio was ever assigned. No wonder they had been boosted through so precipitously, back at the orbiting station! If the guinea pigs were to be used at all, it had to be immediately, lest the larger mission be delayed. Report? No more than a pretext to conceal from the trio their true insignificance.

So Cal's notion that Earth would patiently wait for his delayed report had been wishfully naïve. That was not the nature of the omnivore.

Cal repressed his further thoughts, aware that the agent could ferret them out quickly if suspicious.

They arrived at Taler's camp. A glossy-fabric tent had been pitched in the forest, stark contrast to the ancient ginkgos surrounding it. Inside the tent sat another agent operating a radio. Yes—they were in touch.

"Taner," Taler said, introducing his comrade.

Taner spoke into the mike. "Calvin Potter secured. Fungoids loose."

Secured? Another line of conjecture opened up. An ugly one. He had not been even nominally rescued—he had been taken prisoner. And they were searching for the mantas.

Why? Why indeed! Here was a world for the taking—provided the mantas didn't take it first. Any two of them could sporulate by committing suicide, and cover the planet with the very population the Earth-government abhorred: advanced fungoid entities. That would ruin it for colonization, by certain definitions, and reduce the spoils to ashes.

Perhaps it would be better that way. The manta, at least, was an honorable creature.

Taler turned to him. "I see you comprehend our purpose, Dr. Potter."

Oh-oh. He had forgotten, for the moment, the uncanny abilities of these men. By studying his reactions to stimuli—

217

and words themselves were stimuli—they could virtually read his mind.

"Precisely," Taler said. "Now it will be easier for us all if you choose to cooperate. Where are the other members of your party?"

They would run Veg and Aquilon down soon enough anyway—perhaps already had. Presuming the two had survived the quakes. A speedy pickup—yes, Taler was testing him in much the manner old-time police had verified the performance of their drugs or lie detectors by asking preliminary questions to which they knew the answers. "I left them on a small island in the eastern bay, together."

"And the fungoids?"

That was another matter. "I told them to get lost."

"You are a clever man, Dr. Potter."

Cal smiled grimly. "Common sense suggested that where there were two such highly trained agents as yourselves, others could also be present. Since I actually asked the mantas to observe my encounter with the carnosaur but not to interfere, I am reasonably certain that I have been under observation by them. Since it does not appear to be to their advantage to have these creatures captured by you, it was natural that I express my sentiment."

"However obliquely, and with insufficient precursive tension to alert me in time. Two fungoids were in the vicinity," Taler admitted. "They departed when you amended your prior instructions by suggesting that they 'get lost.' Our personnel were not quite quick enough."

"It would have been messy," Cal said, "had I suggested instead that they attack."

"Correct." Taler pulled aside a flap of the tent and revealed beneath it several heavy cables. These divided and subdivided and fed eventually into the material of the tent itself.

Suddenly Cal was very glad he had warned the mantas clear. The tent was a network of filament! The moment sufficient power was applied, he was sure, the entire surface would flash like a nova, blinding every sighted creature nearby. The agents would have some kind of protection—polarized contact lenses, perhaps—but the mantas

218

would have been destroyed. Alive but dead, for the sensitive eye was virtually their sole sensory apparatus.

That showed how well Earth understood the manta metabolism, now. For in death the bodies of the mantas would dissolve into spores, and in country like this it would not be possible to be assured of destroying every drifting bit of life. Living mantas were no such danger, and a blind manta would be innocuous—unable to strike either in life or death.

"Now we shall have to run them down the hard way," Taler said, showing no malice. "That may mean considerable damage to the area."

Cal knew the agent meant it. But the matter was out of his hands now. "What about the others?"

"We picked Vachel Smith off a rock in the ocean, and one fungoid accompanied him voluntarily. They are confined aboard ship in good condition. Taner is about to go after the girl and her companion. I see you did not know your associates had separated."

"I hadn't known any mantas had rejoined them, either. Well, at least I'll have company in the brig."

XX: ORN

The island was still dark as Orn roused the sleeping quilon with a careful nudge of his beak. Something was wrong. There was an alien presence he could not fathom— the same horror he had experienced the first time he had encountered the giant mams and supposed, erroneously, to be an aspect of their own strangeness.

She woke nervously, brushing her forelimbs against his under feathers, touching the warm egg for reassurance. He knew that gesture. It meant that she feared for the egg, that some danger threatened it. And that was why he had alerted her, for he did not like this odd visitation. Would she sense it too?

"Circe!" she exclaimed. "You came back!"

She saw it! And—she was not frightened. Her reaction, her sounds, were of relief and welcome, not apprehension.

"Veg—Cal—are they safe? Where are they?"

She was trying to make contact with it! She was friendly to this un-creature. It could not, then, be a threat.

Braced by this realization, Orn concentrated on the spot of greatest disturbance. If the quilon could perceive something there, so should he. His eyes were better than hers, and his nose too.

All he found was an unfamiliar growth of fungus: a tremendous toadstool. He could not read its life history, for it deviated too far from the lines he knew. It had not been there when they fought the Elas. But it was the nature of these things to sprout very rapidly.

It moved.

Orn looked to discover what had dislodged it, but observed no cause. There was no wind, and no animal had brushed against it. The ground had not quaked. The water had not washed ashore.

"They're safe!" The quilon was happy. She liked to see the toadstool move.

"Is the water clear now?" She was making query-noises. Orn was able to comprehend more and more of her mannerisms and read her intent. But he could not determine her precise concern. She was smarter than most mams, but fell short of Ornette's level, and was subject to meaningless and transitory expressions.

The toadstool disappeared. Astonished, Orn left the egg momentarily to probe the ground where the thing had grown. It was as though it had been lifted away by the wind—the wind that wasn't there. Surely the quilon had seen the phenomenon. Plants never moved of their own volition!

"Circe is checking out the region. We'll have to move off this rock, Orn, and we can't do it while the reptiles are about. I think I can manage the egg, provided the water isn't too deep and nothing attacks us. Circe can guide us—"

Orn wondered whether this continuous noise could have been what drove the male mam away. Certainly it was

220

irritating, when there was the problem of foraging while guarding the egg against both known and unknown menaces. Already that chatter had brought upon them a disastrous visitation by the Elas.

The toadstool reappeared, blown like a frond in a gale. Orn was able to see it clearly now that he was aware of its properties. These were contrary to all that his memory told him. But gradually he was able to accept that this fung had somehow evolved entirely separate from his own ancestry. Just as the ordinary animals had split from each other and developed over the millennia into dissimilar lines, so had this. Perhaps it had happened entirely in this valley, unvisited by any of his own line. Thus its utter strangeness, that had rendered it virtually imperceptible to him except as a vague horror, was not really so sinister. A creature with metabolism resembling that of a plant, yet as active as an animal. A creature without wings that flew. Now that his mind had conjured the necessary evolution of the species—a fung that reached for organic food, then jumped for it, until it had become dependent on such motions for sustenance—he could accept it.

Just as a mam could become as large as a small rep, and make perpetual noises, so could a fung become a flying toadstool.

The thing had planted itself in the ground again, and the quilon was making her noises at it. Perhaps the two odd species, mam and fung, had evolved together, and somehow understood each other. Such a connection would be no more remarkable than what he had already observed in this changed world.

The quilon faced him. "Circe says there is now a deep and treacherous chasm between us and the main island. The fault must have opened up there, and we can't cross it unless we swim. But I can't swim holding the egg. I mean I might try it, but the cold water would kill the embryo. But Circe says the bay between us and the mainland is shallow, maybe only chest deep on me. The quake must have pushed up the bottom in a ridge parallel to the fault—well, no use trying to explain *that* to you. She can show us the best route across, so we can wade. And she says there are no big reptiles in the immediate

221

area right now, and no sharks; they're all gathering around some battle several miles away, where there's a lot of blood. Something like that—I'm not sure. There's a sleeping duckbill by the main island, and he won't bother us anyway. But the tide's coming in; we have to do it right away if we're going to, otherwise it'll be hot by the time the water's low again, and the sea predators will be out in force."

Orn ignored her chatter. It was dawn—the best time for hunting, because most of the reps were torpid, though not the sharks. He would have to forage for the mam as well as himself, since she had to warm the egg. He had observed that she did not consume fish, sticking instead to tubers and berries from the island. He could cross over now and sniff out some roots for her, then feed himself.

The toadstool flew out over the sea again. The quilon stood up, lifted the egg—*and walked into the water!*

Orn squawked and fluttered after her, appalled at her folly. The cool sea would deaden the life in the egg! But she only made vocal noises at him, refusing to be summoned back.

He was helpless. Any measure taken against the quilon would surely immerse the egg—the very thing he sought to protect. He could not carry it back himself; he had to wait for her to do so. He realized that she meant no harm—but she did not seem to comprehend the danger. How could he make her understand?

She stepped cautiously away from the rock, the water rising to her removable hip-plumage. She held the egg against her fleshy breast with one forelimb, balancing with the other. She was moving away from the main island, following a course suggested by the motions of the flying toadstool.

Orn started swimming, being too light to maintain his footing at this depth. The quilon, well over half immersed, continued toward the mainland. She wasn't even trying to get to the island!

He had no notion how to abate this bizarre exploration. Had he known the mam was prone to such action, he would never have left her with his egg. Now all he could do was parallel her course and hope she would turn back before the egg was lost. He would have to kill her if she sacrificed it through her stupidity—but he did not want to do that.

The sea beneath him was clear. Small fish circulated temptingly, and he was hungry, but he could not go after them now. He could not see through to the bottom, for it was quite deep, though where the quilon walked it was unusually shallow. Memory told him that earth faults under the sea were sometimes like that: one side high, the other low, or two ridges separated by a chasm. But how had she known?

She was in now almost to her head. The egg was precariously lodged on her shoulder, nestled in the yellow mane that descended from her scalp. Both her forelimbs were raised to shield it. This was not adequate coverage; the egg would soon grow cool there, even if the water that was already plastering her artificial fur to her bifurcated udder did not rise farther. He swam closer, though he could do nothing.

The quilon stopped. "Too deep. I can't keep my footing. If I lower my arms, I'll float, and the egg will unbalance me—"

Sometimes such sounds seemed to signal a change of intent. Would she turn back now?

She worked her way back until the mane drew entirely out of the water. She held the egg close before her, warming it though her torso was wet. Then the toadstool came near, bouncing on the surface, and angled away in a slightly different direction. She followed it.

Again she went as deep as she could go, and again she uttered her frustrated sounds and retreated. The toadstool circled, seemingly unable to point the way again. *Now* would she give up this hazardous enterprise and return his egg to land and safety?

Safety? Even the mainland, with its rampaging reps, was safer than the hideously exposed bit of rock they were stranded on. Had it been possible to move the egg even to the main island—but the canyon in the sea prevented that.

Then Orn realized what the quilon and her obscure acquaintance were attempting to do. Shallow water leading toward the mainland, while the tide was low—

He went into action. He dived, spreading his wings against the water to provide the impetus that would send him under. He explored the bottom with his beak and eye.

Ahead of the quilon the ridge descended, then rose again to a level he thought she could navigate. If she could cross that deepest portion, she could travel a long way toward land—perhaps all the way. But she could not pass the hollow without immersing the egg. Perhaps only four lengths of her body, about four wingspans, separated her from the resumption of navigable shallows.

This was not the type of thinking Orn's mind was made for, but his long apprenticeship in solitary survival, coupled with the present pressing need, sharpened his abilities. There were problems memory could not solve, and this was one such: how to get the mam female across the gap without dunking the egg—and soon enough so that the rising tide would not make it entirely impossible.

Had there been floating wood, memory might have sufficed. His ancestors had utilized logs to cross from island to island upon occasion, or from side to side of deep rivers. But there was no log here. Orn himself was the only thing afloat—and only the relative stillness of the water enabled him to maintain his balance. Waves, or any other threat, could swamp him, for he was top-heavy and lacked webbed feet. He was actually better at swimming under water than on the surface, because there his abbreviated wings were effective.

But in this emergency, his abilities might be enough to save the egg. And the egg was paramount.

Orn paddled up and nudged the standing quilon. She was silent now, and water seemed to have splashed onto her face though the egg was dry. There was a certain unhappy handsomeness about her as she stood balked, and he wondered to what extent mams had genuine emotions.

But there was no time for such idle considerations. Orn nudged her again, trying to make her understand. The egg could be saved, if her dull mam brain could rise to the occasion.

For a moment she did not move. Then, slowly, she placed one forelimb across his back, bearing down on his body so that he sank in the water. She was astonishingly heavy, but he spread his wings somewhat and kicked his feet and maintained his position. He could not endure this for long; his instinct and memory cried out against such proximity to a foreign creature. But long enough—

She moved the egg until it rested partly against his back, just above the water. Then she pushed slowly forward. Her body went down, but the egg remained high, its weight borne by his feathers.

At the place the mam had balked before, her feet left the bottom and she floated. Orn paddled desperately to maintain his balance as she lost hers. It was difficult; he was tilting irrevocably over—

Then the quilon's stout legs began to kick in the water, driving them both slowly ahead and restoring joint balance. He steered and she held the egg on his back. A single bad wave, even a gust of wind, would topple them.

The toadstool circled rapidly, as though even its vegetable intellect were aware of the crisis. Orn glanced at it—and saw the suggestion of motion in the distance behind it. Something was coming!

Almost, in his instinctive eagerness to scramble for safety, he dislodged the egg. But he controlled himself after a single jerk and went on paddling. Perhaps it was only one of the sporting cory reps, who were unlikely to stray this far out from shore.

Progress was so slow! Only by poking his head under the surface and noting the locations of the bottom features was he able to determine that they were moving. If a predator rep came upon them now—

It did. It was the Elas, the flippered paddler who had carried Ornette away before. Already it was hungry again, or merely mischievous, and their motion in the shallow water had summoned it from its hiding place. Here within its feeding ground they had no chance at all to escape.

The toadstool broke its circle and went to meet the Elas. Orn could not watch closely, for his balance remained precarious. He saw the fung rise high in the air as though it were a ptera and pass over the lifted head of the rep. Nothing happened—but the Elas emitted a tremendous honk of pain.

Then it was retreating, and the smell of its blood came

to him. Had an old wound reopened as it strained to snap up the toadstool? Or had it merely been frightened by the oddity of the fung, the blood remaining from the wound Orn had inflicted on its neck before?

Orn was satisfied that they were safe again. Joy was no more a part of his nature than was grief, and the security of the egg was what mattered. Somehow the rep had been turned away.

The animal panting of the quilon became loud, and his own respiration was labored. He was, in the aftermath of the rep threat, quite tired. He had been subjected to a double strain—the weight of the quilon and egg on his back, and the fear of the Elas when he was impotent as a fighter. But they were over the shallow section again. He honked, trying to convey this to her, and finally she stopped kicking her heavy-boned feet and pushed her round extremities down until they struck the bottom sand.

The rest of the crossing was easy. Twice more he had to assist the quilon, the rising tide making the portages longer, but now they were both familiar with the routine. The flying fung guided them unfailingly, selecting the best route. Orn was coming almost to like such toadstools.

Secure at last on land, they lay on the pleasant beach, the egg warmed between them. The toadstool also rested nearby, a hump with a single peculiar eye. He could see it quite clearly now, though it remained a most unusual phenomenon.

The quilon had been right; the drive for land had been best. The chick still lived in the egg for he could feel its living presence. With the Elas remaining so near, they would have been perpetually vulnerable on the fragment island. Now they had a chance, and the egg too. The mainland was by no means ideal for nesting, but the island had turned into a death trap.

Orn looked about. He knew the terrain because he had pursued Ornette here during their courtship. Not far back from the shore the snowy mountains rose, riddled with their caverns and gullys and heated waters. Somewhere near the snowline there might be a suitable nesting site. The cold would make it doubly difficult to warm the egg, but this was necessary to escape the predator reps, who ordinarily would not ascend that far.

He stood and led the way, and the quilon followed, submissive now that she had done her task. She held the egg closely against her damp body, enclosing it with her forelimbs so that as little as possible was exposed to the air. Actually, the heat of the day was upon them, so this was no longer critical. The fung vanished into the brush; he spied it only occasionally.

Between shore and mountain was a level plain, an extension of the larger one the Tricer herds ranged on. Here the palms were well trimmed, showing that the huge reps had foraged here recently. Though he did not fear them himself, he was not certain how they would react to the large mam. They might ignore her—but if they did not, the egg would be in peril again. He decided to change course so as to avoid the local herd.

Then he sniffed something else. It was another large mam of the quilon species—a male.

Orn did not know whether this was good or bad. The male had left the female, and perhaps this return meant a reconciliation. But it could also mean trouble. Orn would not ordinarily interfere with mam courtship and mating rites—but he needed the quilon female to transport the egg, and to warm it while he foraged. He could not hatch it alone.

Before he could make a decision, the male approached. It was not the original mate.

There was a babble as the two mams vociferated at each other. The toadstool had taken off at the first whiff of the visitor; Orn smelled it in the vicinity but could not spot it.

The haphazard dialogue continued. Orn picked up the sequence of reactions from the female: surprise, comprehension, anger, fear. She did not like the stranger, but was afraid of what might happen if she made an open break. She suspected the male of malicious intent. Her concern was not primarily for herself, though; it was—

For the egg!

Orn was already charging as the realization hit him. His

227

wings flapped to boost his speed; his beak aimed forward. Headfirst, he launched himself at the strange male quilon.

The creature was not facing him, but from it a bolt of lightning emerged. A terrible heat struck Orn, searing the feathers of one wing and the flesh of that wing and the bony substructure, and lancing on through his body. The wound was mortal; he knew it as he completed his charge.

The female mam struck the intruder with her free limb, but he caught it with his own and was not hurt. This also Orn perceived as the signals of death spread through his running body. The male was swift and deadly and without compassion. He would kill them both and smash the egg. This certainty kept Orn going when he should have fallen. Only by somehow bringing the mam enemy down could he give the egg a chance—even the ugly chance Orn himself had hatched with. His own parents had died defending their nest and eggs from a marauding croc; Orn would die defending his egg from a predator mam. It was the way it had to be.

But he knew too that it was *not* to be. He had thought these mams to be slow and clumsy and not wholly intelligent. He had foolishly judged from the pair that came in peace to mate. This other mam was in his strength, and was devastating. This one would prevail.

Yet he continued, his legs somehow supporting the momentum of his body. He could at least strike at it, perhaps wound it . . .

Then a shadow came upon that scene.

The male quilon had one limb taken by its grasp on the female, the other lifted to ward off Orn. Its stout hindlimbs were anchored in the soil. Only its head was free, this moment, to move about. It turned.

The shadow passed.

There was a gash across the mam's head, where the eyes had been.

The shadow returned. Orn recognized it now. It was the flying fung, moving with dizzying speed.

Fire lanced from the male again, scorching brush and trees but not the toadstool. A second gash appeared, almost circling the mam's throat. Blood pounded out.

As Orn finally collided with his target, only a few

228

heartbeats from the time he had started the charge, he knew that both of them were dying. His weight jarred the male's grip loose from the female. Only she and the fung—and the egg!—had survived this brutal encounter.

"Circe!"

Orn collapsed in a heap with the mam, his blood mixing with that of his antagonist. He no longer had command of his body, but he could hear the female quilon's sounds. She never was silent!

"Circe! We've killed an agent! There may be others in the area, and they'll wipe us all out. They've come to take over Paleo, I'm sure of that. We'll have to cover the evidence. In a hurry."

The toadstool slowed and came to rest. There was blood on its tail.

"The Tricers! Can you stampede them?"

The fung was gone.

Then she was standing over Orn, touching the feathers of his neck with those uselessly soft digits. She still supported the egg. "Orn—you're alive!"

He had not known that death would be so slow. He was helpless, but now he felt no pain. There was only a gradual sinking to the sound of her dialogue, now gentle and no longer annoying.

"No—you can't survive that burn. I'm sorry, Orn. I—I didn't mean it to end like this. I'll save your egg. I'll keep it until—"

Her paw caressed his neck feathers. "The Tricers are coming. I have to get out of here, Orn. With your egg. Those brutes will flatten everything, so no one will know, I hope. How he died, I mean. Keep Paleo sacrosanct. . . .

"I—you were a gallant soul—*are* one—and I love you. You diverted the agent so Circe could—you gave your life for ours, and I'll always remember that. Always.

"Goodbye, Orn."

She was gone, and somehow he knew she would preserve the egg. That was all that mattered.

The ground rumbled and shook. Tricers—stampeding! Orn tried to move, but could not, before he remembered that the effort was pointless. Their sound was loud, their massive hooves striking the ground in a gargantuan rain-

229

drop pattern. They were coming here! The entire herd, charging along the narrowing plateau, converging on this spot, their growing cadence like the shaking of a volcano.

There would be nothing but a beaten trail, after their passage.

Orn was satisfied.

XXI: VEG

He stood on the deck and watched them bring Cal in. Hex stood beside him, in his shadow, impassive as only a manta could be.

The ship was anchored in water of appropriate depth near the mouth of the great swamp. It was a double-hulled military yacht, chemically powered but capable of fifty knots. Veg assumed that the agents had assembled it piecemeal this side of the transport tunnel, since it would have been impossible to beam the entire ship through as a unit. A big job, requiring skill and time, though of course the agents would have been programmed for it. They must have started work the moment the trio set sail on the *Nacre*. He didn't need Cal to tell him what that meant about the importance of the trio's original mission. They had simply been a test case, human guinea pigs, sacrificial lambs or whatever, sent through on the spur of the moment to verify that the transfer equipment was in working order and that men could survive the jump. A few days to allow for any subtle residual tissue damage, then a few more to make sure there were no slow-acting poisons on Paleo. Probably Noodlebrain had thought he was sentencing them to death, and it had been sheer luck that everything *had* functioned properly.

The tiny cutter docked beside the yacht. A derrick hoisted Cal and one of his captors to the deck. In a moment Cal passed across the line marking Veg's area of confinement, and the two friends were together again.

"There's a force screen or something," Veg warned him as they watched the cutter cut east. He still felt the awkwardness of their last discussion. How could things be the same between them, after . . . Aquilon?

Cal nodded. He knew all about such things. If any of them attempted to jump ship or even cross the line on the deck without authorization, the invisible alert screen would trigger automatic weaponry that would blast them immediately. The remains would be netted and englobed in seconds, so that the atmosphere would not be contaminated by their corpses. This was mainly for Hex's benefit, since his demise would release a cloud of potent spores. Earth had learned its lesson in that regard.

" 'Quilon?" Cal inquired.

"It didn't work out," Veg said; then he realized with fierce embarrassment that Cal had not been referring to their sexual liaison. "I left her on the island, when I heard about—" He broke off, aware that that was wrong too. Cal had not asked for help, in his contest with Tyrann.

"So Hex tattled," Cal murmured, smiling briefly.

"Yeah. Circe, anyway." The tension was broken; Cal understood. "How'd you make out?"

"Taler shot it."

"Oh." That was too simple. It meant Cal didn't want to talk about it, any more than Veg wanted to talk about his own adventure. And Cal would have explained about the other mantas by now, the missing ones, if he intended to. Something was going on.

A woman stood amidships, fiddling with radio equipment. She was tall, slender, and blonde—rather beautiful, yet quite unlike Aquilon. Veg had been observing her with covert admiration, wondering what she was doing here on this man's mission.

"Taner reports island evacuated," the woman said, every syllable clear though she did not seem to be striving for precision. "Proceeding to mainland."

Cal looked at her. "Earth is keeping extraordinarily close tabs on its representatives," he remarked. "I've seen three agents so far, with evidence of at least two others, and reporting in at every turn."

231

"They figure Paleo will corrupt somebody, otherwise," Veg said. "The way it did us."

"A telling point. I believe I would have termed it 'enlightenment,' however."

"And a gal aboard too."

"That's nothing to interest you," Cal said with an obscure expression. "That's a female agent."

Veg was shocked. "That little thing? A superman?"

She glanced their way and smiled. "Tamme, at your service."

Veg recalled the things the agent Subble had been capable of back on Earth. He looked again at the girl. He shook his head in negation. She would not last long in a lumberman's free-for-all, whatever her training.

Tamme was watching him. "I *would*, you know," she murmured.

For the third time in as many minutes he felt quick embarrassment. Damn that mind-reading ability of theirs!

She laughed.

Cal looked thoughtful, but did not comment.

"Contact," Tamme said. "Bird and woman. Fungoid concealed." Then she paused, frowning. "Tanar dead."

Taler's head appeared in the hatch. At least Veg thought it was Taler; they were all so similar they were hard to tell apart unless they were together. "So the report was correct. The fungoid can upon occasion dispatch an agent."

"*She* must have had a hand in it," Tamme said. "Shouldn't have sent a man for that chick."

"You have to admit we aren't exposed much to attractive feminine types," Taler replied.

She threw something at his head. The motion was so rapid and controlled that Veg was only aware of the jerk of her full blouse and the flash of metal in sunlight.

Taler moved simultaneously, plucking the object from the air before his face. He held it aloft, a trophy. It was a tiny stiletto—and had he not been ready for it, the point would have skewered his nose.

They were only playing, but they were deadly. All of them. That sudden murder of their companion seemed to mean nothing more to them than an ineffective tactic.

Unless this whole little episode was merely a show to impress the prisoners. Yet Subble had seemed like a decent guy, and he had been an agent not many letters removed. SU compared to TA—SUBble, TALer, TAMme, TANer. . . .

Taler came to them. "It appears there is some difficulty picking up Miss Hunt. We are also interested in the three outstanding fungoids. Is the present creature able to contact others, if set free to do so? There is no need to answer."

No need indeed! Veg was familiar with this type of interrogation. The agent merely asked questions, and gauged the response from the bodily reactions of the listener. There was nothing an ordinary man could do about it.

But why were the agents so intent on capturing all the trio and the mantas? They could survey the planet and make their report without reference to those who had gone before. The trio wasn't important any more, if it had ever counted for anything here at all, and this campaign hardly seemed worth the effort.

Well, Cal would know. Veg would follow his friend's lead.

"If you do not cooperate," Taler said gently, "we shall have to undertake a search-and-destroy mission. That could mean the death of Miss Hunt, too."

Cal did not speak, but Veg's pulses leaped angrily. Aquilon—dead?

"Interesting," Taler remarked. "Dr. Potter is even more enamored of Miss Hunt than is Mr. Smith. But Dr. Potter refuses to be influenced thereby. Since a threat of this nature would therefore be ineffective, I make none; I merely advise you that the element of risk does apply to Miss Hunt so long as she is beyond our jurisdiction."

Taler now addressed himself completely to Cal. "We shall begin with a humane nerve gas. This particular formula should render all mammals unconscious on contact. Reptiles and amphibians will be affected to a lesser extent. Plants will suffer some loss of foliage in the following days and a few will rot. Representatives of the third kingdom—"

"Blinded," Cal said.

Taler signaled to Tamme. "Lift the barricade."

Something clicked off. "You'd better explain it to Hex," Cal said to Veg. "He's your manta."

"I'm not sure myself what's going on. You want Hex to fetch 'Quilon?"

"These gentlemen," Cal said, "want very much to have all four mantas here on the ship, alive, because if any two should die on Paleo their spores could spread and mate and produce many thousands of mantas to take over the planet."

"That wouldn't be so bad. Mantas aren't destructive."

"These gentlemen wish to preserve Paleo for human colonization, however."

Veg smiled bleakly. "Oh. They'd have trouble, with all those mantas."

Then something occurred to him. "*I* don't want Earth to colonize, and 'Quilon doesn't either. We already had that out."

"I have come to agree with you," Cal said surprisingly. "Paleo should be preserved as it exists. But although I decided not to make my report, events have made the issue academic. The agents are now in control."

Veg experienced a mixture of emotions. He was gratified to learn that the schism between them was gone, that Cal was now on the side Aquilon had espoused—but angry that Cal should so readily submit to the demands of the agents. It was not like Cal to yield under duress.

Taler spoke, facing Veg. "Your friend is very clever. He has already outwitted me once, and I am not a stupid or gullible man. No agent is. Now he is planning to betray us again. I must therefore request that you address your manta immediately, without further conversation with Dr. Potter."

The manner was polite. Taler could afford courtesy. Veg knew that he was fully capable of enforcing his demand, and needed no bluster.

But the other remark! So Cal had not surrendered! That was especially good to know. But what had Cal planned? Could Veg figure it out in time?

"Instruct your manta," Taler said, his voice still mild

but carrying just that hint of urgency required to make his point. Further delay would mean considerable unpleasantness. Veg did not fancy himself to be a fool.

But what could he do, except as told? "Hex," he said, and the manta rotated on its foot to face him. "These men have—do you know what nerve gas is?"

Two snaps of the tail.

Veg turned to Taler. "I have to explain—"

"Nerve gas is a substance that can be released into the air," Taler said. "It will fill the entire valley within an hour, barring exceptional atmospheric conditions. It will blind all eye-bearing fungoids without killing them—and the damage is probably irreversible."

"Do you understand that?" Veg asked Hex. He wondered how the agents had developed and tested this chemical, with no mantas to try it on. Could it be a bluff?

To his surprise, Hex snapped once. The mantas were getting better at picking up human speech and grasping its content.

"They will release this gas, if you don't go and tell 'Quilon and the other mantas to come here—to surrender. We can't stop them."

One snap.

"So I guess you'd better—"

Something crackled. Veg saw Cal fall to the deck.

"Remain where you are," Taler snapped. He was facing Hex, who had not moved, and his directive was as much for the manta as for Veg. "Your friend was about to impart inappropriate information to you and the manta. I had to anesthetize him immediately. He will recover in a few minutes, unharmed. Instruct your manta."

"They aren't kidding," Veg said to Hex, furious but helpless. "I don't like it, but I have to tell you to go bring Circe and Diam and Star back here—and 'Quilon too, of course. They'll kill us all, otherwise." Inside he was chagrined that he hadn't been able to follow Cal's plan, whatever it was. By the time Cal woke up, Hex would be on his way, and it would be too late.

"Very good," Taler said. "The barrier is down—but the creature will be covered by our cannon until out of sight.

We are equipped to englobe the remains in seconds. It has one hour before we release the gas—no more."

"One hour, Hex," Veg repeated dully. "So make it fast. I—" He turned to the agent again. "You promise not to hurt any of them, or us?"

"If you cooperate. Our interest is in completing our mission; there is no personal onus. The group of you will be assigned elsewhere, where there need be no restriction on your activities or those of the fungoids. You have my given word. That is not sacrosanct, of course, but is a statement of intent."

Veg remembered Subble once more. The man had kept his word all the way, though he hadn't been obliged to. He had to trust Taler that far.

"It's okay for all of us, if you make it in one hour," he told Hex. "Tell them that. Now get going."

Hex leaped into the air and was on his way, a disk skipping across the water. He was traveling at something like a hundred miles an hour, and in about a minute had disappeared into the foliage fringing the swamp.

Veg lifted Cal to his feet as Taler departed. In a few minutes, as predicted, the little man recovered, though he had a scrape on the head where he had struck the deck. Veg raged to see the injury done, but knew that protest would be useless.

"Sorry," Veg murmured. "I couldn't figure out what you wanted, and the bastard wouldn't give me time to think, and he could read my mind anyway, so I just had to send Hex off."

Cal gripped his hand momentarily. "It's all right."

"I blew it. I'm just not smart enough."

"On the contrary. It was essential that I be out of the way so that *I* couldn't blow it, as you put it. They were already suspicious of me. *You* they assumed were safe."

"I *am* safe," Veg said. "Mad as hell, but safe. And I can't even slug one of them. I tried that on Subble, and got smeared."

"Yes, I'm sure Taler read that fury in you. So now Hex is telling 'Quilon and the other mantas the ultimatum. What do you suppose they'll do?"

236

"What *can* they do? No sense having that gas turned loose."

Cal only smiled.

Half an hour passed before a manta reappeared, alone. It glided in while the cannon tracked it and landed neatly on the deck. It was Circe.

Taler came out immediately. "This is not the same fungoid," he said.

"It's Circe—'Quilon's manta," Veg explained.

"Miss Hunt is ready to be picked up?"

"I guess. The swimming isn't so hot hereabouts."

Taler swung lithely over the rail and dropped into a second cutter. In a moment he was speeding in the direction Circe had come from. Veg wondered how he was so sure of the way, then realized that the sharp perceptions of the agent would make location easy. It was her cooperation Taler required, nothing else. Her agreement would bring in the remaining mantas.

Tamme was on deck, her efficient yet feminine manner disquieting. She had sex appeal, and he knew she read his appreciation of that, and read his attempt to repress and conceal his reaction. She hardly bothered to hide her amusement.

Fifteen minutes later Aquilon was brought aboard, along with Hex. She held what had to be one of Orn's eggs in her arms; Veg had no idea how she had come by it. There was a bruise on her cheek that he didn't like to look at, suspecting that he had put it there; but that was the least of the change in her. She was not the same woman he had known and loved.

"It's been a long time," Aquilon said. "Four nights and three earthquakes since we three were last together. . . ."

"Three nights, two earthquakes," Cal said.

"You must have been very busy, not to notice. *Four—*"

"Now don't you two start fighting again," Veg interposed quickly. "Could have been ten days and nine earthquakes, for all I remember, and what difference does it make?"

She smiled, becoming the girl he had known. She held no grudge against him.

Still, they stood there somewhat awkwardly. Veg knew

237

he really hadn't managed things very well. First, siding with her against Cal (and had it been sex that decided him?), then trying to go back to Cal when the man didn't want help, and getting stranded himself. Finally, he played the betrayer to them both by sending Hex off ... no, he had no congratulations coming.

Suddenly he realized that the hour was up—and Cal's two mantas, Diam and Star, had not come in.

"Release the gas," Taler said. Tamme, who seemed to handle more than radios, opened a chest and brought out several sealed cannisters. Frost glistened on them; they had been stored cold.

"That's pointless now," Cal said. "The two mantas are already dead."

Taler studied him. "You play a dangerous game, sir."

Cal nodded. "There is a world at stake."

Tamme spoke into her mike. "Parley has failed. Two fungoids have spored. Too late for enclosure. Proceed with alternate." She returned the cannisters to their compartment.

"What happened?" Veg demanded. "I thought they were coming in!"

Aquilon touched his hand in that way she had. "They knew what the invasion by the Earth omnivore meant. So they ... died, and Hex cut them up and spread the spores while Circe reported back here to the ship. By now those spores are all over the valley. They can't be wiped out."

"But I told Hex—"

Taler cut in, seemingly without malice. "Dr. Potter was aware that Miss Hunt would not honor that request—and that she would correctly interpret its real meaning. Had Dr. Potter been conscious at the time your manta left, I would have fathomed his sensation of victory, and thwarted his plan. As it was, I picked up nothing from him except his nonspecific chord of emotions. In my confidence, I failed to read him later, and I attributed Miss Hunt's confused state to apprehension concerning her treatment at our hands following her involvement in the termination of Taner. Therefore I did not question her, assuming that the remaining mantas were on their way

238

separately." He smiled with good-natured rue. "I have not before been so readily outwitted by a normal man."

Veg's mind was spinning. Cal had been walking a tightrope while juggling flaming torches barehanded! So many complex factors were interacting. This was a type of contest alien to him, and one he had certainly not appreciated at the time. "Why did 'Quilon and Circe come in, then?"

"Two sets of spores were sufficient," Aquilon said. "No point in having us all die."

"But we didn't follow through on the bargain," Veg said. "We didn't bring in all the mantas. So the agents don't have to give us any break. Maybe they'll kill us all, now."

"Does it matter?" Aquilon inquired dully, staring at the egg she held.

"Revenge would be pointless," Taler said. "Mr. Smith's bargain was made in good faith; it did not occur to him that the others would not honor it. We agents are realistic, not recriminatory—otherwise we would have brought you to accounting for the damage done by the three fungoids back at the Earth station, and particularly for the one that escaped entirely. But we chose instead to learn from the experience, and so we followed you as rapidly as was feasible."

"You mean you didn't plan to come here anyway?" Veg asked, wondering just how bad a mistake that manta break at the station had been.

"Not this particular party. The original expedition was to consist of normals—extraterrestrialogists, geologists, paleontologists. When we realized the potentialities of your fungoids, this military unit was substituted." Taler faced toward the mainland, as though watching for something. "You have demonstrated that as a group you are too valuable to waste. Future agents will be programmed to avoid mistakes of the nature of those we have made here, and you will be reassigned as agreed."

Veg shook his head dubiously. "So you're letting Paleo go, after all that trouble?"

"By no means. Our alternate program to salvage the planet for mankind is already underway. Observe."

They looked across the water. Smoke was rising from the valley—a wall of it on the west side, near the trio's original camp. The breeze was blowing it east.

"You're burning the enclave!" Aquilon exclaimed, horrified.

"The spores, as you pointed out, are beyond recovery. It is necessary to destroy them and the habitat in which they might prosper. We are doing so."

"But the dinosaurs! They have nowhere to go!"

"They are part of that habitat," Taler said. "This will hasten their extinction, yes."

She stared at the smoke, stricken.

"You can't get all the spores that way," Veg said, similarly appalled. "They're tough. Some will ride high in the sky, where it stays cool. Some will settle in the water—" He stopped, wondering whether he had said too much.

"Some spores will survive, inevitably," Taner agreed. "But the point is that they require hosts for their maturation. By depriving them of these—chiefly the omnivorous mammals of the valley—we are making it impossible for them to develop there. Some will drift beyond the mountains—but as you saw, that landscape is barren, and their numbers will be diffuse after the hurdles of fire and snow. The ocean is not a conducive habitat, either, since the fungoids are land-based. The probability is that a long-range program of survey and extermination will prevent any fungoid menace from erupting."

"The whole valley!" Aquilon said. "How could it possibly be worth it!"

"Perhaps you should have considered that at an earlier time. We were prepared for this contingency, but it was not our desire to destroy the enclave. You forced it."

"I didn't know!" But it sounded to Veg as though she lacked conviction. She certainly should have guessed that the omnivore would not be easily balked.

"Dr. Potter knew."

He was right, Veg thought. Cal would certainly have anticipated the consequence of his plot. Had he betrayed Paleo after all, making dupes of those, like Veg and

Aquilon and the mantas, who would have saved it? Veg did not look at him.

"Some will escape," Cal said. He sounded worn. "The spores can survive for many years, and there will be an entire planet to hide on. In as little as a year some will mature sufficiently to respore, and there will be no way to control that secondary crop of mantas. It will be cheaper to vacate Paleo than to police it effectively. Your superiors will realize that in time, and act accordingly. This valley had to be sacrificed for the sake of this world."

"You are gambling with genocide," Taler said. He turned to Veg and Aquilon. "If I were this man's companion, I would be afraid."

Veg watched the smoke rising, knowing that Cal had foreseen this and probably planned on it, and understood.

XXII: QUARTET

Aquilon stood holding Orn's egg: a nine-inch shell containing all that remained of a gallant pair of birds. She had wrapped a soft blanket about it, but could not be satisfied that it was warm enough. She kept turning it so as to hold a new face of it against her body, lest any side chill. This was an unreasonable fear, for the air was warm and the egg's requirements were not that critical; she suspected it could survive up to half an hour in isolation at normal temperature, and perhaps more. All it needed was a general, mild warmth, such as that provided by a clothed human body.

Tell that to my female psyche, she thought. Orn had died protecting her—because she held the egg. It was her egg now, never to part until hatched. There could never be enough warmth for it.

Smoke shrouded the dinosaur valley. Soon the enclave would be a mass of embers—all because she had tried to

241

fight the ruthless agents. She was a murderess now; it had been at her behest that Orn and Circe had attacked that agent Taner, who so resembled Subble. Almost, when she had seen him first, she had capitulated. But then she realized what his presence meant. . . .

Cal thought it was worth it. But his analytical brain was sometimes frightening. Even human colonization, with all its inequities, would have been better than this. Why had he set it up this way?

Everything had turned out wrong. The night of love with Veg had aborted; she knew now that she did not love him. Not that way. She had loved Orn, in a fashion—only to see him die. Such a noble spirit! Now there was only the egg.

She could not get close enough to it. She cradled it with one arm and reached under the blanket with the other, pressing her hand between its rough surface and her own abdomen. She found the catches on her blouse and disengaged them, opening her bosom to the egg. Still it was not close enough. She released her brassiere and slid it up over one breast and then the other, letting it cling just beneath her shoulders while her softly resilient breasts pressed yieldingly against the shell Then, almost, she felt close enough.

The fires were rising. Open flame showed in patches at the west fringe, licking at the cycads. Obviously it was not a natural conflagration; it ate too readily at green wood, consuming living fern and horsetail as well as ground debris. Tongues of it snaked out over the water, sending up gouts of vapor. No—this was the incendiary product of man, the omnivore. Like its master, it destroyed every living thing it touched, and despoiled the nonliving.

She suspected, intellectually, that Cal was right. Earth had been ready to move in on Paleo from the start, and the actions of the trio had had little bearing on that decision. Only if they had turned up some imperative reason for caution would this rape have been blunted. Carcinogenic vegetation, poisonous atmosphere, super-intelligent enemy aliens—one of these might have done it. But dinosaurs? They were merely a passing oddity, a paleontological phenomenon. Animals.

242

Animals. Suddenly she realized what it meant, this fire, in terms of life, of feeling. This was not merely the destruction of an anachronism. These were living creatures.

Veg and Cal beside her had field glasses, and both were using them silently. She was occupied with the egg, her naked flesh embracing it, giving it warmth, drawing some subtle comfort from it. She would not be helped, Paleo would not be saved, nothing useful would be accomplished, were she to witness the enlarged optic details of the fall of the reptile kingdom. She needed no glasses. She saw the distant orange flickering, the smoke smudging up, and that was already too much. The camps they had made, the raft, Orn's body . . . everything, incinerated at the behest of the omnivore.

She turned about, glancing at Charybdis to the south—and saw the smoke there too. They had not overlooked any part of the enclave! Yet she had not seen any agents traveling about to start those devastating blazes.

The water rippled. Things were swimming past, outward, fleeing the heat, though surely there was nowhere to go. Fish, reptiles—and the latter had to come up for air. *Ichthyosaurus* with the monstrous eyes? No, this was a paddler, *Elasmosaurus*. The same, perhaps, that she and Orn had fought. Was that a scar on its neck? Was it blind of one eye?

It passed the ship, hasty, frightened, pitiable.

Fire bathed it. The reptile struggled in the water, burning, dying, and the odor of its scorching flesh was borne to her across the brief distance between them. She did not need to turn to see the agent with the weapon. That would be Tamme, an omnivore with female form. Naturally these butchers would not allow any large swimming reptile to escape, for it might conceivably serve as host for a microscopic manta.

She hugged the egg. How could she sit in judgment on her species? She herself had killed, useless gesture that it turned out to be. She was an omnivore too.

The dream of bliss was cruelly ended. The idyll of Paleo had been revealed as genocidal naïveté. What

243

good was it now to feel sorry for Elas, the one-time enemy plesiosaur? It was less vicious than man.

She had known it before. She had seen this on earth, this savagery.

She held the egg, wondering whether it would not be kinder in the long run to dash it against the deck.

Veg focused the glasses on the fringe of the valley, fascinated in spite of himself. The fire burned everything, even the ground, even the water. The lenses brought every detail within arm's reach.

Amazing, how quickly and uniformly the fires had started, spaced to spread across the entire valley. They must have fired incendiary shells, and must still be firing them, because new centers of flame appeared at intervals, hastening the death march of orange.

He had seen such carnage before. They had burned his own forest, back on Earth, and for the same reason: to get the manta. The omnivore (now he was thinking in manta terms!) was ruthless. He had thought to foil it, here on Paleo, but that never had a chance to work.

He sneaked a glance at Aquilon, keeping the glasses to his face and pointed forward. She stood beside him, wild and beautiful, holding the egg she had saved. A blanket covered it and her shoulders, though the air was warm. Through an open fold he thought he saw—

He snapped back to the glasses. A trick of vision, surely. But, bewilderingly, his eyes suddenly stung, and the glasses seemed to cloud for a moment. He remembered his night with Aquilon, the joy of which had faded so quickly. It was as though he had expected more than a mere woman and was disappointed to have found her, in the dark under a tarp, to be less than ethereal. It seemed to him now that it could have been anyone he embraced then. *Should* have been anyone . . . but her.

He saw now that he wanted a dream Aquilon, not the flesh 'Quilon. And the dream had been sullied. And his friendship with Cal had been demeaned.

The reptiles were charging into the water, trying to escape the fire, but it pursued them. Tricers, Boneheads, Struths and Ankys, drowning simultaneously, inhaling water and flame. With them, he was sure, were many more mammals, too small to show up amid the giants. And birds, and insects.

Veg was not, despite his pretenses, a violent man. But had he had any real opportunity to wipe out this shipload of killers, he would have done so.

He saw a large duckbill, *Para*-something-or-other, smash through the smoke and dive into the sea. For a moment only its bony crest showed above the surface, and it seemed that smoke plumed back even from that. Then the dinosaur came up, reared skyward—and a jet of flame shot from its nostrils. It had taken in some of the chemical, and its lungs were afire. A true dragon for the moment, it perished in utter agony.

And farther out to sea the head of Brach emerged, clear of the fire. But the stupid brute was charging the wrong way again, going toward the conflagration. Back! Back! he mouthed at it, to no avail. Monstrous, it lumbered out of the water, fire coursing off its back outlining neck and tail and pillarlike thighs. The tiny brain tried to make sense of the agony surrounding fifty tons of body, and could not; burning brightly, Brach keeled over like a timbered redwood tree and rolled with four trunks in the air.

For a long time Veg watched the spasmodic twitching of Brach's smoking tail, until at last that smoke seemed to get in his own eyes, and the stench of it in his nose, and he cried.

Cal watched the destruction of the reptile enclave with severe misgiving. It was true that he had foreseen this, even precipitated it, but the cruelty of the denouement was ugly. Certainly the extinction of most major lines of reptiles was inevitable, here, regardless of the actions of man. One could no more halt that natural process than one could turn back the drifting of the continents. But the dinosaurs did have the right to expire in their own time and fashion, rather than at the fleeting convenience of man.

The masses of herbivorous reptiles had thinned, the majority already perished in the flaming ocean. Now the carnivores, unused to fleeing from anything, were coming into sight. *Struthiomimus*, birdlike predator; several young *Tyrannosaurs*; then a real giant—

He refocused the glasses. That was no carnosaur! It was an ornithischian dinosaur, a bipedal herbivore. *Iquanodon*! But of what a size! Sixty feet from nose to tail tip, as scaled on the range measure of the field glasses. Larger than Tyrann full-grown, and heavier in proportion, for the gut was massive. A total weight of twelve tons, at least. A herbivore *would* be heavier-set, of course; the digestive apparatus had to be more voluminous. . . .

If a biped that size—the largest ever to tread the earth—had hidden unsuspected in the valley, what other treasures had been concealed? The lost opportunities for study. . . .

Yet it had to be. He had intended to set the manta spores loose before the Earth mission arrived, knowing it *would* arrive. But he had misjudged how *soon*. He had debated with Veg and Aquilon, putting it all on record so that the investigators would know he had intended to summon them. And he *had* so intended—but he had meant them to arrive too late. They would have discovered that Veg and Aquilon, despite their stand, were innocent. That the mantas had traveled with *him*—and apparently acted without his knowledge and against his wishes. Acted to take Paleo for the third kingdom, for the manta. Cal himself would have been gone, presumed dead, for the plan did not tolerate any interrogation of him by agents. Thus the Earth invasion would have been balked, and the other two either deported again or simply left on Paleo, but not punished.

But in his vanity he had delayed, seeking to vindicate his right to make such a decision for a world. And in so doing, he had thrown away his *chance* to make it. And so he had been caught, and had had to play the game the hard way, making it expensive for everyone. Perhaps if he had not suppressed his real thoughts and intentions, had not constructed his elaborate justifications for the sake of verisimilitude—

Yet it changed nothing. The age of reptiles was finished here, whether man came or not. And the battle was for

Paleo, not the class of mammals or the class of reptiles, or even the kingdom of animals or fungus.

No, the battle was not even for this world. He could have advised the mantas long before the actual enclave had been discovered. The enclave was nothing, Paleo was nothing—nothing more than the convenient battleground. There would be a million enclaves, a billion Paleos, and trillions, quadrillions, quintillions of *other alternate worlds*. That was what the confirmation of the parallel-worlds system meant. He had known, despite his earlier words to Aquilon, that it could not be the paradox of time travel. Paleo had to be one of an infinite series of parallels, each differing from its neighbor by no more than an atom of matter, a microsecond of time. The two went together, space and time displacing each other in a fixed if unknowable ratio. No alternate world could match Earth *exactly*; no two alternates could jibe precisely, for that would be a paradox of identity. But they could come close, *had* to come close—and Paleo and Earth were close (or had been, prior to the crossover), almost identical physically, almost identical temporally—even though to man's viewpoint sixty-five million years was not close, and an intelligent flightless bird was not close. Such distinctions were trivial, compared to those between potential other alternates.

Perspective. If Aquilon liked Orn, she could find millions like him, in those quintillion other frames of reality. And millions of other Aquilons *were* finding those Orns.

Yes, it was vast. A sextillion worlds, each complete in every detail down to the atomic level. A septillion worlds, octillion, nonillion decillion—there were not numbers in the mind of man to compass the larger reality. Infinity trailing behind Earth, ranging back to the age of reptiles, the age of amphibians, the age of fishes, the age of invertebrates—all the way back to the primeval formation. Millions of contemporary Earths discovering millions of Paleos, raping them. . . .

Sooner or later those parallel crossings would intersect, and Earth would meet Earth with an insufficient spacing between them. A decade perhaps, or a minute—and there would be unique war.

Better that this Earth ravish this Paleo, delayed by the manta. Better that the lesson be learned that way, now. Coexistence had to be learned, and the very hardest coexistence was with oneself. Earth might get along with an alien world, but not with another Earth. The rivalry would be too immediate, too specific. Without bloody experience of the Earth-Paleo nature, the later and major confrontation would be disastrous. As the three-year-old might fight with the two-year-old for a favored toy, and gradually learn to interact more reasonably, so Earth would fight with Paleo.

But it remained hard to abide, the brutality of this first meeting. If only there were some way to come at maturity (individual, species, world) without passing through immaturity. . . .

Memory. It began far, far back in the half-light, wetter and warmer than much of what followed. He floated in a nutrient medium and absorbed what he needed through his spongy exterior. He reached for the light, a hundred million years later, needing it . . . but brushed against the enclosing shell and was restrained. He had to wait, to adapt, to grow.

There was warmth, but also cold. He moved restlessly, trying to achieve comfort, to get all of his suspended body into the warm section of his environment. And he remembered that too: somewhere a billion years ago he had struggled between freezing darkness and burning light, and satisfied his compelling hunger by growing into an absorbtive cup, a cylinder, a blob with an internal gut, by extruding fins and flukes and swimming erratically after game. He formed eyes, and gills, and a skeleton, and teeth, and lungs, and legs.

Ornet remembered.

POSTSCRIPT: CALVIN POTTER

The Cretaceous enclave of a world otherwise representative of the Paleocene epoch of Earth captures one of the more remarkable episodes in the history of our planet. For more than two hundred million years the reptiles dominated land, air, and the surface of the sea; then abruptly all but a few forms vanished, vacating the world for the primitive mammals and birds.

Quite a number of theories have been advanced over the years to account for this "time of great dying" but none havo been completely satisfactory. It has been suggested for example that "racial senescence" was responsible: the notion that species, like individuals, gradually age and die. No evidence supports this, and it fails to explain the survival and evident vigor of reptiles such as the turtles and crocodiles, or the much longer tenure of creatures like the horseshoe crab. Another theory was pandemic illness: perhaps a plague wiped out most reptiles without affecting mammals or birds or amphibians. Apart from the fact that disease simply does not work this way—it can decimate, but seldom exterminate, a widespread and varied population—the gradual diminution of numbers of species in the late Cretaceous argues against this. Why should it attack one species at a time, then later strike many others simultaneously? Various types of catastrophes have also been proposed—solar flare, worldwide flood, etc.,—but again, the selectivity of such an occurrence is not explained, and no record of it is found in relevant sedimentary deposits. The rocks show an orderly continuity from Cretaceous to Tertiary, wherein the great reptiles disappear and, later, the small mammals appear. The changeover could not have been violent.

More recent theories have been more sophisticated. Did world temperature become too cool for most reptiles, so that they gradually became torpid and unable to forage effectively? This would account for the survival of the warm-bodied mammals and birds. But a substantial cooling would have been necessary, and there was none at the time, as illustrated by plant life. Could the opposite have happened: a devastating heat wave? Again, the record denies this.

Radiation? A science-fiction writer suggested that fluctuations in Earth's magnetic field should periodically permit the planet to be bathed in increased radiation from external sources, increasing the mutation rate of animals disastrously. If a magnetic lapse occurred when radiation from a nearby supernova struck, there could indeed be biological havoc. But why only among the reptiles and certain sea creatures? Radiation is one of the least selective forces.

There was a radical change in vegetation during the Cretaceous period. The angiosperms—flowering plants—suddenly became dominant. Did the herbivorous dinosaurs find the new vegetation, particularly the grasses, too tough to chew and digest? Another science-fiction writer thought so. But this plant revolution came before the extinction of the dinosaurs, and many of the hugest reptiles flourished for millions of years amid the flowers. They were able to adapt, and the dental equipment of *Triceratops*, for example, shames anything developed since short of a lumbermill.

Could the mammals have competed so strongly with the reptiles as to exterminate them? Direct physical oppression seems an absurdity, for the dinosaurs held the mammals in check quite readily for a hundred million years. One has only to visualize a pack of mice attempting to bring down *Tyrannosaurus*. Mammals might, however, have eaten reptile eggs—but again, it is strange they would wait so long, then be so completely effective. The swimming reptile *Ichthyosaurus* gave live birth, so should have survived. And why did the land-laid eggs of the turtle and crocodile escape?

No—to comprehend the decline of the great reptiles,

one must first grasp the geologic cycle of which they were a part. No form of life exists in isolation, and evolution and extinction is never haphazard. Definite conditions promoted the ascendence of the reptile orders while suppressing the amphibians and mammals. The later reversal of these conditions demoted the reptiles in favor of the mammals and birds. The dinosaurs were doomed to transience by their very nature.

The surface of the Earth has always been in motion. One facet of this is termed "continental drift." The continents owe not only their positions but their very substance to the convective currents of Earth's mantle. This turbulence brought up the slag and guided it into floating masses that accumulated considerably. Though normally separate, at one point several came together to form the segments of the supercontinent, Laurasia/Gondwanaland.

Such a situation has occurred more than once in the past. It is marked by a particular complex of phenomena: subsidence of mountains, the intrusion of large, shallow bays or inland seas, diminution of tremors and volcanic activity, and extraordinarily even climate. In sum: a very quiet, conducive environment for life.

In such case, the competitive advantages of amphibianism or internal temperature control are academic. When the temperature of land, water, and atmosphere at sea level varies only from 10° F. to 20° F., day and night, season to season, century to century, warm-bloodedness is a complication irrelevant to survival. Indeed, it may be moderately detrimental, since it requires a higher rate of metabolism and therefore makes food intake more critical. The mammals perfected this control, involving the development of a hairy covering (to retain body heat), compact torso (same), sweating mechanism (to cool that compact furry body when necessary), improved teeth, limbs, and posture (to hunt and feed more effectively, to meet the demands of increased appetite), live birth (because infant exposure would be fatal), and sophisticated internal regulatory mechanisms. But while the mammals struggled through the innumerable false starts and the tens of millions of years necessary to accomplish all this, the reptiles were simply growing large and savage. The birds

251

undertook a similar program, and were similarly overshadowed by their flying reptile cousins.

Thus developed the age of reptiles, extending from the Permian period through the Triassic, Jurassic, and Cretaceous: two hundred twenty million years. The reptiles were not as complicated as the birds and mammals, but they dominated the world-continent.

But eventually this tremendous land mass began to break up, as the convection currents formed a new pattern. North to south, east to west, the continent was sundered. The Americas were shoved away from Europe and Africa; Antarctica broke from both, and from Australia. A crack in the land widened into a chasm, to a strait, to a channel, to a bay, and finally to a sea: the Atlantic Ocean. This was no overnight occurrence; it took millions of years. Though there were many severe tremors associated with the upthrusting of matter through this rift and the other rifts of the world, they posed no immediate threat to life on land. The severance of the Americas became complete just before the end of the Cretaceous; the other continents separated at other times, but geologically the fragmenting was rapid.

The consequences of this breakup were multiple. The ocean floor was re-sculptured, disturbing ancient breeding and foraging grounds. Enormous quantities of continental debris were dumped into the oceans, for a time affecting the chemical properties of the water. Volcanism was restimulated, affecting the atmosphere. And the motion of the fragments brought about stresses leading to new orogeny: tremendous mountain ranges like the Rockies and Andes, that remade weather patterns and dehydrated inland plains. The physical restructuring of the world inevitably brought about a shift in climate, and this in turn affected life.

The plants reacted massively. Forms that had been minor suddenly had a competitive advantage: the angiosperms, or flowering plants, that did not leave their reproduction to chance. The increased winds and mountains and oceans and deserts worked against random fertilization. The older gymnosperms did not become extinct, but assumed a minority role in the new ecology.

This change in vegetation necessarily affected the animals. The arthropods—chiefly the insects—radiated astonishingly because of the offerings of the flowers, and the spiders followed them. The insectivores—mainly mammalian and avian, together with the reptilian lizards and amphibian frogs—multiplied in response, for this food supply seemed inexhaustible.

The large reptiles were only indirectly affected. They were not insectivores, and even the flying ones were adapted to prey on fish, not flies. Reptile herbivores were capable of adjusting to the new foliage, or surviving in reduced numbers on the less plentiful old-style plants. The variety, but not the vigor, of their species declined, while the carnosaurs continued much as before. But their young began to be crowded by the burgeoning other life. Full-grown mammals and birds, hunting in packs or flocks, began to deviate from their normal diet and prey on newly hatched reptiles, and so added a factor to the ecological balance. This was an annoyance rather than a calamity, for even new-hatched reptiles were more than a match for most other species, but it presaged the new order.

The revised geography struck far more specifically. The ponderous ornithischians could not thrive in steep mountains or dry deserts or icy wastes, and were restricted by the violence of the landscape. As these untoward conditions developed, they migrated from large sections of the new continents, and the carnosaurs of course accompanied them. The disappearance of the vast continental seas and swamps severely limited the range of the massive sauropods and the paddlers of the shallows. Unkind wind patterns ravaged the pteradactyls. But many suitable places remained, and the net effect of the change was to concentrate the reptile orders in smaller sections of the world and reduce their meanderings, not to bring them anywhere near extinction.

The climate was another matter. The overall temperature changed only slightly, becoming cooler. This by itself was unimportant. What counted was not the average but the range. The so-called temperate climate developed: actually about as intemperate as the world has ever

253

known. The even seasons shifted to hot summers and cold winters. An individual summer's day might range from 50° F. low to 100° F. high. A winter's day could begin at that low and drop fifty degrees. The reptile biology simply was not equipped to handle such extremes. A heat wave in summer could wipe out enormous numbers; a prolonged freeze in winter did the same. The warm-bodied creatures, in contrast, were ready, and only a fraction of their number failed to adapt. This, more than anything else, drove the reptiles as a group to the tropics, and reduced their territory drastically.

And here the most direct aspect of the continental breakup came into play. For the individual land masses were not contiguous. They were now isolated by deep water. *The reptiles could not migrate far enough.* North America, for example, drifted too far north to have a tropical zone, and was completely separated from South America for some time. Stranded, the reptiles were subject to the full ravages of geography and climate, and they expired. Some few survived for a time in local enclaves, but such existence was tenuous. These extremely confined areas were subject to volcanism and recurring tremors and drastic alteration by shifts in the prevailing winds or drainage. Inevitably the reptiles there were destroyed, whether in a few hundred years or a few million.

The dinosaurs could have survived all the other changes and met the challenge from other classes of vertebrates— had they been able to travel freely over the world, for there was always suitable pasture somewhere. But the fragmentation of the original land mass restricted them at the very moment, geologically, that they could least afford it. Far from being coincidence, this was inevitable. The age of reptiles on land was finished.

The sea reptiles had their own problems. Those tied to the shallows who laid their eggs on land, such as *Elasmosaurus*, expired with the others, for the shallows were gone. Those fully adapted to deep water, such as *Ichthyosaurus*, suffered severe competition by flourishing sharks and, more deviously, by restriction of their diet. For an earlier revolution had occurred in the water: the teleosts, the so-called bony fishes, had appeared. These had stronger skeletons than did the earlier types, and possessed an air bladder modified from a one-time lung that enabled them to match the density of the surrounding water and float at a given level without muscular effort. For the first time, vertebrates were able to compete specifically with the invertebrate ammonites, who for hundreds of millions of years had possessed this controlled flotation ability and thrived. The fish, however, were superior swimmers. This did not eliminate the ammonites, but it did restrict them. When the continental breakup ravaged the oceanic geography and chemistry, the ammonites lost out. Those swimming reptiles who preyed exclusively on ammonites followed them into oblivion.

Thus, medium by medium and type by type, the life of the world was transformed by the breakup of the master continent. It was not that the birds drove out the flying reptiles, or that the teleosts and sharks drove out the ammonites and certain corals and swimming reptiles, or that the angiosperms drove out the gymnosperms, and certainly the mammals did not drive out the land reptiles. But the conditions of each habitat changed significantly, and shifted the balance to favor new species. Those forms of life that were ready for harsh extremes of geography and climate and chemistry prospered; those that were not did not.

But what of the few surviving reptiles? These were the ones who *were* equipped to endure the new regime. The crocodiles and turtles were able to forage either on land or in the deep sea, so neither the sharks nor severe temperature extremes could eliminate them entirely. They were able to migrate from an unkind continent to a kind one, and did so, and have lasted until the present. The duckbills might have joined them, as they were strong swimmers and fast runners on land—but they had to feed on land, so could not remain in the water for weeks at a time. The snakes and lizards were small enough, and suitably shaped, to reside on and in the ground and trees; for them the arthropods and small mammals represented an improved diet, and deep burrows shielded them from winter's cold and summer's heat. They survived largely because they were small enough to utilize such shelter; the dinosaurs' specialization in large size worked against them fatally.

Have there been other extinctions as the continents drifted into new configurations? Certainly, many of them, though few as impressive as this one. There will surely be more. When the land moves, life must follow. The real mystery is not the great dying, but why this natural course remained a mystery for so long. . . .